LOUISIANA
VAMPIRES

LOUISIANA
VAMPIRES

Compiled by
Lawrence Schimel &
Martin H. Greenberg

FALL RIVER PRESS

Compilation © 2010 by Lawrence Schimel and Tekno Books

This 2010 edition published by Fall River Press by arrangement with Tekno Books.

Book design by Suraiya N. Hossain

Fall River Press
122 Fifth Avenue
New York, NY 10011

ISBN 978-1-4351-1849-2

Printed and bound in the United States of America

1 3 5 7 9 10 8 6 4 2

✠

CONTENTS

CONTENTS

INTRODUCTION

> ━◦┃◦◆━◦━◎━◦━◆◦┃◦━ ◄

NO OTHER PLACE IN THE UNITED STATES HAS BEEN ASSOCIATED WITH vampires as strongly as has Louisiana. Which is not, perhaps, unexpected, considering the location and history of the State, and its inhabitants— from its original Native Americans to the successive French and Spanish colonization, its purchase by the United States, and the mix of African and Haitian slaves and immigrants. To this amalgam of peoples from so many different cultures, each brought their own superstitions with them. And few creatures of the night are more haunting than the vampire, returned from the dead to prey on the living, found in one form or another in almost every culture.

So it is not so surprising that the vampire, or many different vampire variations, found a home in all levels of Louisiana society, from the white European gentility to the black slaves. And from these many traditions that make up Louisiana, the vampire has come to be one of the commonalities that cuts across the social strata, the way sex or money can, thereby making it part of the image of the state, an image that has been exploited and made use of in countless books and films.

And few places in Louisiana have as much power in our collective imagination as New Orleans, not so much a city as the myth of city, whose allure draws thousands of visitors to it each year. While most of southern life (and fiction) tends to focus on small-town existence, despite the presence of major cities like Nashville or Atlanta, New Orleans has long been the exception. At times, it has been less a city than a nexus of commerce and culture, of decadence and excess, perched at the mouth of the Mississippi. It is a place where people come to find things, or perhaps to lose themselves.

And it is a place where, time and again, no matter where they come from or where they're meaning to go, people find vampires. Or sometimes, vampires find them.

Gathered here in this anthology are stories in which some of today's hottest writers explore this fertile territory, from the bayous to Mardi Gras, from the famous Latin Quarter to anonymous small towns. You'll find tales of decadence, of talismans, of past glories and of eternal promises. And of course, of the War, which in the South is always only that one unavoidable war.

But whatever the setting, whether gothic or contemporary in tone, the one thing you can be sure of is that these are tales steeped in the region, rich with local details and superstitions, stories sure to leave you itching to look over your shoulder in unease even as you're still reading.

—Lawrence Schimel

✝

A NIGHTWALK IN HELL

FERELITH DAWSON

><+>>—☉—<<+><

Part the First: 1862

IT WAS NIGHT IN NEW ORLEANS. THE FULL MOON ROSE LIKE A SHIELD OF beaten gold, casting deceptive shadows over the slum quarter of the Crescent City.

Little moved here after dark. The Union army was enforcing General Butler's curfew.

A shadowy figure moved out of the midnight blackness, sliding in and out of cover, satin-shod feet making no sound on the wooden *banquette*. It gained the safety of a doorway that smelled of sweat and urine, and looked up.

There was light in the second-story window of an shabby old hotel across Gallatin Street—a flickering light, like flames.

He is there. And he is waiting for me, even if he does not know it. And then we shall begin.

SEVERIN VERLAC TURNED away from lighting the last of the long beeswax tapers and turned to the window. The wooden shutters rattled faintly as he opened them, and he looked out over the Crescent City. A fog was coming up off the Mississippi, encouraged by the night. The moon's light made the fog an almost tangible thing.

A living ghost in the pale moonlight.

Almost . . . almost I could believe I were not in New Orleans, but in Paris. In la belle Paris with la très belle Liane . . . But he was not in Paris with Liane, and never would be again. Liane was dead for all time.

His Liane, whose only crime had been a desire to visit her beloved New Orleans, city of her birth. And his crime had been that he had arrogantly, thoughtlessly, permitted her to travel here without him. So Liane had been trapped in New Orleans alone when war had been declared, and the city blockaded by the Union's navy. And then General Butler had come, and then Butler's infamous Order 28 . . .

"... *it is ordered hereafter when any female shall, by word, gesture, or movement, insult or show contempt for any officer or soldier of the United States, she shall be regarded and held liable to be treated as a woman of the town plying her vocation.*"

Order 28 had outraged public opinion across the world. Severin could imagine how it had outraged Liane; how it had inflamed the volatile mixture of pure Creole and royal Africa that flowed through her veins. He *knew* what had happened: proud Liane had been arrested, locked up for the night in a jail cell with slatterns and prostitutes.

Arrested on a complaint from one called Vulmaro. Arrested for a night and released by day, thrown out into the street, helpless under the lethal sun—

Severin's hand clenched on the shutter; wood splintered under his fingers. Surprised, he looked at the shattered wood and then brushed splinters from his hand before turning away, back to the tawdry room now lit by clusters of candles in heavy, ornate candletrees. The candlelight mellowed the room, gentled it, allowed it the illusion of being again what it once had been: beautiful, serene . . .

Illusion, Severin thought. *I deal in illusion.*

His gaze turned to the table. Resting on it, in solitary splendor, was a single ruby-and-silver chalice. Candlelight coaxed faint red sparks from the lining and gilded the ornately chased silver cameos on the sides. The cup stood alone on the bare table, stark as memory. Liane had given him that cup the night he had changed her, offered the silver chalice up to him filled with her own sweet hot blood . . .

Severin walked over to the table, ran a finger lightly along the rim of the cup. *Soon. Vulmaro will come, tonight or tomorrow . . . He cannot afford to delay, with Butler falling out of favor. Vulmaro must be growing . . . impatient.*

Severin had planned his campaign with the most exquisite of care; planted his hints, his clues, his trail, with the most exquisite skill. Vulmaro would take the bait, swallow its poison whole. *Yes, he will come. He has no choice.*

Severin Verlac smiled.

HER NAME WAS Cendrine—at least it was now, and what she had once been called now concerned her rather less than her master's lightest whim. She pulled the red skirts of her strumpet's gown away from a patch of dark mud as she watched the ancient hotel.

M'sieur Vulmaro wants this one. And he means to have him. He has hunted him as hard this past year he hunts the Devil—No!

She would not think of what else her lord and master hunted. It was too dangerous.

Just as it was too dangerous to think of herself, and what she had been before Vulmaro had stolen her away from the Ursuline Convent. Stolen her because he had heard rumors of her Gift, and desired its power for his own use . . .

And now he has what he desired. The thought was flat and cold as ice. Vulmaro had trained her well, and now she was nothing. Only Vulmaro's creature. Forever.

Forever doomed to a world of corruption and evil; of power thrown as carelessly as a child tosses a ball. Once there had been hope—a faint candle in eternal dark—that Vulmaro's ambitions could be stopped. The Voodoun knew what Vulmaro was, and what he tried to do. And they had tried to stop him . . .

Fires in the darkness, and voices raised in chanting, raising power for the Light—and then screams, as soldiers poured into the waterfront alley and the whole world shuddered before exploding in rage and fire. Vulmaro had known, warned by something she dared not guess at, and now those who would stop him burned. She had closed her eyes, only to endure the fire with other senses, a fire glowing upon the black water and swirling up into the black night, burning her inside and out . . .

Burning her forever. Forever . . . .

Cendrine shook her head clear of memory, still looking up at the lighted window of the hotel. These thoughts wouldn't help now. What mattered was that Vulmaro had won. Vulmaro was firmly in his Dark Master's power. Damned to burn forever.

As she was damned.

Once Vulmaro had hunted her; she had been easy prey, soft and certain in her piety. Now she was neither soft nor pious, and Vulmaro used her to hunt Severin Verlac, loosed his chained huntress to seek this new quarry, to mark and hold for her master's pleasure. *But I seek a pleasure too, and it is not true that in the dark, all cats are gray . . .*

A late, unwary pedestrian passed by, his feet making sucking sounds in the glabrous mud. He smoked a cigar; it glowed, a small fire, in the uneasy darkness of Gallatin Street.

In the shadows, Cendrine waited, her eyes gleaming, ready to do whatever she must to reach her goal. But she was unnoticed in the darkness, and so the cigar-smoker passed by, unmolested. Once he turned the corner into Hospital Street, Cendrine walked, cat-dainty, across the reeking mud of Gallatin Street and into the hotel.

SEVERIN VERLAC WATCHED the door, other-than-human senses alert. He felt a tension in the air, like the oppression before a storm.

There was a faint grating sound as someone tried the door, and a startled pause as the intruder discovered the door had not been locked. The door swung inward, and Severin stepped forward to greet his guest, only to pause, faintly surprised, when he saw the young woman standing in the doorway. Then he smiled, for he knew who and what she was—and what she once had been. Verlac planned carefully for his hunts.

The woman stepped inside, and pushed the door shut behind her.

"M'sieur Vulmaro will see you tomorrow," she said flatly. "I will see you tonight."

Severin raised one eyebrow, amused by the fragile-looking creature's presumption. He took a step toward the door, but she did not seem to notice any implied threat.

"Don't try to leave, Severin Verlac. I advise against it."

"I would not dream of abandoning such a charming companion," he said, with only the faintest trace of irony. "But you seem to know my name, mademoiselle, while I am in ignorance of yours."

"You may call me Cendrine." There was an odd hesitancy to her voice; Severin permitted his interest to be aroused.

"Cendrine." *So he renamed you for ashes and servitude, little nun,* Verlac thought, and smiled, remembering the true ending to that fairy tale. Aloud, he said, "A lovely name for a lovely lady. Will you take some refreshment?"

"If it pleases you. I have come to talk to you."

"And I remain to listen. Of course." Severin smiled, and bowed over her cool pale hand.

CENDRINE WATCHED HIM as he busied himself in a cabinet by the side of the cold, disused fireplace.

Count Severin Verlac did not appear to her inner sight.

For as long as memory served her, Cendrine had depended on that extra sense. Everything appeared to her in it—everything living—an endless cosmic dance, endlessly informative, linking her with Creation in a holy bond that told her not only what was, but hinted at what might be as well. It was her Gift.

It was what had driven Vulmaro to take her, to corrupt her; to enslave her God-given Gift for his own use.

But Verlac was *not*. When she closed her eyes, she *knew* she was alone in the room—more alone than she would have been had he been a dead man, or a zombie. It was a terribly disorienting thing to know that Severin Verlac was there—to see him and hear him, to feel the air currents he disturbed brushing against her skin, and to *know* that he was not there at all.

"He takes the forms of the night . . . he does not die . . . and they say he can control men's souls . . ."

Two of Vulmaro's Servants had died to bring Vulmaro that information. Another had died so that Cendrine might know it.

Verlac came toward her, carrying two goblets. They were of black glass, or stone, and the ruby cameo he wore on his left hand glinted against that backdrop like a splash of blood.

"Some wine, Mademoiselle Cendrine?"

She took the cup, set it down on the table untasted. It stood in the shadow of the red-and-silver chalice like a silent promise.

"What sort of creature are you, Verlac?"

SEVERIN VERLAC SET his goblet down on the mantle over the cold fireplace and walked toward her. He stopped, rather too close to her, and did not reply. When he did, at last, it was as if an invisible spun-glass web had shattered.

"Creature? That hardly seems kind, mademoiselle." He stepped back slightly. "Won't you sit down?" He gestured toward a chair beside the hearth.

With an opaque look, Cendrine walked away, careful to come no nearer to him, and seated herself on the indicated chair. Dust rolled up from the cushion, and the color of her gown mocked the brocade with the color it once had been. Severin retrieved her goblet from the shadow of the red-and-silver one and brought it to her.

"You have forgotten your wine," he said. She took the cup from his fingers with every appearance of ease, unable to avoid touching his fingers as she did so.

"It would be a pity to waste it. It is French, blockade-run. That is rare, these days."

"Stop playing games, Verlac," Cendrine snapped.

"Games are for children and fools. I do not play games," Severin corrected her, equally sharp. Their eyes locked—Severin standing, at his ease, by the mantlepiece; Cendrine sitting, engulfed by the chair. Her eyes dropped first.

"And which do you account Vulmaro?" she asked in a low voice. "I am sorry, M'sieur; you are right. This is no time for games." She paused, summoning her strength, before adding, "I must speak with you, and we have little time."

"Indeed? And why is that?" Severin sipped from his goblet.

"I told you," she repeated with deadly patience. "Vulmaro will come for you tomorrow. He has been hunting for you."

Severin noted the faint furrow between her brows, the unease in her posture. "Perhaps you would be so good as to tell me why?" Severin asked her, nearly innocent. "And why *you* have favored me with your—admittedly decorative—presence?"

He set his cup down again, deliberately moving out of her range of vision.

CENDRINE TURNED TO follow him with her eyes—unwilling to watch him, unwilling to look away. When she looked away, Severin Verlac wasn't *there*. An unnerving opponent, neither alive nor dead. Uneasy, she began to wonder who was the true quarry in this night's hunt.

"If you must waste my time," she began, choosing words of deliberate rudeness, "then know that M'sieur Vulmaro has hunted you for nearly a year. Why? He has heard—rumors—that you possess powers . . . that he might find it convenient to use. And so he has trapped you here."

"Trapped?" Severin's smile broadened, openly mocking. He walked to the center of the room, displaying himself. He spread his hands in a disarming gesture at open variance with his tone and words.

"No one uses me, mademoiselle."

"The port is sealed, the city is under curfew, and Union soldiers patrol the streets." For a moment, she seemed uncertain what to do with her wine cup, then set it carefully on the floor beside her chair. "Unless you can turn to mist, M'sieur Verlac, I would say you are trapped."

" 'Trapped,' mademoiselle, implies that one wishes to flee."

She rose to her feet quickly, clenching her fists. She did not dare turn away from the spectral figure of the Count. He had stepped away from the light the candles threw upon the table as he spoke, and seemed to blend into the dark shadows of the ancient room.

If I cannot see him with my eyes, will he be there at all . . . ?

She walked toward the table, toward him, her heels hitting deliberately hard on the floor to make some sound, give some definition to the room.

"Then you expect to serve M'sieur Vulmaro?" she asked him, and strained all her senses to hear his answer.

"No." Severin walked into the light again. Cendrine stepped back involuntarily, fingers skating across the dull wood of the table as her hands fought to become claws.

"You will have no choice," she told him. "He gives no one a choice."

"And that is why you are here?" Severin was lazily amused. "To give me a choice, mademoiselle?"

"You do not know what serving M'sieur Vulmaro means."

"I have told you, I do not intend to serve him."

Cendrine had been watching Verlac's hands, rather than his face—now she looked up, in bitter humor, and saw that his eyes were red—wine-red, red as human blood. She clamped her teeth hard in her lower lip, and Verlac looked away.

"To be . . . *of* service to him, yes . . . that I will be," Severin murmured, walking past her to the chair she had abandoned. "Out of . . . simple . . . kindness . . . ." His words came slower and slower, and Cendrine felt herself being drawn in; coils of forgetfulness winding around her like time. Then Severin again deliberately broke the mood he was weaving. He shrugged and reached down for the cup she had spurned; she desperately tried to recall the thread of the conversation. She did not think of leaving. She would never know, on her journey back through the streets of the *Vieux Carré*, if Severin Verlac followed her or not.

She did not want to think about that. And Verlac was dangerous; far more dangerous than her master dreamed. Far more dangerous than she had dared to dream . . . .

"If you expect to 'be of service' to Vulmaro," Cendrine said as Severin straightened, "then you *do* have the . . . powers you have been rumored to—to possess."

"Those being?" he asked, holding her cup in both hands and caressing it absently. She watched his hands, unable to dismiss the thought that the most important truth in the room was that Severin held the cup he had given her, and that soon—sometime—soon he would come over and return it to her . . . and this time she would accept the cup from his hands . . . .

"That you are . . . unkillable. That you can . . . change your form, that you . . . ."

"He owns men—he does—he takes them, and they become his slaves."

"Control men's souls?" Severin said. Cendrine's hands twitched against the surface of the table. "And women's too, I suppose . . . . Flamboyant, but true enough."

"And the rest?" Cendrine asked huskily, her mouth suddenly dry.

"Also true. I am surprised my powers were so accurately reported."

"And what . . . reward do you expect for 'being of service' to M'sieur Vulmaro? And why lead him such a chase?"

"I will offer my . . . unique abilities to your *soi-disant* master out of . . . love. Kindness. Compassion, if you will. As for leading him on—" Here Count Verlac shrugged. "Surely he would not value me so much if I simply—came to him?"

No, he would not. Vulmaro desired, always, what he should not even wish for. Goaded past patience by the long pursuit, demanding Verlac's powers for his own, Vulmaro would not wonder about Severin Verlac's motives. So she had been right: this had been Severin's game, Severin's hunt, all along.

Severin's trap.

And she had no way to read him; no way to see truly into his mind and heart. Severin could say anything to her, and she must take him at his word.

"He will not trust you to act in his service."

Severin smiled. "He need not. These powers will be his."

"I told you no one uses me, Cendrine."

She backed away from him, feeling that she could not breathe, that she was drowning. One of the chairs by the table got in her way; she edged around it and held to it, clutching it tightly for strength. M'sieur Vulmaro would own the powers of Severin Verlac—unkillable; older than the night—and with those powers, Vulmaro would build upon the world's bones a universe held in soul-thrall to his will alone.

She saw this end for him and could not face it. An eternity for him, damned beyond any possible redemption, as Vulmaro hunted and grasped and sacrificed all and everything to raw brute power, until there was nothing in all the world save what he permitted to exist. No God, no Devil; nothing but Vulmaro for all eternity . . .

"No," she whispered.

"No?" Severin purred. "But you must admit, mademoiselle, that Vulmaro would find such powers useful."

"No," Cendrine said again. "You can't. You must not; you don't know what he—"

"I know I own M'sieur Vulmaro a . . . great debt. As, I think, do you, mademoiselle. And debts must be paid, must they not?" Severin Verlac smiled, a curl of lip that revealed nothing.

Suddenly memories long ago locked away flooded her mind. *Chaste silence in the company of holy women. The exultation of perfect obedience. Smooth stone beneath her knees. Light falling brilliant through stained glass, painting the Virgin's serene face with rainbows* . . .

"Mademoiselle?" Verlac's voice shattered the images, ripped her back to the shabby room in Gallatin Street. "Yes, I think you too owe our M'sieur Vulmaro a great deal. Now, my child, I have told you that *I* will not serve him. So how is he to possess this boon I offer in payment?"

Verlac smiled again, another meaningless curve of mouth. "You do not answer, mademoiselle? Well, I shall reveal the mystery, and ask a question: Shall I initiate him, or . . . someone in his service?"

The wood of the chair creaked as her fingers tightened on it. She opened her mouth to speak, but the words would not come.

"Still no answer? An easy choice, I would have thought. Especially for you, little . . . sister." Suddenly Verlac's voice was soft, kind. Compassionate . . . .

She struggled against unfamiliar tears; struggled for speech. "And then—and then—"

"And then," Severin said, speaking for her, "I would leave, naturally, having no further business in New Orleans. I am not dependent on the goodwill of either Confederacy or Union. If I should choose not to be found, I would not be. Especially by our dear M'sieur Vulmaro."

She let go of the chair with one hand, half-gestured as though to speak.

"You have my word on that, of course," he added quietly.

She looked up into his face for a moment, dropped her eyes, and let go of the chair with her other hand, stepping away.

Severin looked down at the cup in his hands.

"*Ma chère,* you seem to have misplaced your wine cup again. Allow me to restore it to you." Smiling, Severin stepped forward.

She did not try to stay him as he came toward her. She did not run. He offered her the cup, and she took it in both hands, holding it tightly for fear of dropping it. She did not think she was afraid of what he would do to her. He had promised to leave without seeing Vulmaro, and if he broke that word, she vowed she would find some way to destroy Vulmaro and Verlac both.

Severin touched her bare shoulder, and the cup in her hands shattered.

HE TOOK BOTH her hands in his, quickly, seeking to see if she had damaged herself. She stood docilely, seeming stunned by the sharp shattering of crystal. Finding her whole, he held her hands between his palms. His fingers, long and cool, circled her wrists and toyed with the pulse-points there.

Severin looked down at his new-chosen bride, raising her fingers to his lips to kiss the wine stains from them. Her eyes were veiled, as though she weren't really there with him, and he felt a faint spark of anger.

"I had no idea I frightened you so, Cendrine," he said gently.

"No . . ." She tried to pull her hands free and instead stepped closer to him. "It's only that . . . I cannot 'see' you."

"Then I do not appear to these powers of yours at all?" he asked, interested. He took both her hands into one of his own and slid his free hand, palm flat, along her arm toward her neck.

"Being with you is like . . . being alone," she said. She ducked her head, trying to pull free again and failing. "Do—what you have to, but stop—this."

" 'This' is part of what I must do," Severin told her, tracing the line of her jaw with his thumb while his fingers stroked the back of her neck. "You must not fear it. When I have initiated you, a whole new range of perception will open to you. You will be able to sense me, to know me. You will be mine, Cendrine. Mine without fear. Without force."

He pulled her closer, releasing his grip on her hands and clasping his fingers lightly around the column of her throat. "Mine by choice . . . ."

Her eyes closed, lashes fluttering on her cheeks. He raised his hands to cup her neck and her head went back. The skin of her throat and jaw made an exquisite contrast to the vivid scarlet of her low-necked gown; the garish color made her skin look paler, as pale as though she were fleshed from moonlight. Severin pulled the combs from her hair and her braids came tumbling down in a shining serpentine mass. She shivered, clenching her fists in the velvet edging his coat.

Severin deliberated, looking down at her. He did not want a victim unwilling, or one who came to him out of duty to another. He leaned down, brushing his lips against the side of her throat, feeling the blood hammer in the vein that pulsed there. He could see, almost, the blood coursing through the veins that lay, blue and perfect, just beneath her skin.

He pulled himself away from that hypnotic contemplation with an effort. She stirred, a protest to this interruption forming on her lips.

"Cendrine—look at me," he commanded. Slowly her eyes opened. He saw his own, red sparks, reflected in their dilated depths.

"Do you ask this of me?"

She looked at him. Her eyes seemed to focus, and at last he was certain she was seeing *him*.

"Yes," she breathed, "you are Death."

"No," Severin corrected her, "I am the resurrection and the life."

Suddenly Cendrine smiled, reaching up to him.

"Then come to me, my lord," she said, and drew him down to her.

The candles guttered and went out.

VULMARO ENTERED THE room like a Fury. The blue-clad soldiers who were his escort found reasons not to be near him, and the sharp-faced man in the plumed hat, Vulmaro's aide, followed him into the room at a nervous distance.

They had summoned Vulmaro as soon as the patrol had found her.

Cendrine lay on the rough wooden table as though she had fallen asleep there. Her hair was unbound, trailing off the table like a fall of black water, and her hands were clasped loosely around a cup. Two racks of candles burned, nearly whole, at the head and foot of the table. The soldiers had brought in torches whose light flared the room into stark reality, fading the flickering candle-flames into pale ghosts. Her scarlet whore's gown was the only color; lurid and accusing.

Vulmaro looked around, all motion stilled. The room was a ruin, but it had been a ruin for a very long time. There had been no struggle, no disturbance of its artifacts. He reached out with his hard-won power and found nothing—no trace of any presence save Cendrine's. Her aura dwindled and faded obscurely. She had not left. She had died here.

Three quick strides brought him to the edge of the table. He looked down at her body, reached out a hand toward it, then drew back.

"How long?" he demanded of the nearest soldier. The man looked up, swallowed nervously.

"They found her this morning, sir."

Vulmaro turned away. He saw his aide trying to look inconspicuous. "Captain."

The man started; froze. Vulmaro stepped toward him, speaking in a voice of deceptive gentleness.

"Where is Severin Verlac?"

His aide looked at him beseechingly, frightened doglike eyes ill-placed in his sharp-cut raptor's face. "I—sir—we have patrols searching—"

Vulmaro's fist clenched on the captain's neck. The captain choked, skin mottling, veins bulging in neck and face. He pawed at Vulmaro's arm, the gesture a mockery of supplication. The touch angered Vulmaro; he opened his hand and the man, released, staggered back.

"Find him," Vulmaro suggested mildly. He turned away, and the captain drew a sobbing breath.

Vulmaro returned to the table. He reached out to the corpse, taking it up by the shoulders and drawing it to him. Its head lolled limply on its shoulders; inanimate.

He turned, raising the body in his arms. It swept one of the candle-trees from the table with it, and Vulmaro's boot ground the wax tapers underfoot.

"Find Severin Verlac!" Vulmaro shouted, and flung the Cendrine's body savagely at the hearth. It struck the bricks with a dull thud and slid into the cold fireplace, a slack shattered jumble of red and white.

No one dared say anything at all as Vulmaro turned and stalked from the room.

✝

Part the Second: 1863

The Spanish-built Cabildo still functioned quite efficiently as a prison. Vulmaro knew this well, now. He had been inside the Cabildo precisely one month today.

The moon is full again, he thought irrelevantly, watching the faintly golden disc break free of New Orleans's rooftops. The view offered the illusion of freedom, but it was only that.

Vulmaro turned his back on the outside world and walked into his suite. A fire burned in the grate, warming a room nearly indistinguishable from the best the St. Charles Hotel could boast. Even a prison offered a variety of accommodations to its clientele; Vulmaro could afford to pay for the best.

For fires and furniture and books and meals brought to him daily from Antoine's. For his own clothes, opulent irrelevancies of an aristocrat of leisure.

For the illusion of the life that was no longer his.

With the recall of Butler, Vulmaro had fallen from eminence. Without little Cendrine and her occult powers, Vulmaro had found himself oddly vulnerable. He had relied too long upon others to do what he should have done himself; he realized that now, accepted it. Once he was free, he would remedy it. But for now, he waited in the Cabildo. Waited for judgment.

He turned away from the fire, no longer diverted by its lies, and returned to the barred window. The moon hung almost white against the darkening sky, and the first faint stars appeared, competing with the city's lights for primacy in the heavens.

Behind him, his room filled with shadows.

"M'SIEUR VULMARO?"

He heard the words behind him and spun around, startled. He had heard nothing, sensed nothing. He looked in the direction of the voice, but none of his senses, mundane or occult, could detect any presence but his own. He advanced, wary.

"I have found you," Cendrine said, "I have found you at last, Monseigneur." She stepped forward, into the firelight, the long black gown she wore a rustling shadow among shadows. Funeral robes, rich and formal. He had buried her in that gown a month ago, when the moon had last been full.

Vulmaro backed away a step, breath escaping in a startled hiss. She stopped, tilting her head in an achingly familiar gesture. The fire shadowed her black gown red, painted flames on her midnight hair, struck sparks from the golden cross lying on her breast. A phantom in flames. A phoenix.

"You buried me," Cendrine told him.

"You were dead," Vulmaro he reminded her, then, irritated by his own words, turned away from her unreal image. Dead; this must be only her ghost. Ghosts had no power over him. It was *he* who held power, *he* who controlled. He would not let her—not let *it*—unsettle him.

"No!" she protested. "I wasn't dead! I was only . . . I wasn't dead!"

There was no answer. Ignoring her, Vulmaro watched the moon.

CENDRINE STARED AT the indifferent back of the man who had torn her life into ruin. With hesitant steps, she padded over to him. He did not move, though he must hear her. She reached out to him.

"Vulmaro . . . please?" Her fingers sunk into the deep velvet of his dressing gown.

She felt his muscles tense, but did not expect the blow that knocked her sprawling. She rolled to her knees, glaring up at him through the dark curtain of her hair.

"You should not have done that," she told him. Her eyes flared red.

"You are . . . *real*," Vulmaro said in slow disbelief.

Cendrine got to her feet. "As real as Severin Verlac."

Vulmaro's arms fell to his sides. He reached out a hand to her and let it drop. Cendrine folded her hands before her waist and regarded him as primly as the nun she had once been.

"I found him," she said. "I went to him. That night—I could not let you have him, what he offered—"

"He killed you. I saw your body."

She frowned, impatient. "I am—not dead. I am—like him. And I can free you now—it took me so long to find you, but it will be all right now. Now you will be free of your sins, poor man."

"Why do you call me that?" Vulmaro demanded, hand making a reflexive gesture, as if groping for a weapon.

Her eyes followed the gesture, flicking from his hand back to his face. She smiled, smoothing the black gown against her hips, moving forward.

16

"Is it not my right? Am I not your chattel—and you, my lord and . . . master?" She stumbled slightly over the last word and licked her lips, never taking her eyes from his rigid face. "I am free now. Come, I can free you too." She held out her arms to him.

"No." The flat denial stopped her, the knifelike gesture that accompanied the word cutting through the space between them like a sword of light. She bit her lower lip, puzzled, not quite understanding.

"But—"

"I do not know what Severin Verlac has done to you, but I do not propose to share in its folly. After I am free of this prison I shall—"

"*No.*" She lashed the skirt of her burial gown around her like folded wings. Vulmaro regarded her with interest and irritation.

"Whatever else you are, you are still mine. You will do as you are told," he said flatly.

Her chin went up; she glared at him with a look that was red ice.

"No. Not now. Not any—" She broke off, manner changing. "Please, M'sieur Vulmaro," she began again, "you don't understa—"

He summoned power then, reached for her with a whiplash of energy that belled the curtains veiling the barred window and sent the burning logs spilling out over the andirons. She felt the force brush her; a pale echo of what she expected, unable to check or harm. Truth at last; the truth that set her free.

Her master was completely powerless against her.

THE WOLFEN FORM struck him high in the chest, bowling him over. Its gleaming fangs skated over bone, sank deep into flesh and velvet. It jerked its head sideways and glared triumphantly down at Vulmaro with scraps of crimson velvet and bloody linen hanging from its dripping jaws.

He knocked the beast back, baffled when his strength failed to hurl the creature against the opposite wall. Ghostly in the smoke and firelight, the wolf gathered itself and lunged again, growling, this time shoving its nose up under his throat with a horrid gobbling sound. Redsilver pain shot through Vulmaro as beast-jaws closed on his throat and wrenched sideways. He felt his life pumping away in hot bitter gouts.

17

Small hands touched his brow, tracing a symbol upon his forehead in his own dying blood. Then consciousness fled with breath and life's blood.

CENDRINE KNELT ON Vulmaro's chest and stared at the cross she had drawn with his blood. Blood; a roomful of it. Blood dripped down her face, clotted her hair, turned the bodice of her mourning gown slick and viscid. Blood starred the Persian carpet, dark counterpoint to the coals of fire flaming out from the hearth.

She pressed slippery scarlet hands to Vulmaro's cooling cheeks, staring down at the body in horrified fascination. With trembling fingers she touched the ruined flesh of its neck, then raised her fingers to her lips and licked them.

He's dead. He's dead and he won't rise. He's dead and I killed him.

The door to the room burst open. Cendrine turned, leaping to her feet, to face two men in blue uniforms; they held guns in their hands. Smoke from the smoldering carpet coiled up around them—she knew they couldn't see her clearly. Yet.

An honor guard. An honor guard to see him to hell. Her lips drew back in a snarl.

The carpet burst into flames.

No, Cendrine!

She hesitated, turned, and ran.

SEVERIN VERLAC STOOD at the gate to Jackson Square and watched the Cabildo. The moon was well-risen now; moonlight painted the city below in shades of turquoise and indigo, transformed gaudy New Orleans into a somber city of ghosts and shadows.

Severin was waiting.

He had gone to her tomb in Saint Louis Cemetery twice—too soon and too late. The second time he had returned to the elaborate basalt memorial, she was already gone. He had tracked her, after his own fashion, as she hunted the one who had owned her in life—just as he followed the news of Vulmaro's disgrace and imprisonment once Butler had been recalled, and another military governor of lesser cupidity installed over rebellious New Orleans.

Payment, M'sieur Vulmaro. Payment in full. And payment for her own debts, as well.

Vulmaro knew now, if knowledge there was after true death, what it meant to lay hands on things that were Severin Verlac's.

There was a flicker of movement across the square. A wolfen form flashed into view, the moonlight painting its fur pale silver as it bolted from the Cabildo at top speed. Long ago, and for a brief time tonight, it had been a girl called Cendrine.

She had done well. Alone and without help, she had sought Vulmaro and found him, learning to live and survive in her new form as she did so, proving her . . . worthiness. And she had returned to Vulmaro, as a dutiful servant must, to offer him one last service before rejoicing in her freedom.

Severin smiled. The mark of a man is in those he can bind to his service. And there is more in that binding than the ties of duty and convention. There is honor.

You destroyed yourself, Vulmaro. I had very little to do with it.

Drawing his cloak around him, Severin waited for the wolf to reach the spot where he stood.

CENDRINE LOPED ACROSS the moonlit plaza, her pace slower now. Her non-human senses brought her the scents and rhythms of the night. The night was her home and her protection; she had no fear of any attack the children of men might make upon her.

She reached the statue of Andrew Jackson and stopped in its shadow to shape-shift, the pain at what she had done already less sharp. Vulmaro was dead. And she was . . . not-dead. And her responsibility to God and his wishes was ended with this final lesson she had given him. She sat up and shook her hair back, stretching. Now she was alone. Alone . . . She tossed her head again, uneasy, not certain she liked the idea. Vague comprehension of the length of the existence before her pressed in on her. She twined her hand in her hair, shaking it free. All of eternity.

Alone.

"Cendrine."

She looked up and saw him. The moon silvered his dark hair, frosted the fur trimming his cloak. She could feel his presence, more real and vital than anything else, and for such knowing the vanishment of her secret gift seemed a small price to pay.

He held out his hand to her, signet ring black in the moonlight. "Come with me," he invited.

She stood and walked to him, knowing she had a choice, that she went to Severin freely, and of her own desire.

"My lord," she said, taking his hand.

Severin swept his cape around them both and they were gone.

✝

Coda

The two Union soldiers who had gone to Vulmaro's prison-room agreed there was no point in worrying the Provost with crazy stories about wolves and women clad in black. They didn't know what they'd seen; the smoke, the fire, must have confused them. They were perfectly clear on that point, when questioned.

They were not questioned hard. It was perfectly clear that the notorious Vulmaro, dealer in devils and murder—and worse, in the eyes of the Orleannais, collaborator with General Butler—had crowned a lifetime's evil with the mortal sin of self-destruction.

After the hasty inquest, his mutilated body was hastily buried in unhallowed ground, and left to rot.

"AND FRIENDS TO RESTORE US AGAIN"

JENNIFER STEVENSON

ALWAYS FELT IT WAS SIMPLY TERRIBLE THE WAY HE DROVE THAT MOTORCYCLE so fast, it was bound to cause an accident." Elva trailed off with the voice of the very old and feeble, though she was only sixty-five.

Maxine bit her lip. 'He' had been Toussant, Maxine's younger son, and Elva had forgotten who she was talking to again. Elva would feel really bad if she realized. But she wouldn't realize.

Elva breathed heavily over the phone. "You still there, daughter?"

She swallowed. "It's Maxine, Elva. You getting good eats there?"

"Maxine! How nice to hear from you! The kids take me out for lunch now and then, thank you. Tell Bobby I don't get any decent shrimp out here. All bitsy tasteless things like pink rubber. I miss Kettle's boil."

Bobby was dead too, gone five years now. "I miss *you*, Elva," Maxine said through the lump in her throat.

"I miss you too, Maxine." Elva's voice failed and sank to a thread. "I wish you were here. Without you or anybody I know, I'm just going invisible. Don't even know myself. I need familiar faces. Someone to bring me back. That song, you know, that old Chris Caswell song—"

Maxine closed her eyes. Not that song.

"Home, home, wherever you roam," Elva quavered, "though night and storm come between us, home, home, morning will come—"

"—And friends to restore us again."

Together they drew a long, shaky breath. Elva said, "Call again. I'll try to be more lively." Maxine heard shame in her friend's voice. Maybe she'd remembered after all, realized how Maxine must feel. "That was an awful thing. Bobby dying so young."

Maxine said with difficulty, "I love you, Elva."

"Love you, too," said the faint voice. There came a clatter and the click of the line going dead.

Maxine hung up the phone and wiped her eyes carefully on the underside of her apron. Her mascara made black smudges on it. She wiped her hands, patted her cheeks, and sailed into the dining room, flipping her checkpad open as she went.

"Arny, whatcha having?"

Arnaud didn't need a menu. "Just the boil. I finished the book, Maxine."

"Didja now?" she congratulated him. "Hold your horses, I got to finish up with these folks." She hustled over to number three by the window, a nice looking couple. They paid and left a good tip. She smiled them out the door. Then she headed back to Arnaud's table and put her fanny down.

"Okay, tell me." Arnaud would be crazy, but at least he wouldn't be Elva's kind of crazy. Her throat still felt tight.

"Really finished?"

"Yep. Sent it off to Swamp Gas Press this morning. Five hunderd and fifty pages of raw truth."

Maxine smiled. "You nervous?"

"Gawd yes." Arnaud worked his skinny neck. She'd known him and his two sisters for years. The sisters were not floating so far off the ground as Arny. They had told her that their parents tortured them all, but Arny particularly, and because he loved their parents best he had made up this crazy story to cover it up: his great work, the account of his childhood abduction by space aliens. The sisters got factory jobs when they were only sixteen and escaped their daddy's hickory stick. They hated their parents with a clean, pure, sane fire. They didn't even bother to pity Arny anymore. They were jealous. His delusion had brought him a balm they couldn't have. He stayed loyal to his folks, who rewarded him with whatever twisted affection was still theirs to give, plus a roof over his head.

If only Maxine knew who she ought to hate, or where her anger and fear lawfully belonged.

Besides, it wasn't fear or hate or anger she felt. Oh, no.

She felt a rush of heat in her heart, spreading down into her panties and up into her head, making her dizzy with a sense of *being loved*. Whoever you are out there, I love you, she thought.

This again. Couldn't be change of life, she'd done that already. Seemed like she walked around all the time now with the heat in her heart, feeling foolish, just as she had felt thirty years ago when she was so in love with Bobby that it seemed the whole world must see it. Everyone must have seen and thought how indecent it was for her to wear that naked face of love out in public. It reminded her, too, of the way she felt when she was pregnant the first time, working her first year in this old greasy spoon, her big belly proclaiming not only her waiting condition but the condition of love that had got her into it. She'd lived on Kettle's gumbo and the boil in those days, they were so poor. A wonder the kids hadn't come out with claws.

Arnaud came in twice a week for shrimp boil. His mutant memory seemed to throw off new wrinkles every day. Maxine never let on that she noticed.

Kettle rang the bell. "Arny's boil is up. Maxine, you gonna marry him? You gettin' prettier and prettier."

She scowled at the cook, who was also the owner and founder of Kettle's. His grin and the whites of his eyes showed through the long, low, narrow window into the kitchen.

"Talk sense," she gruffed. "Little twit loses another marble every day."

She brought Arny his shrimp and sat with him while he peeled them and ate, laying the herb-gummy shells on the newspaper. Why he ever wanted to grow that stringy old beard, she thought, not listening to him but remembering what a pretty child he had been.

She thought about how that boy had grown to become this sorry creature, eaten up by his folks' meanness and his own terrible love for them. To live at all, he had to let them do it.

And that loyalty made him stupider every day. Like a baby that's born knowing the language of God and yet forgets by making room in its head for the human speech it needs to survive. She watched Arny's hands carry shrimp to his little red mouth. Frankly she couldn't stand the smell of the stuff sometimes. His jaw worked steadily, turning shrimp into Arny.

Bobby used to tell stories about shrimps to the kids. Swore they was all true. He ought to know, wasn't he a shrimp fisherman, and didn't he know all their secrets? On and on he would yarn about their graceful cotillions in the warm fresh waters of the bayous, all their legs waving and eyestalks coyly twined together. And down came Daddy's nets, dragging them off in their millions to Momma's boil down at Kettle's. How he'd talk. *How you talk, Bobby.* She swallowed.

She watched the shrimp go down Arny's hatch, boiled, pink, and legless. A shame to destroy the thingness of the food, which had life and beauty of its own after all. But we must eat, mustn't we? Would never do to let it stay shrimp once it's down there in the belly. No, it's got to forget shrimp cotillions and start believing in Arny.

"Piece of peach pie with that?" she said.

"Sure."

She got up while Arny was about the personal business of sorting shrimp shells out of his beard. She took the pie out of the cake display case and cut it. "An instant on the lips, forever on the hips," she said, putting it in front of him. She wiped the knife and put the pie back into the case. The shrimp forgot their dances. Did the peaches remember the tree? She stared idly at the tower of plexiglas, its sides scratched and milky, bearing revolving shelves of impossibly perfect, beautiful cakes and pies. The shelves inside turned and turned. The inside light glistened on glazed strawberries and the black richness of the chocolate cake, like flesh made edible. She ought to feel hungry. She'd been missing meals.

Arny dug into his pie. Apparently he was through talking about his book for today. He said eagerly, "How about this granny killer? I hear he got another one last night."

Maxine made a face. "Now, Arny, I don't want to hear about it. That sensational crap." *Now he's off again.*

"They say he talks to 'em and then he *scares* 'em to death somehow. At first they thought it was bitin' their tongues out 'at did it."

"Hush!" Mouth set, Maxine got up.

Arnaud's face turned toward her, spilling the juicy stuff in spite of her anger. "Now the cops think they all died of heart failure," he called back to her as she left the booth.

"I'll get your coffee," she said firmly, and stumped away.

Still she brought Arnaud his cup, and if she set it down with more of a smack than usual, she also left more cream and refreshed the sugar bowl. The world was getting worse and worse to live in. No sense losing more of your friends than you must. She felt a rush of fondness for Arny even as she hurried away from his table lest he start up again with his litany of horrors.

"Need anything, Kettle?" she said through the narrow window.

"Cut me s'more okra." The bowl came up on the ledge, with a cutting board and knife. Maxine got to work. Kettle's nappy white head came and went on the other side of the window. "Tell you something about the philosophy of gumbo."

"What." She could use some of Kettle's philosophy. Take the taste of Arny out of her mouth.

"Why they's bay leaf in it."

"I haven't the faintest," she said absently, trimming and slicing okra one pod at a time.

"Your bay is your laurel leaf, see." Kettle's knife whacked steadily in the kitchen, cutting corn-on-the-cob into sections.

"Crown of heroes and fallen kings. It's for glory, and also forgetfulness, 'acause glory is fleeting."

Forgetfulness. Maxine almost cut herself on the paring knife. Again she heard Elva's voice fading, fading over the phone. She put the knife down, rubbing her trembling hands together in her lap.

"*Mi abuela,* she used to say the bay and the shrimp was put together for a reason," Kettle continued. "To make us forget the past and live for the present. Your bay is most efficacious in the presence of shrimp, she used to say. Gets rid of tragesangre and the fly by nights, 'specially when you adds garlic."

"How—how's that?" Carefully she went back to her trimming and slicing.

"Oooh, well, your tragesangre is eaten up inside with little bugs. They didn't have penicillin in those days, you know. He eat the leaf of the laurel, your bay leaf, along with your shrimps, and them little bugs fall asleep and he forget all about coming into your house at night. Forget everything but your goood cooking. Then he grow old and die like the rest of us."

"It is good," she said, remembering her first taste of Kettle's shrimp boil, smiling into Bobby's eyes. The taste of bay leaf was as strong as wine that day. *Caught them shrimp myself. Best in the bayous. Go on. Eat up, pretty lady.* Long time ago. She couldn't remember the last time she'd really tasted it. Flavors were going on her, along with colors, faces, and names.

"You don't eat so much of it these days," Kettle remarked. He didn't sound offended. He peeked through the window again. "Slimming. Gettin' younger every day, Maxine."

"I got to powder my nose," Maxine said abruptly. She slid the bowl of cut okra onto the ledge and laid the knife and board beside it.

In the Ladies, she pressed unnaturally cold hands against her closed eyes, trying to remember what Bobby used to say about Kettle's philosophies and Arny's funny stories. So funny. So strong and faithful and loving, and so funny, he always made a joke of the past so it didn't hurt. She'd lost them all—Sukey to drugs, Bobby Junior in the war, Toussant in the motorcycle accident. And then Bobby himself.

Now Elva. That one hurt almost worst of all. Elva had been her buddy since the wedding, thirty-five years ago, and they'd kept each other sane through some mighty interesting times. She'd lost her Raymond the year before Bobby died. Then she'd begun to get forgetful, then wandering, and then the doctor had said Alzheimer's, and her kids came and took her away to Chicago where they could look after her. Maxine was appalled at the swift change in her friend's condition.

The feeling came to her again that her life was fading away from under her before she was ready. She was only fifty-nine. This shouldn't be happening to her yet. She shouldn't feel that all the meaning was leaking out of it. *The world is turning into an awful place.* Now somebody was killing old women on Jackson Avenue, as if the ordinary and personal shit weren't enough.

She had to face it, something was wrong. Her appetite was failing. She didn't sleep well any more. On top of it all was that feeling she got, like today, like a yoyo reaction to all the grief and loss and fear, that someone out there loved her deeply and was calling to her. Someone close enough to whisper in her mind's ear, silently, sweetly, truthfully, *I love you, I love you, are you out there somewhere, I love you.* At night she dreamed over and over of climbing a stair, or running through a woods, or jumping out of a tree house, or swimming madly across a drowned quarry. Toward something. Toward someone. *I love you.* A growing sense of love and peace and arrival. Even in the daytime now she suffered an occasional feeling that some bubble deep in her deepest waters was rising with a light or a jewel in it, toward the surface of her mind.

The woman in the mirror stared blindly at her. She did look younger. She felt younger. Her whole body shouted like a teenager's; hell, even Arny was looking good to her. She was fifty-nine, a widow, and her hair had been streaked with white when Bobby Junior died seven years ago. The woman in the mirror looked smooth. Her hair was black as a crow's wing.

Am I going to die soon? she wondered. Am I going blind, or just losing my mind? Is it like this for Elva?

While she stood there with her hand pressed unthinking to the starched lacy bosom of her apron, the feeling came again. Warmth, relief, a feeling like getting a good hard hug from someone she loved. *Is that you, Bobby?* she wondered, as often before. No answer. It was as if the sun were poking its fingers right through the building, through walls and all, touching her heart with one loving finger.

She stood like that, forgetful, until Kettle came and knocked on the Ladies' room door.

LATE IN THE night Maxine drowsed as she looked through her old photo album. Bobby smiled out at her, his arms around the kids. *Don't get distracted.* She was looking for a particular snapshot, one she had told Bobby was of herself at age thirteen. It was a lie, she remembered now. The snapshot wasn't of her. She'd found it in the street. It was one of a dozen lies she'd told him that first year when she was so in love and she didn't want him to question her past. While she worked, awake, fuddled with loneliness and pain, she forgot they were lies: the flyspeck town near Bowser City where she'd grown up and everybody who knew her had been wiped out by a flood, the school records burnt with the school, the burglary at the Y that had taken everything but her purse and the clothes she stood up in that day. That magic day she walked past Kettle's and saw him through the window, shoveling gumbo into his grin. The day she fell in love. That day she remembered clear enough. But the stories she had told, mostly gabbled out that very day while he grinned at her across the table, they'd stopped feeling like lies. Over the years she'd begun to believe them herself. They had pushed aside the truth she worked so hard to hide, pushed it clean out of her head. And now they were fading. She dropped off to sleep with a sense of double loss. No lies left, and nothing to put in their place, either. In her dreams, she paged through the album looking for familiar scenes. Who were these people? Why so many empty pages?

27

"Maxine, I don't know what to tell you. Do you want the tests or don't you?"

She wrung her hands. "Lordy, Doc, I just don't know. What if it is Alzheimer's? What good would it do me to know?"

He pressed his lips together. "You got family here?"

"Not any more. You know that, Doc." She swallowed, tears blinding her. "Buried 'em all."

"You're mighty young to get Alzheimer's," he said. "You look better than last time I saw you. Are you finally getting some exercise like I suggested?"

Blinking, she said, "Ain't there some kind of memory drugs? Help you, help you *keep* it?"

He took her brown hands in his clean old pink ones. He was the one who had tried to save Toussant. He had stood by her while Bobby wheezed his last in the oxygen tent. "Keep what, Maxine?" he said gently.

But she couldn't speak. The feelings, she thought. The color and taste of the past. It's all fading, like cotton candy on my tongue.

There is treasure buried in you. You have to find it! Please try! Try to find it! he hissed. The old woman only stared wildly, pressing her hand to her mouth. Come, kiss me, he begged. He took her in his arms. She didn't struggle but she didn't give in. Kiss me. He bit her cheek, her lip, her tongue. Blood filled his mouth. Her heart fluttered against his breast, tripped, paused, cracked. By then he knew that she was the wrong one again.

Night fell on Jackson Avenue. Maxine lay in her too-wide bed, sinking eagerly toward the darkest part of sleep, listening for the voice of love. Just as the last ferry hooted out on the water and the first fishing boat hooted back, she heard it. *Beloved.* She sighed and rolled into the empty gully in the mattress on Bobby's side of the bed.

You again. They walked the west levee along Lake Pontchartrain, like other lovers. *It won't be long. Just a little while,* she pleaded, she begged. *They don't last. They can't, poor things. Will you wait for me?* A surf of invisible sunlight rushed through her, into him and back, making her heart thunder. *You'll forget me,* he said. *You'll remind me,* she said.

28

"LIKE COTTON CANDY. Like a dream, Hermana."

"That's bad." Hermana Rosa seemed to force every word out, as if her magic could escape through her mouth if she didn't keep it shut.

"I know you got some kind of herbs. Something. For memory," Maxine said, prodding with the cautious urgency of a woman trying to get a spider out of her sink. She had never asked a four-eye for help before. The old lady had gumbo on the stove. Maxine could smell the bay leaf. She put her handkerchief to her lips.

Hermana Rosa looked her up and down. Without moving, she seemed to withdraw all over. *She knows*, Maxine thought, her bones filling with cold lead. *I've got something horrible and she knows and she can't help and she's not even gonna tell me.*

Hermana Rosa's lips worked. "Which?"

"Which what?" Maxine gasped.

Impatiently, angrily, as if Maxine should not be forcing her to speak so many words, the old four-eye pronounced, "Do you want to remember, or to forget?"

Maxine stared. Fright was paralyzing her. Distractedly she said, "I don't know. I don't know." She picked up her handbag and waded through her fear to the door. The old lady said nothing, not even when she walked out without paying, shutting the door behind her.

MAXINE WAS UNSURPRISED to find the granny killer in her kitchen. He stood up from her chair and came toward her, wearing black and holding his hands out like a priest greeting the parishioners one at a time. "My dear," he said, just like a priest.

"Oh." The sun burst in her heart, showering her body with joy. "Oh."

He took her by the hands and led her under the light fixture, reached up, pulled the chain. Maxine stared round-eyed into his face. He stared back. He put his hand to her chin, tilting her face to the light this way and that. "It is you," he breathed. "Poor love. Did you think I had forgotten?"

Her mouth gaped open and shut like a fish's. "Oh." She trembled. "Oh." The past became the present, the lies forgotten became truth remembered, and she sighed with relief to be in his company again.

"You're not as old as I expected," he said tenderly, brushing a tear off her cheek. "I looked everywhere. They were all so old."

"I quit—I quit eating gumbo a while ago. Oh, where have you *been*? I've been going crackers!"

He took her in his arms and put his mouth on hers. *Oh finally*. He bit her lip, her tongue, and she bit his. Blood filled their mouths. She remembered, remembered.

When they had drunk their fill of one another he pulled his head back to look in her eyes. "Was it worth it? Your shrimp fisherman?"

She fingered the hair on the back of his neck, smiling into his face with half-shut eyes. It was like smiling into the sun. "I guess so." There would be no more hunger now. They had before them an eternity of comfort and trust. Permanent love, which once she had lost but now had found. Every breath tasted of it, as if the air were full of fiery love liquor. Her body heated from the heart outward. "It fades on you. Like a dream. Like cotton candy."

He smiled back. "Wouldn't know. I never touch the stuff."

✝

THE BLACK OPAL CROSS

Jennara Wenk

>─┼─❬>─❭─○─❬>─❬─┼─❬

THE CROSS WAS SET WITH BLACK OPALS, LUMINOUS DARK FIRES imprisoned in rich worked gold. A ruby hung pendant from the bottom of the opal cross. The ruby had come over the seas, from faraway India; the image of Kali-Mata, the Drinker-of-Blood, was carved into the stone's crimson depths. Perhaps the ruby had once belonged to a princess, or a priestess. Now the precious stone hung from the black opal cross, vice bound to virtue, and it belonged to a young and virtuous lady. But youth is a transient thing.

And virtue lies in the heart of the beholder.

TO PLEASE HER family, she had married a very desirable *parti* in 1867, the year that she was seventeen and he was thirty-four. A perfect match, family and friends had murmured. The groom twice the bride's age; a man of property and maturity to support and guide the giddy young girl's life.

The restrictions of Reconstruction did not prevent the wedding from being a delightful affair. Everyone said the wedding had been delightful; in her snow-white satin and swathings of lace and illusion, the bride had more resembled a fairy princess than a mortal girl, and the groom had been quite respectably somber and solicitous. After the ceremony in St. Louis Cathedral, the young bride most piously and properly sent her bouquet of pure white roses to lie upon her mother's marble tomb in St. Louis Cemetery. Then, with a sinking heart, she went upstairs to change into her going-away dress. For in defiance of Creole custom, which dictated that a newly-wed couple spend a week in romantic seclusion, her new husband was taking her North to honeymoon in New York. He had business interests there, he said. And she would like to shop on the Ladies' Mile, and see the sights. She did not contradict this assertion; already she had learned it was far better not to argue with him.

About anything.

IN MANY WAYS, she possessed the ideal husband, or so she was told. And she dutifully agreed that he was sober, respectable, and reasonably generous with her pocket-money. And that he was considerate; marital duty was demanded of her only thrice a week, and the act did not occupy much time. There was no reason for her eyes to dull and her mouth to droop—

"You read too many novels," her husband said. "Put that blasted book down and go out for a walk. It'll do you good. And don't forget to take your maid this time! I have my position to think of, you know."

Obedient, she laid down her book and silently went to take a walk. She did not, particularly, desire to go for a walk, for the day was sultry; the heavy hot air still and dead.

But she had even less desire to contradict her husband. And a walk would take her away from him, and from that house, with his blessing. So she walked the Quarter's banquettes at a sober, proper pace, and tried to forget that sooner or later even the longest healthful walk must end back at her husband's door.

IN 1880 SHE was thirty years old and had been married for thirteen years. These two occasions coinciding, her husband took her to dine at Antoine's and presented her with a *carte blanche* to Dulaine's so that she might select her own gift—

"More sensible that way; get just what you like and send the bill to me. Within reason, mind," he added, for his generosity had diminished somewhat as the years passed. However, he rarely criticized her for failing to present him with living pledges of her affection.

She thanked him, politely, and agreed that she would, of course, be moderate in her desires.

As always.

BUT DESIRE CANNOT always be regulated like a clockwork toy. Thirty is a dangerous age for a woman, and thirteen is a chancy number for anyone.

And suddenly wakened passion is a force far more powerful than habit. Moderation, in the face of it, has no chance at all.

THE CROSS LAY waiting upon a pale bed of velvet as rich and thick as country cream.

"Russian gold, madam," the attentive clerk assured her, "and black opals from

Australia. The ruby is Indian, I believe—would madam care to see?" Without awaiting an answer, he reached into the glass case and lifted out the velvet pad. "Please, madam—indulge yourself."

As if mesmerized, she reached out and slowly gathered the archaic cross into her hand. The gold was cool; the opals sleek as oiled silk. She held it up and light poured through the ruby drop. The gem was red as heart's blood, and within its crimson depths a strange figure seemed to dance in fire—

"There is some Hindu god or other carved into the ruby, madam. An intaglio piece, you see—fine work, very fine. If you will allow me—" The clerk reached for the cross, prepared to display the piece to its most saleable advantage.

"No." She drew back, her fingers closing over the glowing ruby. The jewel seemed to warm under her touch, throb to some unheard rhythm. After a moment she knew that the rhythm was the beating of her heart. She opened her fingers and stared down at the black fire of the opals and the deep sullen extravagance of the ruby and knew she could not leave them.

No matter what the price.

Without looking away from the ruby, she asked, "This is not a new piece. Why is it here? Who could bear to part with it?"

"Well, madam, you know how it is— " As if suddenly deciding that perhaps madam did not, in fact, know how it was, he stopped and began again. "The former owner spoke of casting bread upon the waters." The clerk ventured upon a tactful curve of his lips; a customer's wit, however small, must be appreciated.

When she only stared at him, he swiftly added, "And was quite anxious that the piece should only go to one who—who would appreciate its true nature." These last words were said almost by rote, as if memorized but not understood. Then, brightening, "But perhaps madam would prefer to see something less—unusual?"

"No," she said. "I will have this. You need not wrap it—I wish to wear it now." Reluctant to release it, she set the cross down while she untied the thin black velvet band she wore around her neck. She unpinned the bunch of white silk violets from the velvet and slipped the cross onto the ribbon. A moment later she had retied the velvet ribbon around her slender throat, and the black opal cross settled upon her prim fawn-colored basque. Below the cross the ruby rested patiently.

And within the ruby, Kali danced.

HER HUSBAND WAS not pleased; she had not expected that he would be. The black opal cross was a precious item, very costly. By no stretch of imagination could it be considered within reason. And, as he pointed out with great restraint, the ornament was far too extravagant in other ways. "It's too—" he struggled for the proper word to express his criticism; found it and flung it before her. "Flamboyant. Yes, it's far too flamboyant. You don't want people to think we're one of those *nouveau* families, now do you, my dear?"

She stood there with her head bowed, accepting his judgment, but her hand cradled the cross at the base of her throat. The ruby shifted against her palm, a smooth caress of gem against skin.

"It's something an—an *American* would wear," he added. "Not a Creole lady. And certainly not my wife."

There was silence between them for a moment. She sensed that he wished to order her to return the cross to Dulaine's, or never to wear it. But he could not, quite, square either order with his limited sense of fair play. He settled for muttering, "It's too gaudy, far too gaudy; trust a woman to choose the worst and most expensive."

She took this as permission to keep the black opal cross, and after that she wore it daily. But never openly. The cross and its ruby drop lay hidden beneath her modest bodices. And beneath the chaste concealment of muslin, of taffeta, of silk, the crimson jewel warmed to her skin, tuning its rhythms to the steady beat of her waiting heart.

WITH HER MARRIAGE, she had put away childish things, including hopes and dreams. But now she dreamed again, by night; lurid illusions of sensual delights from which she woke languid and ravenous, remembering nothing of the dream. On other nights the dancing goddess called her into the ruby's fires, urging her to shed her dying skin and dance until the world was forgotten; dance within the fire until the end of time.

She woke from these dreams limp and exhausted, her skin flushed and her eyes fever-bright. Her maid exclaimed over her, and wished to call the doctor, but she refused to have him come to poke and pry and press laudanum upon her. Mornings after did not matter; nights of extravagant dreams were worth the price they exacted.

HER DREAMS HAD begun when the moon was dark; the night the moon rose full she could not sleep. She closed her eyes, but no dreams came to her. At last she gave up the effort and lay restless in her soft bed until she could bear it no longer. Night was torment without the solace of her new dreams.

Sighing, she rose, and in the darkness pulled on the muslin-and-lace peignoir that matched her nightgown and tied the blue ribbons in neat bows at the neck and waist. Then she lit her bedside candle. The hands of painted china clock showed midnight. The candle's light showed a stranger standing by her window. The stranger's body blended into the shadows of the window's heavy velvet curtains. The stranger's eyes burned ruby fire.

"I thought you would wake tonight." The stranger moved forward, towards her, and the single candle flame painted shadowfire over starlight skin and hair the midnight gold of a hunter's moon.

She was not afraid, nor surprised. This seemed inevitable; foretold. "Who are you?"

"Don't you know?" Her visitor held up a moon-pale hand, dangled the black opal cross from its velvet ribbon. "You chose to summon me, after all. I'm glad it was you; I think we'll get on."

"Why?" The single word conveyed infinities of meaning. Why her? Why now? Why come and wake her at all?

"I'm—lonely. Yes. Eternity is a very long time . . . " The vampire seemed to drift across the floor towards her; perhaps footsteps were simply muted by the thick-woven carpet. Suddenly she was looking into eyes that shimmered dark rainbow fire, mirroring the opals on the cross.

"You know what it is to be alone. That is why you called to me."

She began to protest, to swear she had not; the lie caught in her throat.

"Or perhaps it was I who called to you." The cross was swept high, to glitter in the uncertain light. "No matter. We are together now. Will you take back my jewel, now that you know it is my gift?"

The burning ruby hung between them; she stared past the dancing goddess into the vampire's hungry eyes. Prudence told her to refuse, to turn her back on this outrage to sanity and decency. Prudence spoke in her husband's voice.

"Come to me," the vampire said in a voice that sang of loss and longing, and at the sound thirteen years of crystalline perfection shattered and fell away.

Shuddering away the remnants of her defenses, she held out her hands, and waited. Smiling, the vampire slowly lowered the opal cross into her outstretched hands, wound the velvet ribbon around her slender wrist. She closed her fingers over the cross, and closed her eyes as cool fingers traced the winding ribbon banding her wrist.

The seeking fingers paused over her pulse, drew across the blue line of the vein. "You have a strong heart, little one."

"I have had need of it." Within the knot of her fingers the ruby throbbed hot, as if she held a glowing coal within her grasp. Sudden impatience seized her and she twisted her arm to clutch at the other's hand. "It is late; past midnight. Soon it will be dawn. What are you waiting for?"

The vampire smiled, and now elegant, elongated teeth gleamed against reddened lips. "Nothing, my love. Nothing at all."

NIGHT BY NIGHT she grew stronger, more luminous, as if the vampire drew out poisons with her living blood. In those dark hours she learned to revel in passions she had not known she held prisoned within her. And in her lover's gentle arms she learned to take as well as to give.

But she could not be drained of her blood, no matter how delicious the sensation, or she would die. And she had no desire to die now that she had begun to live. She explained this most carefully, and her vampire lover laughed and kissed her white throat above the black velvet band that held the opal cross.

"Oh, my dearest love—there are other joys than those of the body. I will teach you these as well."

And so through the quiet night hours she learned the joy of speaking freely, without necessity weighting her words. The joy of discussing books, and music, and art, as an equal. The contentment of shared silences.

The sheer intoxicating pleasure of friendship.

BUT NOW SHE saw past the cage bars to the freedom that danced elusively beyond. The illusion of liberty no longer sufficed. One October night she tried to put her longings into words, and discovered she had only tears to offer.

"Hush." Her lover bent over her to kiss away the salt tears that streaked her face.

"You are an autumn child; you should not be melancholy."

"But autumn *is* melancholy; it is the dying season."

"Autumn is the promise. The nights grow long and the wind blows strong from the north." A low laugh, rich and seductive as the swirl of leaves on autumn wind. "And the hunter's moon ripens, and gives way to the bright, bright stars. It is time for you to come into the night with me, beloved. These walls need not keep you captive. Have faith. Trust me."

The vampire's moon-white hand was held out to her, waiting with timeless patience for her answer.

She put out her hand almost blindly, and felt slender fingers curl strongly about her own. Something flowed between them, a cool promise of dark comfort settled over her like thick velvet. A pressure on her hand urged her onward; resisting, she touched the opal cross, traced the ruby's oval warmth. *Come into the night . . .*

Come—or be bound forever within these tidy prison walls. *Have faith*— She chose, and leaned forward to kiss her choice upon blood-bright lips—a lover's pledge before she followed through the open window into the wild night beyond.

THEY HAD ONLY the darkness from midnight until dawn. That time was safe for them both. Sometimes during the day she longed for more; the sight, the sound, the touch of the beloved. A hint that their shared world was no fairy tale, no delusion to vanish silently away, leaving her forever bereft.

But she could possess few such moments, and cherished them when they came. Flowers came for her: golden roses; pansies like soft purple velvet; white violets tied with a silver ribbon. Books came too, white cardboard parcels tied with pink ribbon as if they were boxes of chocolates. But these candy-boxes contained novels she had never heard of, brought her works of history and philosophy and poetry. The books she read avidly, stretching her mind to the task, so that she too might fly free upon the wings of ideas and the enchantment of words.

Her husband noted the floral tributes without comment, and of the books said only that reading was a waste of time for a woman. "You'll give yourself brain fever and ruin your eyes and your looks. Go put on something nice; I'm taking you to the theatre."

THAT NIGHT THE Theatre d'Orleans presented a melodrama; a hoary old piece from the antebellum days when cotton was King and the South a land of dueling cavaliers and fainting belles. A vampire stalked an innocent maiden. The vampire was all mindless menace; the maiden mindless chastity. With a suitable half-smile curving her lips, she watched the gaudy stage with sightless eyes, and thought of her own blood-lover, a creature of feral elegance and cultivated charm. An undying wonder whose mind shone bright as winter stars.

At play's end, she applauded, polite little pats of one kid-gloved hand upon the other. Then she rose and allowed her husband to steer her through the theatre lobby toward the waiting carriage. He stepped aside to allow her to step up into the padded interior. She set her foot upon the iron step, and then her breath caught in her throat and her heart beat sudden savage delight. Beyond the crush of people leaving the Theatre d'Orleans, a shape emerged from the blackness of a building's shadow.

She knew it as she knew her own body; totally, without the hesitation of thought. Black velvet cloaked the watcher, shrouding the face and figure from strangers' eyes. But beneath the gaslight was a flash of moon-pale skin against the blackness, and a glimmer of hunter's moon hair.

"Come, my dear, get into the carriage. Ladies should avert their eyes from such creatures."

Docile, she permitted him to hand her into the waiting carriage. As she settled the constricting mass of her skirt, she glanced across the street once more. The figure stood there still, shadow among shadows. Only the eyes moved; burned fire to match the gem lying crimson upon her white skin. She touched the ruby talisman and wondered what her husband saw when he looked upon her beloved.

She wondered what he was meant to see.

"YOU SEEM CHANGED, my dear. You look—different." Her husband frowned at her over the expanse of white linen that separated them; they dined formally, even when alone. When she did not answer, he set down his fork. "I must ask you—have your feelings for me altered in any way?"

She bowed her head, lowering her eyes modestly. "My feelings for you have not changed."

"I think they have." With great deliberation, he took up his glass of red wine and drank. Then he set it down again, too hard; the dark wine splashed onto the linen cloth, blotching its whiteness with garnet roses. "It is not easy to say this, my dear, but I have heard rumors that your behavior is less than exemplary."

Her head came up; she pressed her hand to the cross hidden beneath the frothing lace of her chaste collar. "Rumors?"

He would not meet her eyes. "And while I hesitate to pay heed to servant's gossip—I beg you to remember Caesar's stricture to his wife. However virtuous you *are*, you must also *seem* so."

Servant's gossip—those dark nights of bright passion, endless revelation; had they been overheard? And if they had—what business had a servant outside her bedroom door at midnight?

The ruby's pulse sent a searing flash of inspiration; she knew. One of the maids, one of the two handsome parlor-maids, slithering down the back stairway to serve the master's lust. The considerate master, who did not wish to inflict that lust upon his wife, who was, after all, a delicate highborn lady who required the same care and consideration from him as a china doll . . .

"Yes," she said, "I see." She saw, clear-eyed, that no matter what the parlor-maid had told the master, he would say nothing more. He would simply expect his wife's dutiful compliance, expect her to conform once more to domestic virtue so that he might retain his outward dignity intact in the world's fickle eyes.

"To ensure that no one can say a word against you, I have decided that from now on, we shall share a bedroom. Have your maid move your things tomorrow."

Ice crept slowly through her blood until she sat frozen, unable to respond. Across the length of the table, her husband finally lifted his eyes to watch her. When she neither moved nor spoke, he picked up his wine glass once more. "Good. Good. I knew you'd be sensible, my dear. Now we'll not speak of it again." And looking into the winter chill of her eyes, he raised the wine glass to his lips.

This time he drank in great unmannerly gulps, as if eager to hasten its soothing warmth into his veins. Wine slipped from his mouth and trickled down his chin to stain his collar dying rose. She watched the slow progression of the red liquid down his neck, and then lowered her eyes to stare at her plate once more.

"I am tired," she said after he set down his empty glass. "If you will excuse me, I will go up to my bed."

"Of course, my dear," he said, and his voice was a little too forced, too eager for her to be gone.

She smiled, a tight controlled curve of her lips, and went upstairs to spend her last night in sanctuary.

SHE LOCKED THE bedroom door behind her, and kissed the precious key. One last night—

Slow-moving, as if she dreamed, she crossed the room to unlock her window and open it to the night. Still in the silence of dreams, she turned down the gaslights and lit the candle waiting beside her bed. Carrying the candle, she drifted over to sit before her vanity table. There she set the candle before the mirror, and laid the key to her bedroom door beside her silver-backed hairbrush. After a moment she unbuttoned her bodice and folded back the collar until her face was framed by lace and the black opal cross was revealed against her skin. Bending her head, she reached behind to untie the velvet band, and held the jewel up to catch the candle's light.

The candle flame kindled the fires sleeping within the ruby's depths; if she stared into them long enough, the throb of her heart became the beat of drums, and the little goddess carved within the ancient gem began to dance.

And as the goddess danced, the woman called to her beloved with the strength of silent despair.

And was answered.

NO SOUND BUT a whisper on the air, and a reflection appeared behind hers; a starlight form that shimmered, shifted, as if she saw it through running water rather than on silvered glass. A slender moon-white hand lifted to stroke her hair. "You are sad, my love; you weep. Why?"

She turned into the comforting arms. "You came. Oh, you came to me—"

"You called me, and so I am here. We are blood kin now, you and I. Now smile for me; sorrow does not suit you, my autumn girl."

She clung to her vampire love with arms strengthened by despair. "I shall die; I cannot bear it when we are apart. Every day is torment to me now."

"You know the day is not for me." A kiss, lips tracing lips. "But we own the nights. When you mourn the day, remember the night to come."

"No—" Reluctantly, she pushed herself away. "You must listen. My husband has become suspicious, he thinks I have taken a human lover. At dinner tonight he told me—told me—"

"Hush, there is no need for tears. Come into my arms and I will kiss them away, and you will tell me what this toad who calls himself your husband told you."

She crept into the comforting arms, sighed against cool skin. "That I must sleep in his bedroom now. With him. *Every night.* I won't; I can't; I shall die—"

"Of course you shall, but not for many happy years, my love. Now kiss me, and stop worrying. You do not belong to him—"

"—I belong to you."

Firm hands stroked back her hair, gentle fingers brushed away her tears. "No. You are my dearest love, but you belong only to yourself. Certainly you do not belong to that soulless man."

"But he—"

"Hush. Do not worry, my love. I will visit him, and I do not think he will last long." A laugh, low and sure in the shadowed dark. "No, not long. Soon your husband will be no barrier between us."

She reached out and touched skin smooth as moonstone. "Do you promise? I cannot live without you."

A pale hand caressed her throat, traced over the velvet ribbon to the black opal cross. "I swear it. On this, I swear." Moonsilk hair slid over her skin as her lover bent to kiss the pendant ruby; lips moved from the gemstone to her skin, pressed against the pulse of her throat.

"Oh, yes," she whispered, burying her hands in hair soft as night. "Yes." And then there were no more words, or thoughts, only the brief cold pain and then pleasure soaring through her like hot wine in winter.

THE MIDNIGHT PROMISE was kept; gradually her husband paled, and then became too weak to leave his house. Later, he could not leave his bed, and soon after that, he died—peacefully, in his sleep, his puzzled doctor told the new widow.

"He did not suffer, ma'am—you have only to look at his face to know that. Never have I seen such Christian submission to the Lord's will." The doctor assumed a properly respectful expression in the face of sorrow and stood aside to let her pass into her husband's room.

The doctor was twice right; her husband was dead, and his sightless eyes seemed to stare past her into bliss unimaginable. Dead, he was smaller, shrunken. She looked at him for a long time, trying to remember why she once had feared him so.

But that memory was fading swiftly; soon, like him, it would be gone. She lifted her hand to touch the ruby hanging from her opal cross.

"Thank you doctor," she said with all the gravity the occasion demanded. "You are quite right. He seems almost to have welcomed what came for him."

"You're a brave woman," the doctor told her, and offered to take a message to the undertaker's, as that establishment was only a few steps from his surgery.

Bowing her head, she accepted this offer, and thanked him again before she pressed her lace-edged handkerchief to her trembling mouth. It would not do at all for the doctor to see her smile.

A FEW DAYS later she stood beside his family's tomb in St. Louis Cemetery and watched as the black lacquered coffin was carried inside, to the waiting darkness. Gone. He was gone.

And she was free. The ruby hidden beneath the sober black of her widow's mourning pulsed ecstatic knowledge through her blood. *Free*—

The men carrying the coffin paused just before the tomb's door; a discreet cough from the priest hinted that there was something she must do, an action she must take. Drawing a deep breath that lifted her bosom against the confines of her raven-hued bodice, she took a step forward. "Goodbye," she said, and opened her black-gloved hand. Two red roses dropped onto the polished coffin. Bowing her head she stepped back again, suddenly thankful for the mourning veil that masked her face. For a new-made widow must observe the strictest propriety. Certainly she must not, under any circumstances, display to the critical world a countenance glowing with the radiance of purest joy.

TOO MANY PEOPLE accompanied her back to her house to console her; too many people wished to aid her mourning. She was patient with them, and no one knew how fiercely she longed for them to be gone, or how passionately she desired nightfall. She sat with her hands folded on her black skirt like resting doves, and murmured the proper responses, and waited away time with the concentration of a hunting cat.

Afternoon, twilight, evening.

Night, and blessed solitude.

The house was empty at last—save for the servants, who did not count—and so at last she was free. With a sigh of delight, she bade the butler lock the house against the night—

"And any of the servants who wish it may have tomorrow as a holiday. I shall not want anything, and I do not wish to be disturbed."

The butler bowed and began his nightly task of checking each door and window. Bowing her head slightly, she gathered up her skirt and began to climb the stairs to her solitary bedroom.

SHE CAREFULLY LOCKED her bedroom door behind her before going to a window. Before she could look out into the summer night she had to fling back three layers of curtains to reach the closed window: dark blue velvet, pale blue silk, ivory lace.

The moon was rising full over the Crescent City, soaring over the rooftops like a monstrous pearl, laving slates and spires with glowing light. The night was an enchanted country.

Turning away from the window, she glanced at the china clock upon her vanity table. Late, growing later; it was time. Without hesitation, she moved to stand in the center of her bedroom. For a heartbeat she wrapped her fingers tight around the black cross, felt a faint rhythm pulse deep within the ruby's fire. Then she put her hands to the collar of her mourning gown and slowly undid the fifty jet buttons fastening her basque.

She pulled off the basque and let it drop to the thick-carpeted floor, then unhooked the swaying skirt. The skirt fell away in a rustle of stiff bombazine, pooling like black water at her feet. Then bustle and petticoats; corset cover and the stiff armor of the corset itself; garments peeled from her as if she were a snake shedding dead skin.

She bent to unbutton her black kid boots. The buttons slid easily through the holes, the shoes slid easily from her slender feet. Her hands moved up her legs; her garters fell away in a flash of silver buckles. Only the black cotton stockings remained. She put her hands on the stocking-tops and peeled the heavy stockings down her legs, balanced first on one foot, then the other, to yank them off. The stockings joined the rest of her clothing in the tumbled heap on the floor around her.

Now she stood as she never had before: naked to the air. The only thing she still wore was the black opal cross on its black velvet ribbon band. Below the cross the Kali ruby lay red as blood on her white skin. Ancient feelings uncoiled within her, wanton and libertine. Sinful.

Sin was the night air drifting cool promise over her white skin. Sin was anticipation and hope of fulfillment at last.

Sin tasted sweeter than any honey upon her tongue. She shuddered with delight and lifted her hands slowly to her tightly pinned hair.

She pulled each jet pin out slowly, lingering over the motion; savoring the gradual release as her freed hair began to slide loose and tumble down over her shoulders. More of the cruel pins dropped to the floor, and more, and her hair suddenly fell in a swathe of silken warmth down her back. She ran her fingers through her wild hair, letting the strands drift about her like dying leaves.

Motion caught her eye; she half-turned and saw that it was only the mimic of her reflection in the looking-glass. Reflection of a stranger: a naked woman clad only in a black cross and her flowing hair.

A woman waiting for her demon lover.

She touched the tip of one finger to the blood red gemstone below her throat and watched as the woman in the looking-glass mirrored the action. *Beloved*, she thought, *I am free at last. And I am waiting for you. Only for you, forever.*

Moving with the deliberate grace of a fastidious cat, she went from light to light, turning down the gaslight, blowing out the candle beside the bed. When the only illumination was the moonlight through the windows, she crossed to the wide casement that looked out over the roofs of New Orleans and threw back the bolt that locked out the night. Suddenly reckless, she flung the window open, heedless of whom might see; the night wind caught at her hair and made soft tendrils dance upon the midnight air.

Her fingers stroked the black opal cross, caressed the ruby hanging below it.

Now they would be together forever, and no man would ever again have the power to rend them asunder.

Forever . . . Smiling, she leaned out into the full moon's light and called to her beloved. Only a whisper on the moonsilver night, but she knew the words would be heard and heeded.

"Come to me, my love. Come to me, Carmilla."

Then she waited, with a smile on her lips and the night-call glowing in her eyes. Below the black opal cross Kali's ruby pulsed black fire, a beacon in the moonlit darkness.

And its eternal promise shone as bright as blood.

✝

A BRIEF JOURNEY

BILLIE SUE MOSIMAN

I KNEW NOTHING OF MY CONDITION UNTIL MOTHER WOKE ME ON THE morning after my adventure and the light scalded my skin and nearly blinded me forever. I remember groaning, first feeling the pain in my lower throat where I'd been bitten, and then opening my eyes just a little and seeing the horror of the light. My skin steamed, as if I'd been set into a cauldron of boiling water over a high fire, and with my new-found extended senses, I could hear the minute seams and cracks running zigzag lines down my exposed arms.

I screamed out abruptly, and with such pain that I frightened my mother. She leapt back from the bedside and began to shake, muttering, "What is wrong, Pepita? What is wrong with you?"

I turned my head from the agony of the light streaming through the open windows and crawled to the edge of the bed, scrambling to the floor on hands and knees. I scuttled like a centipede from the room into the dim hall to huddle in shadow, wrapping my arms around my knees. I could feel the new wounds on my arms begin to instantly heal, could hear them mending, could smell my mother's breath tainted with fresh bread where she stood rooted to the spot in my room. The commingled scents caused me to retch, but nothing came up. I wanted to die, but I knew I couldn't. I wouldn't. Not now.

It was only then that I knew what I was, had become, would continue to be, forever.

The night before, against house rules, and despite my parents' admonitions that I *must not* climb down the magnolia tree near my bedroom window again to leave the room, I ventured forth into the starry midnight. The plantation slaves told me that I was a disobedient girl and that catastrophe would befall me if I did not change my ways and listen to my parents. But something in the dark lured me. I could not sleep, tossing and turning in my softly rustling sheets, my sweaty face washed with moonlight, my mind tortured with a passion to be out of the house and beneath the stars. I stood under the wide umbrella of the magnolia, shivering in my nightclothes, barefoot, wondering what manner of evil overtook my faculties night after night this way. What did it want, this voice calling in my head, dominating my thoughts? What was I to do for it? I was but a girl, twelve years old. What good was I to this powerful thing that called to me out of the darkness? Why didn't it possess my parents instead. They were wealthy and smart and had the years to deal with its biding.

I sped across the dew-damp grassy lawn to the closest servant quarters where my maidservant slept with her husband, who was our livery man, and her children, who worked the cotton and ran errands for my mother. I dared not knock and wake them all. Instead, I clambered over the open sill and slid my feet along the dirt floor in order not to step on a sleeping child. I found the corn-husk mattress in the corner and felt for Samay's hand. "Please," I whispered. "Help me, Samay!"

She rose up and clutched at my hand, dragging me into her arms. She was a slight woman and smelled of warm milk and the hide of cows. Besides her duties as my personal servant, she attended to the milking before sundown, lugging the large buckets of milk to our house where she poured it into crocks and the big churn for the kitchen servants.

"Pepita, why are you here?" She stood from the bed and picked me up into her strong arms to carry me out the door into the night so that our talking would not disturb her family.

"Samay, something calls to me to come out. It . . . it wants me. I'm afraid."

She turned her head, looking around at the barns, the livery and horse stalls, the main house, the kitchen set separate and behind the house. "Who calls you?"

"I don't know his name, but he tells me I must come. I think he must be the devil! I can't help myself, Samay. If I don't do as he says, he swoops into my window and . . . and . . ."

"What? What does he do to you, Pepita?" There was urgency and fear in her voice now.

"He . . . tastes me."

Samay sucked in her breath and stooped so that she could look me in the face. "How does he do this? What do you mean he 'swoops' into your room?"

"He sort of glides in, on the air. I am paralyzed and cannot move or make a sound. He takes blood. From here." I leaned my head to the side and showed her the marks. I'd had to hide them beneath my collars for a week now. I had been too afraid to tell my mother about the devil. She had sent away my Great Uncle into the heart of the city to a place for people sick in their minds when he began to spit on the floors and look from the corners of his eyes.

Samay moved close in the darkness and inspected the marks on my neck. Then she said a prayer in the language of the Arcadians and stepped away from me as if I might have a plague. "It is the Destroyer," she said. "He's come here to take us all."

She turned then and sprinted for her quarters. Startled, I ran after her. She alerted her household and suddenly there was a lantern and the children crying.

"Samay! Help me, please, help me."

"You go away," she said, cringing from my touch. "You are the Destroyer's disciple and no one can save you now."

Tears sprang to my eyes to be so betrayed by one who had cuddled me as a baby, bathed and dressed me, sang me to sleep in the evenings. I ran from the room, crying, heartbroken, now truly alone. And I ran right into his waiting arms as I rushed around the side of the barn for the fields. He lifted me up and crooned to me that the time had come for me to join him. His eyes were coal fire, his breath stinking of the grave.

I struggled but a little until his mind overtook mine and I lay limp in his arms, offering up my neck as sacrifice, hoping this would be the last time and that I could sleep then until Gabriel came from heaven and blew his horn to raise the quiet Christian dead.

MOTHER CAME INTO the hallway and said, "Pepita, we must take you to the priest."

So she knew I was possessed and that I needed help. "Yes, Mama. I need the Lord."

They had him come to the house later that day. We sat alone, he and I, in the parlor. I kept my hands in my lap and did not want to look into his eyes. "Father," I said. "I am lured out at night and have been bitten by a creature that may be the devil."

"Oh, my poor child." Father Comities crossed himself. When he reached into his black satchel for the cross and a glint of stray sunlight fell over it, shattering my face with brilliance, I cried out in agony and suddenly I was above my chair, floating in air, my feet dangling free.

Father stood, knocking over his chair in his haste, holding up the cross against me. My voice changed into deep timbre and I said, against my will, words I never would have said had I not been possessed of evil. "Begone, blind mealy bug, begone before I take your life for looking upon me without bowing down before your god."

I drifted to the floor, growled menacingly at the stunned priest, and ran from the presence of the cross like a breeze slipping between the rooms, up the stairs, and through the small door at the top of landing that led into the attic. I searched out and found my grandmother's trunk beneath the stored debris of castoff furniture. I opened the lid, withdrew old batches of letters tied with stiff dry ribbon, and there, on top of my mother's wedding dress, I crawled to lie, lowering the lid over me. They would not find me here today. And when night fell, I would know what it was I had to do. Surely, I would.

DARKNESS. UTTER AND unabated. Stuffiness and the scent of age, of sweat wept into satin and dried, trapped there. Scent of rusted metal hinges and straps, of wood slats warped and covered with the dust of years.

I rose, throwing back the trunk lid, and stretched my arms toward the bare rafters. A moonbeam threw a shaft of warm honey light across the planks of the floor.

Ravenous. Shrunken by hunger I glided to the door and let myself out. Listening. To life sleeping, dreaming in peace.

Out the rear exit to the path leading to the kitchen. There, in the cupboards, I rummage for food. I find cold biscuit and the cracklings from bacon. I stuff it all into my mouth and hardly chewing, swallowing, stuffing more into my mouth like a dog. I rush to the crocks and cup my hands to bring milk to my lips. I slurp, disgusting myself, driven by need.

Finally filled, I sit down on the floor and wipe my face with my hands, then wipe my hands on my skirt. I put back my head and look up at the shadowed ceiling, searching for God, wishing for an end to the nightmare.

A lurching of my stomach bends down my head and I grip at my middle with my hands. It's coming up and I can't stop it! I swallow hard, trying to keep it down, knowing I'll be hungry again if I lose the meal I've just consumed, but my stomach twists, cramping, and the sickness is too much. I retch onto the floor nearby and push away, coming to my feet, crying at this thing that won't even let me take in food. The voice in my head that guides me now says, *Go to your mother. Go to her and feed.*

I creep down the path to the house, glide up the stairs and to my parents' bedroom. They sleep as if I have not been missing, as if life were just as it always was. I crawl under the covers on my mother's side of the bed. In her sleep she puts her arm around me and I ease her wrist toward my lips to kiss it. Her flesh smells like apples and green mint and water from the creek. I tentatively touch that scented flesh with my lips and then feel a strength and power never before experienced as I open my mouth, slide my tongue along the tiny pulsing vein of her arm to the crook and sink my teeth down, down, down into blood-red nourishment.

After only a few moments, the blood rushing down my throat, my actions reach the center of my being. As if shaken from a dream by someone in authority, by someone who would save me, I awaken from evil in revulsion, jerking free of my mother's arm, sliding from the bed like a wraith and to the window where the lace curtains ripple in a breeze. I turn back only once to see them, my parents, still asleep and unknowing in their bed, and then I leap through the window to freedom. I must find a way into the world and away from those I love or else I will take them with me down into the darkness of the lonely and rejected.

At the road bordering the edge of my father's property I hear a wagon approach as I walk-glide. I glide to the center of the roadway and stop the team of old nags merely by commanding it with my mind. I inquire of the driver about a lift into the city. I am heading for New Orleans where I can meld into the chaos of humanity and lose myself. I make up a patent lie about being separated from my mother, who is no doubt frantic over my whereabouts. He takes me onto the seat and, though he edges away as if he knows something is not right with me, he indeed drives his nags harder to get us both to the city in record time.

He fails. I see the dawn kissing the night curtain's drawn edge and my skin begins to crawl in anticipation of pain. I fidget on the seat and watch the driver beat his horses unmercifully now, his own fear nearly as great as mine. I smell that fear and it is as distinct and chilling as a cold hand sticking up from a grave, decaying. "Hurry," I admonish him, "before the sun peeks over the rim. Hurry, man, if you wish to see another end of day."

It's too late, the nags are too broken and slow. They trot as fast as they can, foam dripping from their mouths, but they can't get me to the safety of the city's buildings in time. I can feel the skin tightening into drum-work over the bones of my face and arms. I can feel blisters rising like small blind suns rushing toward implosion on my hands and forehead and cheeks. I say to the driver, "Curse you, old man, curse you with more poverty for your bad choice of horse flesh." He stares at me in horror and I know he can see the changes taking place, the deterioration from the first of the sun's rays. I leap from the racing wagon and bound like a four-legged animal for the woods and cover. Where, where, where can I hide? I see a burrow in the ground and fly headlong into it, digging wildly with my fingers to dislodge more earth and make a place for myself. I startle a sleeping hedgehog and dispatch it with one blow from my fist. I am a giant now, I think, in a little girl's body. I could slay a kingdom and not find a hair on my head harmed. The revelation causes a burble of joy in the center of my chest and I feel as victorious as a warrior who has slain armies.

Finally I am deep enough, a ton of earth heavy over my head, my legs tucked beneath me, and as the sun most assuredly rises into the azure sky as it has all of my life, I am safe. Safe enough to rip a hole in the small animal's gut cavity and drink of its slippery warm blood until I am satiated and grow sleepy.

NEW ORLEANS BUSTLES with trade and mankind busy in endeavor. I slip between walls and alleys, glorying in the cool fragrant dark, the sounds of banjos and pianos, the ripe rich scent of newly baked French bread loaves and pots of spicy jambalaya.

Along one corridor between buildings, I spy and consider a man staggering under the weight of strong drink, but his smell gags me. On a street in the Quarter I contemplate an obese woman who leans against her open door, smoking a cigar and calling out roughly to men across the street. But she is too large; she might present a physical problem until I am better versed in enforcing my will.

Along the docks I wander, looking for a host to feed me. I am always hungry, always preying on warm bodies, beset by a gluttonous rage that seems never to wane. There is a ship from a foreign land docked, a gangplank leading up to the deck. I can see the country's flag fluttering intermittently in the wind. I wait until I am sure they are all asleep in their bunks and then I crawl up to the deck like a cat, on quiet feet that do not really touch the rough planks, and I go in search of breathing that is regular, soft, and full of promise.

In the quarters for the working sailors I take the first man I come to, a thin lad not many years older than I. He is dressed in long johns, but is shirtless, and I see his hairless chest rising gently, falling, rising gently again, his heart pumping steadily just beneath his ribcage. He is possessed of youth and radiant health.

His eyelids flutter in sleepy discomfort as I near him and lift his arm into my lap. I lean down, clip the white skin beneath my teeth and, taking all the time I need to make it impossible for him to resist, I engage his mind with my own as I suckle from his wrist until he has passed over from this world to the next. When I am sure he is dead and his body cools past the point a living soul could occupy it, I put his arm back over his now silent chest. I touch my fingers to his forehead, a sort of blessing for providing a meal to me, and then I slink away in the shadows, to the deck and the open air, and down the gangplank to the docks and eventually the city again.

I don't even miss my parents or the life I lived with them. In retrospect, now one day beyond that life, it seems to me that it was a dull existence, without aim or meaning. I am truly now what I was meant to be. I feel no remorse and no rebuke to my master who made me. He must have known exactly what he was doing. He chose me above all others. I must prove to be good at living on my own, free of encumbrance, like a wild thing, a thing that cannot be tethered.

BEFORE DAWN NEARS I search over the city for a place to rest. There are no natural animal burrows here. It is cobblestone and brick, lanterns and gas lamps. If there are trunks in attics, I haven't time to find them. But I must go to ground somewhere, somehow. It is strange to me that I know what I must do before it is too late to find a way. I am guided internally by a little voice that watches over me.

I chance upon the cemetery at the edge of the metropolis and see the crypts that are placed aboveground, above the high water table. I glide among the stone angels, the solemn cherubs, the rows and rows of rectangular concrete coffins placed right on top of the earth. I test one stone door and know it will shatter if I use force upon it. I stand beside the coffin of a child my size and length and realize if I am able to lift the seal, I might never reposition it in place again once inside and lying down.

Despairing, warily watching the pink glow in the horizon, my skin crawling again in anticipation, I come finally upon a crypt with a wooden door instead of stone. I feel along the door's edges, all the way around, seeking a chink, a place where I can get a grip. I find one on the hinge side, in the center between the hinges, and I push my fingers in. Startlingly, my fingers transform; they flatten and elongate. I rejoice inside and sink my hand further between door and stone crypt, prying. The hinges creak, then burst from their moorings. The door slides upon gravely ground toward me and from inside the first waft of death inflates my nostrils. This dead one has not been in its crypt long. It has not yet finished falling to dust. It still has flesh upon its bones, and muscle and . . . secretions.

I glance behind me at the coming of the light and know I have no choice. A being such as I has little to complain about, least of all how death smells just weeks after it has overtaken the body. I slip through the opening, drag the door back into place, shutting out the horrible light, and find myself in dark as deep as the burrow. I move slowly to the coffin, place my hands on the lid, lift it in one swift stroke, and with one hand feel for the corpse. It is rubbery to the touch and there is a slime along the eye sockets. I prop the lid open and reach in, get my hands beneath the shoulders and legs, and with my new-found might, I wrestle the dead weight from the satin bed. I drop it a little way from me, satisfied that it cannot rise and walk, cannot reprove me. I climb into the coffin and lie back, sighing. Sleep comes dreamless and deep, a death sleep no different from the one all the dead around me enjoy. I am confident I will go undisturbed and safe until the hunger once again opens my eyes and causes me to walk.

BECAUSE THE FOREIGN ship's sailors are so easy to take, I make them my stalking ground. Who can they complain to about these night deaths? New Orleans lawmen will tell them it is not their affair, that they have no authority to take over the case. And I have hidden, listening to their talk in the late nights. The language is mellifluous, but would be unintelligible to Americans. I do not know where they are from, somewhere in South America, I guess from the accent, but I do know they don't wish to draw attention to themselves. They are waiting for a shipment to be loaded for export—fine bolts of cloth, spices, cotton bales, cypress wood from the nearby swamps that is resinous and aromatic. I hear excitement in their voices after the second death, and I detect fear, it's in their sweat and in their tone of voice, but they do not know, I'm sure, what is going on and what is responsible for the deaths of their comrades.

After feeding (careful to leave my victims dead as I have no urge to create more like me), I roam the city streets delighting in the opulence. Velvet-, lace-, and brocade-clad ladies and gentlemen stroll in the park beneath trees hanging with Spanish moss. Beautiful pocket gardens grace old mansions and intricate wrought iron circle the balconies on upper floors. Gates leading right from the sidewalk or street lead to doors decorated with heavy leaden-glass panes and beyond, in candlelight, I can see lives being lived so alien from my own plantation experience that I stand mesmerized, watching for hours as people take their dinners from gold-rimmed plates and drink dark wines that remind me of blood from crystal goblets.

I will have all that, I thought. If I please, I will one day have everything that these rich, cultured people enjoy and I will revel in my ownership. I will have my own crypt built in the backyard where I will teach a servant to watch over me. I will live here in this city forever and be loved and feared by many. I will outlast generations, see them come and go, and I will move into the future to embrace whatever it holds for me.

I had no idea that I would never see that day come. For it was during my fourth feeding from the foreign ship that I was caught.

I might have become lazy in watching for a trap, so hungry was I that night. I might have become too ambitious and took one too many risks going back again and again to the same feeding ground. I think now it was destiny, for that is what caused me to be a bloodsucker and it is what drove me to the city, and it no doubt was what caused the captain to lie in wait for me through the early hours after midnight.

I came aboard as always, noiseless, gliding above the gangplank, the deck, and down the narrow black iron stairs to the sleeping hold below. I chose the man nearest the exit, in the same bunk where the first youth had lain. He was in deep slumber, snoring lustily, his big hairy naked chest rising like a whale in the ocean. I lifted his arm and brought it to my lap. I waited to see if he would waken, slipping gently through his mind and claiming that part of it that would raise alarm unless I paralyzed it.

From behind me the captain approached and not until he was nearly upon me did I know there was trouble. A wire slipped quickly around my throat and I was yanked back onto my heels, my arms flailing to regain balance. I must have let out a cry because the entire hold's sleeping occupants woke, shouting and gathering around me. I twisted to face my captor, the wire digging deep into my neck. I saw the wire was attached to a pole that kept the captain at a distance from me so that I could not reach out and give him a killing blow. I bared my teeth and then opened my mouth in a mighty roar. He was unshaken. I stared into his dark eyes and tried to slide behind them to find his mind and cripple it. He did not blink, nor did he let go of the pole that held me fast. I couldn't control him. I couldn't get to the center of him.

"I know what you are," he said in heavily accented English. "You are to come with me."

In his language he ordered his men back to their bunks. They grew calm and wandered back, away from us. The man I'd chosen for my feeding grinned up at me as if he knew a secret. I hissed at him and kicked at his bunk, but he just laughed like a man who has lost his mind.

The captain dragged me up the stairway by my neck and I fell to my knees once on the deck. He did not wait for me to regain my feet, but continued to drag me several feet until he came to the bow. There he stopped and I scrambled up, furious that I should be treated so shabbily. Did he not know what I could do to him? What power I possessed? I would get free and rend him limb from limb for this!

I said, "Let me go and I'll spare you." Though it was a lie. If he let me go, I meant to dispatch him immediately.

He cocked his head and after a pause said, "You will kill me if I let you go. Or you would try."

He could have guessed that from my countenance. I tried to soften my look and I brought up tears to my eyes. "I am a little girl," I said. "My father owns a plantation outside of the city and will pay you anything for my return. I am worth a handsome sum."

"You are not a little girl," he said, scoffing openly. "You are vampire and you have killed one too many of my men."

"How do you know what I am?" I asked, taken by a second surprise. It was my thought that people did not know of us, except for perhaps some of the African slaves, like Samay. Men with white skin had no experience with those like me who lived, but did not live, who slept by day and preyed by night.

"Why do you *think* I know what you are?" He smiled then and I stood immobile as his eyes turned to coal fire.

"You are one!" I shouted. "But . . . but . . ."

"Why haven't I taken my crew, one by one, the way you were determined to do?"

I nodded my head, unsure of the truth of his admission. If he were like me how did he survive long sea voyages without killing every man on board before they reached land?

"I am older than you. Not just in human years, either. I am one thousand and one hundred and eleven years old. I have had more than a century to adjust to my condition and to learn how to survive without detection. You are just a baby," he added in a superior tone.

"How do you do that?" The years he claimed to have lived astonished me, though I did not yet believe everything he said.

"Survive without touching my crew? Over long months on the sea?"

I nodded, interested now that I knew I was not the prisoner of a mortal.

He suddenly pushed forward on the pole and it loosened the loop of wire around my neck. I whipped it over my head, breathing deeply, freely. He dropped the device and stepped forward to me as if we were to embrace. I opened my mouth to protest, I put up my hands to keep him at bay, but he was too quick. He had me in his arms, my own arms pinned at my sides, before I could delay him. He looked down into my eyes and communicated with his mind, as my master had done, and it was then I knew everything.

I knew of the multitudes he had murdered, the women and children and even infants he had drained of their lifeblood. I knew of pyramids and legions of soldiers on an open dusty plain, of Africa's ivory coast, of England's moors, and of South America's rich varied forests filled with wildlife. I knew that he did not feed on his men because he brought with him, in chains, younger vampires than himself, those like me who were new to the life and uneducated about the tricks and schemes necessary to live one thousand, one hundred, and eleven years.

"You won't die now," he said out loud. "I'll save you for the voyage home. I have two more in chains in the lower chamber of the ship. A stupid woman and a stupid man, both like you, southern neophytes sneaking onto my vessel to kill and frighten my men into deserting me. But no more, no more! They will keep you company until we finish loading and leave this city far behind. You see, I love the sailing life . . . "

I spat into his face. He grinned and let the spittle drip down onto his chin without letting me go.

"I love the sailing life," he repeated, "and I must have the humans to work the ship, to load the cargoes. And—listen carefully my pretty one—I very much love ending the lives of other vampires who compete with me and engage in unfortunate practices like making more of us. I weed out the weak, my dear child. I am a natural disaster to your kind. I am your stake through the heart, girl. I am your violent, blistering sunrise. I am your real death."

He carried me down another set of iron stairs deep and deeper into the belly of the gently swaying ship. He unlocked a thick iron door and pushed me inside. I could hear his maniacal laughter as he re-bolted the door again.

I stood shaking in fury at what ill luck had befallen me. I had a future in the grand mansions in the French Quarter! I had a life unending before me. I had strength and cunning, a safe crypt in the cemetery with a real satin coffin. I had so much to live for!

"Welcome to hell," a woman said out of the darkness.

"Join us in our defeat," a man said after her.

I hung my head and felt my anger subside to be replaced by melancholy. The truth seized me and made me wail. I was as helpless as had been my victims. I was nothing more than a feeding for a hungry creature who sailed the great sea.

I knew what I was and would be. I could not fight my fate no more than I could derail it when my master swooped into my plantation bedroom window in the heat of a sultry summer night when the magnolia bloomed in all its splendor. I had nothing to do but surrender.

"Hello," I said in a controlled voice. "I am glad to meet you, friends. May I ask how he keeps us alive until we are . . . until we are needed?"

"With the dregs of blood he buys while onshore. I think it is from the slaughterhouses. From swine and cattle. It is vile."

"Well at least we will not starve and consume one another before he is ready for us," I said, taking my place on the damp floor in the dark, wrapping my arms around my knees. "I would not like to drink from my own kind the way he does."

I thought of my mother and the way she put her arm around me in her sleep. Of how Samay fled from me. Of the priest and his cross. As a child, merely a child, with childish concerns, I had played with dolls and tea sets. I was losing my past rapidly. It was graying into mist in my mind as if it had all been a long, involved, and detailed dream. But nevertheless I mourned it.

"Do you hear something?" I asked, my head coming up as I listened intently.

"It's the bell," the woman said. "Tolling our leave-taking."

"The ship is finished loading? We're going to sea?"

"Yes," she said simply. "There's nothing to do now but wait."

I lay back on the cold hard floor, feeling the ruffle of deep water washing against the bowed outer hull beneath me. I closed my eyes, willing the sleep to come. It would be soon enough that I would see the light again. Soon, too soon, soon enough.

✠

FAT TUESDAY

RUSSELL DAVIS

❖ ⟩ ❖ ⟩ ⦿ ⟨ ❖ ⟨ ❖

'M WRITING IT DOWN NOW. BEFORE NIGHT COMES AND THE CELEBRATION begins in earnest. Right now, this moment, there's a dog barking in the alley outside and he sounds half-rabid. The high notes from his throaty bark vibrate in the cheap glass of my window. I won't look down at him. I had an uncle who went mad. Stark, raving, mad. When they carted him away he sounded like that dog. I'm writing this down now because just waiting would surely cause me to end up like him or the dog. Frothing at the mouth and barking at the moon. Still, I suppose if I were going to go mad, I'd have done it by now. But I can see my hands shaking as I type, and I've been drinking steadily since I last saw him. Wait! I'm getting ahead of myself, and I need to go slow enough to get it right. I will finish this tale clearly for you, though my mouth tastes of rotten flesh and ash, and darkness will come soon enough.

Tonight is Fat Tuesday. You know about Fat Tuesday, don't you? The Mardi Gras? A grand party where the whole city of New Orleans goes stark, raving mad? Just like my uncle, only worse, because very few get carted away. Very few. I'm a writer, Martin Grant is the name, and I've done my homework. Depending on who you ask, Mardi Gras has been around just about forever. The curious, the rich, the simply bored all come here for the carnival season that begins with the feast of the Epiphany on January 6th, and ends on Fat Tuesday with a city-wide celebration. I looked it up, and the whole point of it originally was to party like mad right up until Lent—when fasting replaces feasting. And that's it, you know. Feasting. The word carnival comes from the Latin: *carnivale*. I'm no linguist, but from what I've been able to determine, the word *carnivale* means "farewell to flesh."

I ARRIVED IN New Orleans on the afternoon of January 6th. I changed clothes, ate dinner at a café outside the French Quarter, and returned to my cheap room.

I was pleased with myself. I'd gotten an assignment to write an article about the carnival season and all the strange things that occur during that time. I was living on a relatively decent per diem that covered my expenses. Since good food was my weakness, I took a cheap room until the end of February, figuring on spending most of my money in restaurants. I slept well that night and arose refreshed in the morning. I left the news on while I showered, and the lead story was about a murder victim discovered in an alley outside a jazz bar. I shut off the water long enough to listen to the on-site report:

"Thanks, Chip. I'm down here near the site where the victim was found. Of course, the alley itself is cordoned off by police tape, and no statements have yet been issued. Wait, here comes the county coroner and an investigator—"

A brief pause followed and then I heard a man's voice.

"O.K., folks, we're going to make this quick and we're not answering questions at this time. What we've got is one dead male, approximately 28 years old and identity unknown at this time. As of now we are calling it a homicide. It appears that the victim died of massive blood loss, but we'll have to do an autopsy to confirm that. That's all for now."

A babble of voices arose as the detective walked away, and then the reporter's voice cut back in.

"Chip, that was Detective Jake Soames of the New Orleans Police Department. As you heard, they are ruling it a homicide, but eyewitnesses first on the scene have been saying that it's worse than that. According to them, the victim's throat had been ripped out, much like the killings that started last year at this same time."

Chip broke back in.

"Kris, the murders you're referring to are the unsolved 'Vampire John' killings that started during last year's carnival and mysteriously ended on Fat Tuesday, correct? Have the police or any of the witnesses indicated that there might be a connection?"

"No, Chip, as you heard, the police aren't saying much. And the four eyewitnesses were taken by police a short time ago for questioning . . . "

I turned back on the water. "Vampire John" killings? I didn't recall hearing about them, but it might be an interesting place to start. I prided myself on writing about the underside of public events. People are sometimes blind to what's going on around them, especially in the midst of a party or social occasion. Killings during Mardi Gras? It was perfect.

After I finished dressing, and had a wonderful breakfast of croissants and jam, I made my way to the library. What I found there got me really excited about this particular story. The essence of it was this: during last year's carnival celebration, a serial killer had been wandering the streets. Because of his rather gruesome method of slaughter a local disc jockey had dubbed him "Vampire John." Vampire because all the victims had died of massive blood loss sustained when their throats had been torn out, and John because he was unknown. According to one clip I read, the disc jockey said, "Well, you know, Vampire John, as in John Doe. It seemed to fit." The name stuck.

The killer was never caught, leaving his last victim's body in a city park filled with reveler's on the night of Fat Tuesday, and then disappearing. He killed eight people. I was stunned. This should have made national news, and I'd never heard of it. But then again, New Orleans was the "murder capital of the U.S." so maybe people just didn't get riled up about it. Some citizens interviewed in the articles expressed concern, but most assumed it was just another nutcase loose during carnival. They also thought the police would catch him. I checked just to be certain that my hunch was correct and it was. The detective who worked the Vampire John killings last year was none other than Jake Soames. He was someone, I decided, that I needed to talk to. But first, I needed to visit the county coroner's office and have a chat with Will Baker, the chief forensic pathologist.

WILL BAKER WAS a short, rotund man, who wore coke bottle lenses in his glasses. At first he was tough, acting like he didn't want to talk, but instinct told me to stay with him, and I was right. Given the chance to speak "off the record" he'd tell me his life story. He was also familiar with the whole history, at least the medical side of it, of the Vampire John killings. Once he loosened up, he told me enough to know that this was the story I was going to write.

I asked him about the victim found this morning. "So, the guy died of massive blood loss, right?"

"Yes, from a wound to his throat."

"What kind of a wound?"

"It was," he paused, "well, it appears that his throat was chewed out."

"You mean like the killings last year."

"Exactly like them. I'd hoped the monster who was responsible had left forever, but evidence indicates that it's the same man."

"Which evidence is that?"

He gestured. "Come on, and I'll show you. That is, if you don't get sick easily?"

"Not really," I replied as I followed him down the stairs into the room where he performed autopsies. When we entered, the victim was still laid out on the examination table.

"How long are you gonna keep him there?" I asked.

"Not long. Detective Soames is due by shortly, and I knew he'd want to see the body, so I left it out. Besides," he chuckled, "this fellow here doesn't really mind." He patted the body on the shoulder.

"So what is it you wanted to show me?"

"O.K., first you've got to understand something. When we've been saying massive blood loss, what we really meant was the victims had no blood."

"No blood?"

"None whatsoever except what had spilled down the front, and that was very little. Usually, in case's where there's a major tissue injury, loss of a limb, cut throat, that type of thing, quite a bit of blood actually remains in the body. You don't have to lose it all to bleed to death, you know."

"No blood at all?" I repeated, a little suspicious that maybe Will was having me on.

"None. Now, for the really strange part." He pulled back the sheet. "Come take a look at something."

"The strange part?" I mumbled to myself as I walked over. "What?"

"There's not a lot of tissue remaining here, but under a magnifying glass you can see it," he said, pointing to the victim's neck.

"See what?" I said.

He handed me a magnifying glass which I aimed at the area he pointed to, the very base of the neck. "You see those little swirls in the bloodstains on the skin surface?"

"Yeah, so?"

"Well, unless I'm mistaken, those are tongue swirls. The perp licked the blood off his victim."

I jerked back suddenly. "Are you shitting me?!"

"I don't know, did I eat you?" Will cackled. I was beginning to realize that forensic people had rather bizarre senses of humor. "No way," he said when he saw my look, "I'm as serious as the dead."

"And that's pretty serious," said a voice from the doorway.

I jumped. "Jesus! Are you trying to scare me to death?"

The man laughed. "No, but unless I miss my guess, you're a reporter and my friend Will here is giving away our secrets."

Will blanched a bit. "Not really, Jake. He's cool, off the record and all." He sounded a bit plaintive.

Jake shook his head. "That's what they all say." He turned to me. "So, which rag do you work for and how long till I'm gonna see this in the paper?"

I took in Jake's appearance now that my heart had stopped racing. He was a fairly tall man, maybe 6'1" or so. He wore khakis and a blue shirt. His hair was mussed and brown, and looked like it hadn't seen the good side of a comb all day. His eyes were brown and didn't leave my face. "No," I said, realizing that I was taking too long in giving him an answer. "You're not gonna see this in the paper anytime soon."

"Oh really?" he asked with kind of a sardonic twist of his head.

"Two reasons really," I replied. "One, I'm a freelance writer and so I don't write the story until it's finished. And two, the story isn't finished. Good enough?"

"I suppose," he said. "What choices do I really have?"

"Not many," I said, "But I mean what I say. I won't write the story until it's over. O.K.?"

"Alright," he said.

We exchanged names and a bit more information. I realized that I liked Jake quite a bit. He was a straight shooter, and he played fair with me. You don't find that too often in police officers when you're a writer. I asked him if we could get together again to talk some more, and he agreed, reminding me of my promise to keep quiet. "Besides," he said, "maybe an outside perspective will shed some light on this thing. God knows it's dark enough now."

"Not a lot of leads, huh?"

"We've got the same thing we had last year at this time."

"What's that?"

"A bucketful of nothing."

"Well," I said, "maybe I can dig up something. Do you have anything at all?"

He turned to Will. "Give him the rundown, Will. Unless you've got anything for me that I wasn't expecting, you can slab this guy." He pointed at the body on the table.

"No," Will said. "Nothing new here." He sighed. "I wish there was."

"Me, too," said Jake, as he turned to walk out. "Catch you later, Martin?"

I nodded. "Yep. I'll call you later." I turned and looked expectantly at Will. "Well?"

"Oh yes," he said. "Here's what we've got but it isn't much. Our suspect is quite tall, say 6'2" or better, and exceptionally strong-"

"Wait," I said. "How do you know that?"

"Well, last year, one of the victim's was a pretty heavy guy, about 250 pounds. Based on the bruise marks we found under his armpits, we deduced that his attacker had picked him up. The victim was about 5'6"tall, and that means that in order to pick him up, our killer would have to be substantially taller and stronger. I'd guess he weighs more than that too, but that's a guess."

"What else?"

"O.K., let's see. We think he's either bald, or he wears a hair net, because we haven't yet found a hair at a crime scene. Probably, he's bald because even with a hair net, some hair escapes. He's also got very sharp teeth, like they've been filed." He paused. "I guess that's about it. Doesn't seem like a lot for eight, rather nine, murders does it?"

"No, but it's a start," I said. "Thanks for your time, Will. We'll talk again, I'm sure."

He smiled. "No problem, Martin. Just keep a lid on it will you?"

"Sure thing," I said. "Besides, if I wrote a story about a vampire in New Orleans, no one would believe me anyway."

I turned and left, determined to find this Vampire John before I left New Orleans. And I knew the truth. What we had here was a case of someone who'd gone off the deep end and actually decided he was a vampire. I'd heard about it before. With those thoughts firmly in my mind, I headed out to find some lunch.

THE PROBLEM WITH eating is that when there's time to enjoy it (as I dearly love to do), it's great. Otherwise, it's just something we have to do in order to stay alive.

When I'm really busy, that's how I view it: a necessity and no more. So I ate what should have been a good lunch, and then continued my search. My first visit was to all the crime scenes. This consisted of visits to three alleys in the French Quarter, two warehouses where they stored floats for the parade held on Fat Tuesday, one city park, two downtown retro dance clubs, and one apartment building. All in all, I spent the day looking and waiting for inspiration.

I didn't find much. But I was hoping that when I talked with Jake Soames, I'd get something more than maybe what he'd even told his rather loose-lipped friend Will. I called him, and we agreed to meet at a bar near the station that night. Over cocktails and some seared crayfish tails, he told me a bit more. It was then that I began to realize why Soames appeared so disheveled.

I asked, "Is there anything more you could tell me than Will did?"

"Yes, there is," he said. "But you've got to promise to never use it. Ever."

"Now wait a minute," I said, "I can't even put it in once the case is solved?"

"No," he said. "Not ever."

"Then why tell me?"

"I have to tell somebody. It's been eating at me for a year." He sipped his scotch, and stared at a point just over the top of my head.

"All right, I guess I can promise to keep it out." (Yes, I've decided to put it in now, because it doesn't matter anymore. No one will be able to take retribution on me after tonight anyway.)

Soames talked and drank steadily for some time while he told me his tale. I'm quoting directly from my recorder here:

I'd called it a night. It was two days before Fat Tuesday, last year, and I still didn't have any real solid leads. I didn't used to drink as much, but now, well, it's all I can really do to keep myself sane. I went to a bar, this bar in fact. I like it here because it's a dim, smoky, quiet place. I ordered my favorite, the same as I'm drinking tonight with you: scotch rocks. It burned going down. I'd been here maybe fifteen minutes or so, just thinking, when a well dressed guy sat down next to me at the bar. He wore black jeans, and a cream-colored, raw silk shirt. He had on an embroidered vest with a blue and silver pattern on it. He nodded pleasantly to me as he sat, and motioned to the bartender. He ordered

Benedictine, straight up. Once he got his drink, he sipped it, and leaned back with a sigh. He turned to me and said, "A welcome break, is it not?"

I nodded. "Yes, though I personally can't imagine drinking straight Benedictine."

He smiled slightly. "It reminds me somewhat of home. It is painful to drink, because it stings the vocal cords. I do not mind because it also warms the stomach." His voice was deep, melodious, but very soft. It held the slightest hint of an accent that I couldn't place.

"Well," I said, "to each their own."

"Always," he replied, and then we raised our glasses to that informal toast.

We said nothing for a few minutes, just sat and watched CNN on the television over the bar. Deciding that watching the news wasn't going to help me any, I turned to the stranger and asked, "So, what do you do?"

He looked closely at me, and replied, "It's not important, friend. What you do, that is important."

"What I do?" I said in some confusion.

"Yes," he said. "You are a hunter of sorts. Right now, you are hunting Vampire John."

I stared at him. "Yeah, I suppose you could say that. After all, it's been in the papers. So what?"

He sipped his drink and I saw his jaw muscles clench slightly when he tasted the liquor. "It will end, you know. At least for this year."

"What will end?" I asked.

"The killings. They will end on Fat Tuesday, and not a night before."

"Wait a second, who the hell are you? And how could you know that?"

"An interested party, let us say. All that should matter to you is that the killings will end."

My cop instinct kicked in. "First, you didn't answer my question. How could you know that? And second, of course it matters to me! We've got some lunatic running around the city who thinks he's a vampire."

He was staring at me compassionately. His eyes were gray. I began to relax a little. It's funny, I was thinking to myself, I'd almost started to believe that this guy was the killer.

"Listen carefully to me, Jake Soames. I have watched you agonize over each victim, each lead that went nowhere. You will be unable to catch the killer because I know him."

"You know him?" I exclaimed.

"Yes, I know him well. I know that the killings will end on Fat Tuesday because I am him."

I tensed, started to rise and go for my gun at the same time, his eyes never left mine, and then his voice hit me. No higher than a whisper but it slapped into me with the force of a baseball bat. "Sit down!"

I couldn't stop myself. I sat. "How, wha-?"

"Poor Detective Soames. I'd explain it all to you, if I had the time. But I don't. Already the hunger that claims me at this time of year is growing. Here is the crux of it: There are many kinds of so-called vampires in the world. But all are cursed in some fashion. My curse began so long ago that I doubt you could even comprehend it. You see, when I became a vampire, I was a priest serving in a large church in France. When offered the chance at everlasting life on Earth, I found the temptation too great to resist. God called down his vengeance upon me, as he must all creatures of darkness and evil. My curse is that I must still abide by the rules of Christianity as much as I am able. So, when the feast of Epiphany begins, a frenzy comes upon me. And I must feast. I must drink each night, wholly slaking my thirst. Normally, we are far more reserved than that. This is the truth: I am here, and the frenzy is here. But at midnight, on Fat Tuesday, Lent begins. Then it will be over. Do you understand?"

I nodded, knowing that Lent was a time for fasting. Somewhere, deep inside me, I was screaming for release from his eyes. But he continued.

"I want you to stop hunting me. Go away. Take a vacation. I am told you are a good detective. Eventually, you might succeed in finding me. I do not wish to kill you because you serve a valuable purpose to society. I do not wish to kill anyone, but I must. The frenzy, the hunger, compels me like the voice of an angel. I will do what I must to survive, and no more. But if it means killing you, I will. Am I clear?"

I nodded again, and felt control return to my limbs. "So that's it then? I just supposed to let you walk out of here?"

"Yes," he said, "if you wish to live." His lips parted slightly, and I could see his pointed canines jutting down from the top of his mouth.

"Why warn me at all?"

"Check your facts again, Detective Soames, about the victims. They all deserved to die."

"I'll think about it, how's that?"

"Do what you must, as I shall. For now, I must go. The hunger calls."

"Wait!" I said.

"Be quick, I must leave," he said.

"What's your name, if it's not Vampire John?"

"Roland," he said. "Roland DuMaurier." Then he turned and left the bar. I haven't seen him since.

I ordered another round of drinks and just sat there. Thinking. Soames looked at me. "I know what's going through your mind right now," he said.

"Oh yeah?" I asked.

"You're wondering why I didn't stop him, right then. I wish I knew, but I don't. I could tell you that I didn't believe him, that I thought he was just some nut. And that might be the truth. I could tell you that there was a rational explanation for everything that happened that night: he was a hypnotist, I was tired, the lights were dim, whatever. That might also be the truth. But the truth is, I just don't know.

"The killings stopped, as he promised, on Fat Tuesday. I hoped, then, that he'd leave. He'd find a new hunting ground, and I could just bury it in the unsolved case file and let it go. But he's still here. The frenzy, as he called it, is back. I must stop him this time. I must." Soames shuddered and I realized what a terrible burden of guilt he must be carrying.

"Well, you've certainly got your work cut out for you," I said. "Maybe I can help you."

He turned to me and said, "There is no help for me anymore. I must find him and kill him. Do I believe he's a vampire? I don't know. But I've got to try."

I gulped the last of my drink. "Look, Soames, I've got to spend a little time thinking on all this, do some more digging. Why don't we meet again in a couple of days?"

He shrugged. "Whatever. You know where to find me."

I nodded. "Yeah. And in the meantime, you've got my number. Call me if anything comes up, ok?"

"Sure," he said. "I checked you out, you know."

I smiled. "I was sure you would."

"You're the same Martin Grant who uncovered the Times Square murders, right?"

I grinned at him, remembering how I'd tracked down the Times Square Killer. "The same," I said.

"What did people say that guy was?" he asked.

"A werewolf, if you can believe it," I said. "He used resin-cast teeth to chew on his victims. He'd been a special effects artist before he went nuts. He was quite good at creating a monster."

Soames looked at me, and then said quietly, "And?"

"And," I said, "he was a man. A psycho for sure, but just a man."

"Maybe," Soames said, standing to leave, "maybe our vampire is the same kind of thing?" He sounded hopeful, almost desperate.

I stood also. "Maybe," I said. Then I grinned at him, trying to lighten the mood. "Or maybe he's a real vampire."

Soames didn't smile. "That's not funny, at all."

"Yeah, I suppose you're right. Call me later, will you?"

"Sure thing," he said. And with that, he left the bar. It was the last time I saw him. The next day, they found his body on the steps leading to his front door. His throat had been torn out; he had no blood left in him. The only difference between Soames and the other victims was how he looked in death. Instead of appearing horrified, he was smiling. Knowing what I know now, I can't really blame him.

I COULD TELL you the details of the next four killings but it wouldn't matter. I could explain in detail how the police found the bodies like they had the year before. How I talked with Will Baker, and lots of other people trying to track down the killer. But no one knew anything. There were no clues. Just bodies drained of blood. I did find out that our mysterious Roland DuMaurier had told the truth about one thing. With the exception of Soames, every person who died had deserved it in some way. They weren't all criminals, but they should have been. They were abusers and molesters who'd gone uncaught. Some of them were connected to drugs. It doesn't matter except to illustrate that our killer had spoken at least some truth that night.

I wouldn't have found him, though I suspect he knew I was looking except for one small thing. Luck. Pure random chance. I'd started spending my nights in dark dance clubs. My only thought was that because of the noise, and the crowds, and the ever-present costumes, he might choose to strike again in that type of place. On the night of the fifth killing, now two days ago, I was leaning against a railing that overlooked the dance floor. I saw him then, or at least, what I thought might be him. He looked exactly as Soames described, right down to the vest. But I couldn't see his eyes. I watched him as he danced with a young woman. He seemed out of place to me, his dance moves appearing strange and out of sync with the times. Still, the woman was obviously having a good time. At the end of the song, he leaned close to her, and whispered something in her ear. She giggled and nodded. He pointed to a door leading outside, and they began moving toward it.

I began to push through the crowd, trying not to lose sight of them. If this was the guy, I thought, then I wanted to get to him quick, preferably before he killed the girl. The crowd surged against me and I lost sight of them as they went out the door. The lights began to flash again as the music started to pound. It took what seemed forever to reach the stairs leading to the dance floor. The crowd worked against me. While I'm not certain, I think it took me maybe ten or so minutes to make my way from my vantage point where I had seen them go through the door to reach it myself. I pushed it open.

It led into an alley that was littered with dumpsters and trash. I paused for my eyes to adjust to the dim lights, trying to listen for the sounds of a struggle over the music. I heard nothing, but turned right and began walking down the alley, deeper into the darkness. Suddenly, he was beside me.

I jumped when he laid a hand upon my shoulder.

"You were searching for something?" he asked.

No point in lying I decided. "Yes," I said. "Actually, you."

"Then you have found me," he said. "What is it you want?"

"I knew Soames. He told me about the bar, you, everything."

"That is unfortunate," he replied. He stepped away from me slightly and released my shoulder. "I had hoped that Detective Soames could have kept quiet. I gave him mercy, you know."

"Mercy?" I croaked. "You killed him!"

"Oh yes," he said. " I did indeed. But he was a tortured spirit. I thought to give him a release from pain."

"Tortured, all right! By you."

"You are incorrect. Detective Soames, though a good policeman, was not a good husband. I have watched him this past year. I hoped he would seek help—for all his burdens. He did not. He was a wife-beater, and death was the only mercy I could give him."

"What a deal," I said. "I suppose now, that you're going to try to kill me?"

He took another step backwards, and the light from the street illuminated his face for the first time. "No," he said, "I have already fed for this night."

I could see he was telling the truth. The area around his lips was covered in blood. "Great, how convenient for me!"

"You do not understand," he said.

"What's that Roland?"

"I will feed once more before Lent begins. On the night of Fat Tuesday. I will come for you because you are a parasite. A man who feeds on the pain of others. You are a leech on society, no more. It will be a mercy."

"Me?" I said. "I'm a leech. What about you? You're the bloodsucker here!"

"I have no choice. I am compelled by a hunger I cannot control. You could have chosen."

I looked at him and realized how serious he was. In my mind, I began to plan. I'd keep him talking and then just jump him. He wasn't that much bigger than me. "Well," I said, "I've got to tell you that I'm not feeling tortured in spirit really. I feel fine. Let's just call it good at that, okay?"

I saw him smile, saw his pointed teeth. It occurred to me that his looked really good compared to my friend's in Times Square. He said, "Once again, you misunderstand your predicament. Right now, I do not bother you, because you doubt my reality. When you come to realize, as Detective Soames did, that I am real, that I'm not just a, how do you say, a 'psycho,' then you will be disturbed."

71

"So," I said, "you're a real vampire, huh?"

"As real as midnight, as real as God, as real as death."

"Why don't we find out!" And as I spoke I leapt upon him.

He caught me with just one hand. Looking down into his face, I could see he was smiling. "Foolish man! I do not doubt the strength of your disbelief!" And with that he hurled me across the alley where I slammed into the wall, and fell stunned to the ground.

"I give you your life until midnight on Fat Tuesday. Enjoy it if you can." And with that he turned and convinced me of his reality. He disappeared by turning towards the unseeing crowd at the mouth of the alley, and melted away.

I heard his voice in my head then. "You'll find the girl's body behind the dumpster next to you. Look at it as a reminder if you still harbor doubt."

I got up, found the girl's body, but did not call the police. It occurred to me as I walked back to my room that Will Baker had been all wrong in some of his guesses. He wasn't all that tall, just strong. He didn't leave hair behind because the dead don't lose hair. I re-played the whole event over in my head while I walked, trying to find the holes, trying to look for something that would change my mind and make me believe that he was a phony. All I found was more proof that he wasn't.

So now, I am sitting here. It's almost midnight on Fat Tuesday. I can feel him coming. I can almost taste him in the air. The party on the streets below has grown progressively louder. They are uncaring, lost in their world of revelry and drunkenness. They are feasting before Lent comes upon them once again. And somewhere in that crowd is a vampire named Roland, who was once a priest. And he's hunting me.

He hungers for blood, my blood. And yet, I am not afraid. I could be wrong. It might have been a dream. I might wake up in the morning, my neck intact, my blood still warm and flowing through my veins. I will end the tale here, as it is finished either way. I will lay down on my bed and try to sleep. I will make what peace I can with God and myself. I will say farewell to my flesh before I sleep. The booze doesn't seem to be helping any. My hands are still shaking even now, but I am not afraid. I wonder if my uncle is somewhere tonight, howling up at the moon through the bars of his cage.

This story is finished now. It is time for sleep. I will transmit it to my editor via e-mail, and then I will rest. I am not afraid. Dear God, I am not afraid.

HIS MOUTH SHALL TASTE OF WORMWOOD

POPPY Z. BRITE

"To the treasures and the pleasures of the grave," said my friend Louis, and raised his goblet of absinthe to me in drunken benediction.

"To the funeral lilies," I replied, "and to the calm pale bones." I drank deeply from my own glass. The absinthe cauterized my throat with its flavor, part pepper, part licorice, part rot. It had been one of our greatest finds: more than fifty bottles of the now outlawed liqueur, sealed up in a New Orleans family tomb. Transporting them was a nuisance, but once we had learned to enjoy the taste of wormwood, our continued drunkenness was ensured for a long, long time. We had taken the skull of the crypt's patriarch, too, and it now rested in a velvet-lined enclave in our museum.

Louis and I, you see, were dreamers of a dark and restless sort. We met in our second year of college and quickly found that we shared one vital trait: both of us were dissatisfied with everything. We drank straight whiskey and declared it too weak. We took strange drugs, but the visions they brought us were of emptiness, mindlessness, slow decay. The books we read were dull; the artists who sold their colorful drawings on the street were mere hacks in our eyes; the music we heard was never loud enough, never harsh enough to stir us. We were truly jaded, we told one another. For all the impression the world made upon us, our eyes might have been dead black holes in our heads.

For a time we thought our salvation lay in the sorcery wrought by music. We studied recordings of weird nameless dissonances, attended performances of obscure bands at ill-lit filthy clubs. But music did not save us. For a time we distracted ourselves with carnality. We explored the damp alien territory between the legs of any girl who would have us, sometimes separately, sometimes both of us in bed together with one girl or more. We bound their wrists and ankles with black lace, we lubricated and penetrated their every orifice, we shamed them with their own pleasures. I recall a mauve-haired beauty, Felicia, who was brought to wild sobbing orgasm by the rough tongue of a stray dog we trapped. We watched her from across the room, drug-dazed and unstirred.

When we had exhausted the possibilities of women we sought those of our own sex, craving the androgynous curve of a boy's cheekbone, the molten flood of ejaculation invading our mouths. Eventually we turned to one another, seeking the thresholds of pain and ecstasy no one else had been able to help us attain. Louis asked me to grow my nails long and file them into needle-sharp points. When I raked them down his back, tiny beads of blood welled up in the angry tracks they left. He loved to lie still, pretending to submit to me, as I licked salty blood away. Afterward he would push me down and attack me with his mouth, his tongue seeming to sear a trail of liquid fire into my skin.

But sex did not save us either. We shut ourselves in our room and saw no one for days on end. At last we withdrew to the seclusion of Louis's ancestral home near Baton Rouge. Both his parents were dead—a suicide pact, Louis hinted, or perhaps a suicide and a murder. Louis, the only child, retained the family home and fortune. Built on the edge of a vast swamp, the plantation house loomed sepulchrally out of the gloom that surrounded it always, even in the middle of a summer afternoon. Oaks of primordial hugeness grew in a canopy over the house, their branches like black arms fraught with Spanish moss. The moss was everywhere, reminding me of brittle gray hair, stirring wraithlike in the dank breeze from the swamp. I had the impression that, left too long unchecked, the moss might begin to grow from the ornate window-frames and fluted columns to the house itself.

The place was deserted save for us. The air was heady with the luminous scent of magnolias and the fetor of swamp gas. At night we sat on the veranda and sipped bottles of wine from the family cellar, gazing through an increasingly alcoholic mist at the will-o'-the-wisps that beckoned far off in the swamp. Obsessively we talked of new thrills and how we might get them. Louis's wit sparkled liveliest when he was bored, and on the night he first mentioned grave robbing, I laughed. I could not imagine that he was serious.

"What would we do with a bunch of dried up old remains? Grind them to make a voodoo potion? I preferred your idea of increasing our tolerance to various poisons."

Louis's sharp face snapped towards me. His eyes were painfully sensitive to light, so that even in this gloaming he wore tinted glasses and it was impossible to see his expression. He kept his fair hair clipped very short, so that it stood in crazy tufts when he raked a nervous hand through it. "No, Howard. Think of it: our own collection of death. A catalogue of pain, of human frailty—all for us. Set against a backdrop of tranquil loveliness. Think what it would be to walk through such a place, meditating, reflecting upon your own ephemeral essence. Think of making love in a charnel house. We have only to assemble the parts—they will create a whole into which we may fall."

(Louis loved speaking in cryptic puns; anagrams and palindromes, too, and any sort of puzzle appealed to him. I wonder whether this was not the root of his determination to look into the fathomless eye of death and master it. Perhaps he saw the mortality of the flesh as a giant jigsaw or crossword which, if he fitted all the parts into place, he might solve and thus defeat. Louis would have loved to live forever, though he would never have known what to do with his time.)

He soon produced his hashish pipe to sweeten the taste of the wine, and we spoke no more of grave robbing that night. But the thought preyed upon me in the languorous weeks to come. The smell of a freshly opened grave, I thought, must in its way be as intoxicating as the perfume of the swamp or a girl's most intimate sweat. Could we truly assemble a collection of the grave's treasures that would be lovely to look upon, that would soothe our fevered souls.

The caresses of Louis's tongue grew languid. Sometimes, instead of nestling with me between the black satin sheets of our bed, he would sleep on a torn blanket in one of the underground rooms. These originally had been built for indeterminate but always intriguing purposes—abolitionist meetings had taken place there, Louis had told me, and a weekend of free love, and an earnest but wildly incompetent Black Mass replete with a vestal virgin and phallic candles.

These rooms were where our museum would be set up. At last I came to agree with Louis that only the plundering of graves might cure us of the most stifling ennui we had yet suffered. I could not bear to watch his tormented sleep, the pallor of his hollow cheeks, the delicate bruise-like darkening of the skin beneath his flickering eyes. Besides, the notion of grave robbing had begun to entice me. In ultimate corruption, might we not find the path to ultimate salvation?

Our first grisly prize was the head of Louis's mother, rotten as a pumpkin forgotten on the vine, half-shattered by two bullets from an antique Civil War revolver. We took it from the family crypt by the light of a full moon. The will-o'-the-wisps glowed weakly, like dying beacons on some unattainable shore, as we crept back to the manse. I dragged pick and shovel behind me; Louis carried the putrescent trophy tucked beneath his arm. After we descended into the museum, I lit three candles scented with the russet spices of autumn (the season when Louis's parents had died) while Louis placed the head in an alcove we had prepared for it. I thought I detected a certain tenderness in his manner. "May she give us the family blessing," he murmured, absently wiping on the lapel of his jacket a few shreds of pulpy flesh that had adhered to his fingers.

We spent a happy time refurbishing the museum, polishing the inlaid precious metals of the wall fixtures, brushing away the dust that frosted the velvet designs of the wallpaper, alternately burning incense and charring bits of cloth we had saturated with out blood, in order to give the rooms the odor we desired—a charnel perfume strong enough to drive us to frenzy. We traveled far in our collections, but always we returned home with crates full of things no man had ever been meant to possess. We heard of a girl with violet eyes who had died in some distant town; not seven days later we had those eyes in an ornate cut-glass jar, pickled in formaldehyde. We scraped bone dust and nitre from the bottoms of ancient coffins; we stole the barely withered heads and hands of children fresh in their graves, with their soft little fingers and their lips like flower petals. We had baubles and precious heir-looms, vermiculated prayerbooks and shrouds encrusted with mold. I had not taken seriously Louis's talk of making love in a charnel-house—but neither had I reckoned on the pleasure he could inflict with a femur dipped in rose-scented oil.

Upon the night I speak of—the night we drank our toast to the grave and its riches—we had just acquired our finest prize yet. Later in the evening we planned a celebratory debauch at a nightclub in the city. We had returned from our most recent travels not with the usual assortment of sacks and crates, but with only one small box carefully wrapped and tucked away in Louis's breast pocket. The box contained an object whose existence we had only speculated upon previously. From certain half-articulate mutterings of an old blind man plied with cheap liquor in a French Quarter bar, we traced rumors of a certain fetish or charm to a Negro graveyard in the southern bayou country. The fetish was said to be a thing of eerie beauty, capable of luring any lover to one's bed, hexing any enemy to a sick and painful death, and (this, I think, was what intrigued Louis the most) turning back tenfold on anyone who used it with less than the touch of a master.

A heavy mist hung low over the graveyard when we arrived there, lapping at our ankles, pooling around the markers of wood or stone, abruptly melting back in patches to reveal a gnarled root or a patch of blackened grass, then closing back in. By the light of a waning moon we made our way along a path overgrown with rioting weeds. The graves were decorated with elaborate mosaics of broken glass, coins, bottlecaps, oyster shells lacquered with silver and gold. Some mounds were outlined by empty bottles shoved neck-downward into the earth. I saw a lone plaster saint whose features had been worn away by years of wind and rain. I kicked the half-buried rusty cans that had once held flowers; no they held only bare brittle stems and pestilent rainwater, or nothing at all. Only the scent of wild spider lilies pervaded the night.

The earth in one corner of the graveyard seemed blacker than the rest. The grave we sought was marked only by a crude cross of charred and twisted wood. We were skilled at the art of violating the dead; soon we had the coffin uncovered. The boards were warped by years of burial in wet, foul earth. Louis pried up the lid with his spade and, by the moon's meager and watery light, we gazed upon what lay within.

Of the inhabitant we knew almost nothing. Some said a hideously disfigured old conjure woman lay buried here. Some said she was a young girl with a face as lovely and cold as moonlight on water, and a soul crueler than Fate itself. Some claimed the body was not a woman's at all, but that of a white voodoo priest who had ruled the bayou. He had features of a cool, unearthly beauty, they said, and a stock of fetishes and potions which he could hand out with the kindest blessing . . . or the direst curse. This was the story Louis and I liked best; the sorcerer's capriciousness appealed to us, and the fact that he was beautiful.

No trace of beauty remained to the thing in the coffin—at least not the sort of beauty that a healthy eye might cherish. Luis and I loved the translucent parchment skin stretched tight over long bones that seemed to have been carved from ivory.

The delicate brittle hands folded across the sunken chest, the soft black caverns of the eyes, the colorless strands of hair that still clung to the fine white dome of the skull—to us these things were the poetry of death.

Louis played his flashlight over the withered cords of the neck. There, on a silver chain gone black with age, was the object we had come seeking. No crude wax doll of bit of dried root was this. Louis and I gazed at each other, moved by the beauty of the thing; then, as if in a dream, he reached to grasp it. This was our rightful night's prize, our plunder from a sorcerer's grave.

"How does it look?" Louis asked as we were dressing.

I never had to think about my clothes. On an evening such as this, when we were dressing to go out, I would choose the same garments I might wear for a night's digging in the graveyard—black, unornamented black, with only the whiteness of my face and hands showing against the backdrop of night. On a particularly festive occasion such as this, I might smudge a bit of kohl around my eyes. The absence of color made me nearly invisible: if I walked with my shoulders hunched and my chin tucked down, no one except Louis would see me.

"Don't slouch so, Howard," said Louis irritably as I ducked past the mirror. "Turn around and look at me. Aren't I fine in my sorcerer's jewelry?"

Even when Louis wore black, he did it to be noticed. Tonight he was resplendent in a narrow-legged trousers of purple paisley silk and a silvery jacket that to turn all light iridescent. He had taken our prize out of its box and fastened it around his throat. As I came closer to look at it, I caught Louis's scent: rich and rather meaty, like blood kept too long in a stoppered bottle.

Against the sculpted hollow of Louis's throat, the thing on its chain seemed more strangely beautiful than ever. Have I neglected to describe the magical object, the voodoo fetish from the churned earth of the grave? I will never forget it. A polished sliver of bone (or a tooth, but what fang could have been so long, so sleekly honed, and still have somehow retained the look of a *human tooth*?) bound by a strip of copper. Set into the metal, a single ruby sparked like a drop of gore against the verdigris. Etched in exquisite miniature upon the sliver of bone, and darkened by the rubbing in of some black-red substance, was an elaborate veve—one of the symbols used by voodooists to invoke their pantheon of terrible gods. Whoever was buried in that lonely bayou grave, he had been no mere dabbler in swamp magic. Every cross and swirl of the veve was reproduced to perfection. I thought the thing still retained a trace of the grave's scent—a dark odor like potatoes long spoiled. Each grave has its own peculiar scent, just as each living body does.

"Are you certain you should wear it?" I asked.

"It will go into the museum tomorrow," he said, "with a scarlet candle burning eternally before it. Tonight its powers are mine."

THE NIGHTCLUB WAS in a part of the city that looked as if it had been gutted from the inside out by a righteous tongue of fire. The street was lit only by occasional scribbles of neon light overhead, advertisements for cheap hotels and all-night bars. Dark eyes stared at us from the crevices and pathways between buildings, disappearing only when Louis's hand crept toward the inner pocket of his jacket. He carried a small stiletto there, and he knew how to use it for more than pleasure.

We slipped through a door at the end of an alley and descended the narrow staircase into the club. The lurid glow of a blue bulb flooded the stairs, making Louis's face look sunken and dead behind his tinted glasses. Feedback blasted us as we came in, and above it, a screaming battle of guitars. The inside of the club was a patchwork of flickering light and darkness. Graffiti covered the walls and the ceiling like a tangle of barbed wire come alive. I saw bands' insignia and jeering death's-heads, crucifixes, bejeweled with broken glass and black obscenities writhing in the stroboscopic light.

Louis brought me a drink from the bar. I sipped it slowly, still drunk on the absinthe. Since the music was too loud for conversation, I studied the clubgoers around us. A quiet bunch, they were staring fixedly at the stage as if they had been drugged (and no doubt many of them had—I remembered visiting a club one night on a dose of hallucinogenic mushrooms, watching in fascination as the guitar strings seemed to drip soft viscera onto the stage). Younger than Louis and myself, most of them were, and queerly beautiful in their thrift shop rags, their leather and fishnet and cheap costume jewelry, their pale faces and painted hair. Perhaps we would take one of them home with us tonight. We had done so before. "The delicious guttersnipes," Louis called them. A particularly beautiful face, starkly boned and androgynous, flickered at the edge of my vision. When I looked it was gone.

I went into the restroom. A pair of boys stood at a single urinal, talking animatedly. I stood at the sink rinsing my hands, watching the boys in the mirror and trying to overhear their conversation. A hairline fracture in the glass seemed to pull the taller boy's eyes askew. "Caspar and Alyssa found her tonight," he said. "In some old warehouse by the river. I heard her skin was *gray*, man. And sort of withered, like something had sucked out most of the meat."

"Far out," said the other boy. His black-rimmed lips barely moved.

"She was only fifteen, you know?" said the tall boy as he zipped his ragged trousers.

"She was a cunt anyway."

They turned away from the urinal and started talking about the band—Ritual Sacrifice, I gathered, whose name was scrawled on the walls of the club. As they went out, the boys glanced at the mirror and the tall one's eyes met mine for an instant. Nose like a haughty Indian chief's, eyelids smudged with black and silver. Louis would approve, I thought—but the night was young, and there were many drinks left to be had.

When the band took a break we visited the bar again. Louis edged beside a thin dark-haired boy who was bare-chested except for a piece of torn lace tied about his throat. When he turned, I knew his was the androgynous and striking face I had glimpsed before. His beauty was almost feral, but overlaid with a cool elegance like a veneer of sanity hiding madness. His ivory skin stretched over cheekbones like razors; his eyes were hectic pools of darkness.

"I like your amulet," he said to Louis. "It's very unusual."

"I have another one like it at home," Louis told him.

"Really? I'd like to see them both together." The boy paused to let Louis order our vodka gimlets, then said, "I thought there was only one."

Louis's back straightened like a string of beads being pulled taut. Behind his glasses, I knew his pupils would have shrunk to pinpoints: the light pained him more when he was nervous. But no tremor in his voice betrayed him when he said, "What do you know about it?"

The boy shrugged. On his bony shoulders, the movement was insouciant and drop-dead graceful. "It's voodoo," he said. "I know what voodoo is. Do you?"

The implication stung, but Louis only bared his teeth the slightest bit; it might have been a smile. "I am *conversant* in all types of magic," he said, "at least."

The boy moved closer to Louis, so that their hips were almost touching, and lifted the amulet between thumb and forefinger. I thought I saw one long nail brush Louis's throat, but I could not be sure. "I could tell you the meaning of this veve," he said, "if you were certain you wished to know."

"It symbolizes power," Louis said. "All the power of my soul." His voice was cold, but I saw his tongue dart out to moisten his lips. He was beginning to dislike this boy, and also to desire him.

"No," said the boy so softly that I barely caught his words. He sounded almost sad. "The cross in the center is inverted, you see, and the line encircling it represents a serpent. A thing like this can trap your soul. Instead of being rewarded with eternal life . . . you might be doomed to it."

"Doomed to eternal life?" Louis permitted himself a small cold smile. "Whatever do you mean?"

"The band is starting again. Find me after the show and I'll tell you. We can have a drink . . . and you can tell me all you know about voodoo." The boy threw back his head and laughed. Only then did I notice that one of his upper canine teeth was missing.

THE NEXT PART of the evening remains a blur of neon, ice cubes and blue swirling smoke and sweet drunkenness. The boy drank glass after glass of absinthe with us, seeming to relish the bitter taste. None of the other guests had liked the liqueur. "Where did you get it?" he asked. Louis was silent for a long moment before he said, "It was sent over from France." Except for a single black gap, the boy's smile would have been as perfect as the sharp-edged crescent moon.

"Another drink?" said Louis, refilling both our glasses.

When I next came to clarity, I was in the boy's arms. I could not make out the words he was whispering; they might have been an incantation, if magic may be sung to pleasure's music. A pair of hands cupped my face, guiding my lips over the boy's pale parchment skin. They might have been Louis's hands. I know nothing except this boy, the fragile movement of the bones beneath the skin, the taste of his spit bitter with wormwood.

I do not remember when he finally turned away from me and began lavishing his love upon Louis. I wish I could have watched, could have seen the lust bleeding into Louis's eyes, the pleasure wracking his body. For, as it turned out, the boy loved Louis so much more thoroughly than he ever loved me.

When I awoke, the bass thump of my pulse echoing through my skull blotted out all other sensations. Gradually, though, I became aware of tangled silk sheets, of hot sunlight on my face. Not until I came fully awake did I see the thing I had cradled like a lover all through the night.

For an instant two realities shifted in uneasy juxtaposition and almost merged. I was in Louis's bed; I recognized the feel of the sheets, their odor of silk and sweat. But this thing I held—this was surely one of the fragile mummies we had dragged out of their graves, the things we dissected for our museum. It took me only a moment, though, to recognize the familiar ruined features—the sharp chin, the high elegant brow. Something had desiccated Louis, had drained him of every drop of his moisture, his vitality. His skin crackled and flaked away beneath my fingers. His hair stuck to my lips, dry and colorless. The amulet, which had still been around his throat in bed last night, was gone.

The boy left no trace—or so I thought until I saw a nearly transparent thing at the foot of the bed. It was like a quantity of spiderweb, or a damp and insubstantial veil. I picked it up and shook it out, but could not see its features until I held it up to the window. The thing was vaguely human-shaped, with empty limbs trailing off into nearly invisible tatters. As the thing wafted and billowed, I saw part of a face in it—the sharp curve left by a cheekbone, the hole where an eye had been—as if a face were imprinted upon gauze.

I carried Louis's brittle shell of a corpse down into the museum. Laying him before his mother's niche, I left a stick of incense burning in his folded hands and a pillow of black silk cradling the papery dry bulb of his skull.

The boy has not come to me again, though I leave the window open every night. I have been back to the club, where I stand sipping vodka and watching the crowd. I have seen many beauties, many strange and wasted faces, but not the one I seek. I think I know where I will find him. Perhaps he still desires me. I must know.

I will go again to the lonely graveyard in the bayou. Once more—alone, this time—I will find the unmarked grave and plant my spade in its black earth. When

I open the coffin—I know it, I am sure of it!—I will find not the mouldering thing we beheld before, but the calm beauty of replenished youth. The youth he drank from Louis. His face will be a scrimshaw mask of tranquility. The amulet—I know it; I am sure of it—will be around his neck.

Dying: the final shock of pain or nothingness that is the price we pay for everything. Could it not be the sweetest thrill, the only salvation we can attain . . . the only true moment of self-knowledge? The dark pools of his eyes will open, still and deep enough to drown in. He will hold out his arms to me, inviting me to lie down with him in his rich wormy bed.

With the first kiss his mouth will taste of wormwood. After that it will taste only of me—of my blood, my life, siphoning out of my body and into his. I will feel the sensations Louis felt: the shriveling of my tissues, the drying-up of all my vital juices. I care not. The treasures and pleasures of the grave? They are his hands, his lips, his tongue.

✠

THINLY VEILED

CECILIA TAN

> ⊱ ⊰ ⟡ ⟡ ⊙ ⟡ ⟡ ⊱ ⊰ ⊰

ALISHA'S HEELS TAPPED OUT A LONELY RHYTHM AS SHE MADE HER WAY down the brick sidewalk. On either side of her, generations-old houses stood dark, their windows unlit by the familiar flicker of television or the glow of reading lamps. She clutched her elbows close to her chest as if she were walking into a chill wind, though the night was steamily hot. Trees even older than the houses seemed to reach for her from behind wrought iron fences, kudzu and bougainvillea hanging low. Had the trees always hung like that, or had Hurricane Katrina bent them that way? Or was it just her imagination, turning everything into something sinister?

It's only midnight, she thought to herself, *someone in this neighborhood must be up.* She scanned the houses across the street, and the next block over, but all were dark. She stopped at the gate to number 217 and sighed. She had been all the way around the block, now, looking for someone's phone to borrow, to call Damien and tell him she was here. It would be just like him to call her up halfway across the country, and make a date, and then forget or be late. He'd have some lame excuse and she'd tell him he hadn't changed a bit, and that would be that.

She wasn't even really sure why she'd let her ex- talk her into coming down here. Alisha was a little creeped out by the fact that mere days after the "*unfortunate dissolution*" of her coven, as he put it, Damien had found her and extended an invitation to her. She didn't like to think maybe he had somehow, secretly, had something to do with the fact that she was again alone in the world and looking for a place to fit in.

He was clearly still not here. The house *felt* deserted. Alisha stamped her foot a little inside her shoe, angry at herself for believing that anything could be different about Damien now. On the phone he had seemed so persuasive, so matured. "Alisha," he had said, "don't think about the past. I know your pain and want only to help you."

"No one can help me," she had replied, the taste of ash in her mouth. "I don't need you, Damien."

"Don't be ridiculous. None of us can make it solo. It's too difficult. Listen to me. I have influence here, I can make a place for you."

"No, Damien, you don't have to do that."

"I know I don't have to. I want to. For old time's sake, Alisha. You still matter to me. Of all the people I knew before the Ritual, you are the only one who still matters to me."

"Do you still talk to your mother? Jeffrey? Damien? Hello?"

The house was dark. He was not here. Alisha thought about waiting on the darkened porch, the wind rustling the leaves around her, and decided to go back to the hotel.

He was going to laugh at her, she knew, when she told him why she'd gone back. No reason, really, other than she got scared. Standing there in the dark, on what seemed an eerily quiet street, she had simply gotten creeped out.

Some vampire I am, she thought.

As she walked toward the boulevard, she wondered if Damien had spoken the truth. If he was, as he said—as he *seemed*—so different from the man she had known when they were both alive, could she trust him now? Could she believe him when he said he still cared about her? She fixed her eyes on the sidewalk in front of her, walking quickly and not turning to look at the vacant windows of the houses on either side of her. *What are you afraid of,* she chided herself, *a ghost?*

As the thought entered her mind, she thought she felt something brush her arm, like a spiderweb, and goosebumps rose all across her arms and shoulders. *There's no such thing as ghosts,* she told herself. But once upon a time she would have said there was no such thing as vampires, either. Were the veils between the land of the dead and the land of the living that thin? Becoming a vampire hadn't increased her curiosity about occult things. She kept to what she knew. They had had a good life in Portsmouth, Alice and Belinda with their weaving and...

She gasped, as she felt something as solid as a hand clutch at her arm, and she walked faster. The street lights refracted as she looked at them, casting rainbows from her eyelashes. She could see the tracks of the streetcar, now, which would take her back in to the French Quarter, and her too expensive hotel, which Damien had said he would "*take care of.*" Or maybe she could catch a taxi . . .

The boulevard was empty of cars, not a taxi or even a passenger car went by. Alisha had always heard New Orleans was a party town, where the bars never closed, but this neighborhood of mansions and plantation houses was, for lack of a better word, dead. Not like some of the sections she'd seen, coming in from the airport, boarded-up houses and places where the hurricane's flooding had driven people out, perhaps never to return. It had been a few years since the disaster, but some parts of the city were still abandoned. But here? This was a rich neighborhood, and any damage had long since been repaired, and yet there seemed to be no one stirring within a mile of her.

She walked up to a wood-slatted bench at the streetcar stop, green paint flaking from it onto the concrete, and sat. They said New Orleans had all kinds of people; that was what made it special. Celebrities lived here, and artists, and the rich and old ruling blood of the south, and female impersonators performed strip acts at all hours of day and night on Bourbon Street. It was a city of decadence and tradition all at once. Maybe it would be a safe place, a place of safety in numbers at least, with Damien and his cohort. She tried not to think about how she had lost the others while she tried not to get her hopes up, either.

Damien, when he had been called Jeffrey, in the days before the Ritual and before the Blood, had often promised her things that had failed to come to pass because of his own lack of planning or his lack of understanding. "I just want to make your dreams come true," he would say, like the time she had been telling him for weeks about her plans to spend an evening alone, in meditation, and he'd used that night to plan her a surprise birthday party. "I knew you'd be home," he had said, hurt, when she confronted him angrily about it, after the party was over. He had sulked for weeks after that. Or the day of the annular eclipse. He had picked her up from work, a picnic basket brimming in the car, with just an hour to get far enough north to see it in totality. When they'd run out of gas twenty miles short of the latitude, she had merely sighed in resignation. Jeffrey's dreams were always beyond his scope to realize, somehow.

A streetcar was coming. She stood up in anticipation, the goosebumps returning despite the sticky heat. The bell clanged as if from far away. The single white light on the car shone like a star, growing brighter and brighter as it drew near, until she had to look away, turn her head, as the car drew alongside her. The doors opened and she went up the three steps, her mouth opening to ask the driver if the fare was the same . . .

A well-dressed devil who was recognizably Jeffrey/Damien sat in the driver's seat, grinning. She gaped, aware of her mouth hanging open as she stared at him in a brocade jacket the color of dark wine, demure white ruffles lying flat between his lapels and a satin tuxedo seam of black running down the length of his pants. His hair was slicked back, smooth and black, and he clicked one long nail against the control bar. The Damien she had known as Jeffrey had never put on so much as a leisure jacket in the time she'd known him. Now, he had even grown a goatee, which she might have laughed at if she hadn't been so startled. He looked like a lounge singer from Hell, suave and creepy.

"Jeff—?" she started to say, but quickly switched to "Damien?"

"At your service," he said with a sweep of his hand, and as his arm moved she thought she heard distant bells tinkle.

She stepped further into the car and sat in the front seat, facing him. The train car began to move, and ahead of them she saw a tunnel made of ancient trees. "I went to the address," she began. "When you weren't there, I didn't know what to do. So I was heading back to the hotel."

"Then the hotel you shall have." He snapped his fingers and she thought, for half a second, that there was a flash of lightning, a clap of thunder . . .

She caught herself before she fell, her feet suddenly under her, her toes sinking into the thick carpet of her hotel room. Her arms flailed a bit and she clutched her stomach like a person getting off a rollercoaster. "Oh my god," she said, realizing she was standing in her hotel room, wearing only a slip and her bra. "How did we get back here? Where are my clothes?"

Damien was standing off to one side, the huge window overlooking the river glittering like a wall of black marble behind him, his hands crossed over his chest. "Simple, my dear. You never left. We never left. You have been here all along. You'll find your clothes still in the closet where you put them when you unpacked."

She sat down on the bed, and realized that the air conditioning was going full blast in the room. "We never left."

"That's right. At a certain moment while you were dressing, I merely slipped in and . . . took you away." His grin was the smug sort she associated with street magicians. "You thought you took the streetcar to the Garden District. You thought you walked around the block. But all the time, you were right here." He tapped his right temple as he said "here."

She crossed her legs. "No wonder the houses were all dark."

"Excuse me?"

"No wonder all the houses were dark. You couldn't envision what they would all be like, full of people." She crossed her arms, too, then got up and flicked the air conditioner off.

"Don't be silly," he was saying, but the smugness had evaporated. "I just wanted to scare you a little. And I succeeded, didn't I." As he raised his eyebrow, she heard a distant strain of ominous music.

Alisha sighed. "Whatever, J— Damien. That's very nice. But I thought the point of tonight was I'd meet some of your coven and we'd see whether there's a place for me here, wasn't it?"

His lips folded a bit and he frowned. Now he looked like the man she'd known three years ago.

"Are those clothes real, too? Or are they just another one of your illusions?" She couldn't help but be a touch snide.

"They're real," he growled. "But they don't have to be." He spun once, in place, and when he stopped to face her, his outfit had changed to a severe-looking but no less over-the-top black outfit of leather and studs. "I've become a master of illusion, Alisha," he said, then. "My power has no limits."

"Well," said Alisha, stifling a yawn, "you always were a dreamer."

Suddenly he was there, his hand at her throat, his face inches from hers. "Do not mock me," he said through clenched teeth.

Alisha blinked calmly. "Or what, you'll kill me?" She had been afraid when the danger had been unknown, ghosts, empty houses, whatever might have lurked in the dark, but she had no reason to be afraid of Damien or his theatrics. "You haven't changed, Damien. You're the same dreamer who never gets what he wants now that you were when I left you three years ago."

"No!" He stood away from her now, turned his face to the window. From where she stood, she could see part of the arc of the river, a tugboat passing, green light blinking on its bow. He shrugged as he composed himself. "Alisha. You're only acting this way because you're still hurt, still grieving for your lost coven."

"You don't know anything about them," she said, her voice cold and quiet. They had all been women. Four of them. Alisha had met one of them at a quilting group in Portsmouth, and had become a housemate, and then, after the Ritual, a coven member. It had been a happy household until someone had decided that five women living together was unnatural.

"I know enough," Damien was saying, fingering his ruffles and looking down at the carpet. "I know you're alone. I . . . I'm sorry for being so hasty."

She sneaked a glance at him. He was looking at the polished toe of his shoe.

He went on. "I shouldn't have tried to scare you or intimidate you with my powers. But I wanted so much to show you . . ."

"I know," she said.

"I didn't ask you to come all the way here to fight with you. Will you give me another chance to explain?" He looked up, as if on cue.

Alisha sighed. "Take me to dinner and I'll think about it."

"Dinner."

"You know what I mean."

"Fine." He drew himself up then. "You'll see how easy it is for me. No begging or struggling. Then we'll talk."

Alisha went to the closet and put on the clothes she had picked out once already that evening. A black silk skirt, knee length, with a burgundy silk sleeveless blouse that, annoyingly, matched Damien's jacket. She slung the black silk jacket that matched the skirt over her shoulder, and slipped into flat black leather shoes. Being alone in the world sometimes made her fearful, at other times cavalier. "Lead on," she said, wondering in the back of her mind whether this time the getting dressed was real.

THEY WALKED DOWN Bourbon Street, where midnight crowds milled and wandered from bar to bar with plastic cups of drinks in their hands, modern jazz coming out of one door, reggae the next, karaoke from across the street, and Cajun accordion and spoon-scratch from the one just behind. So many people seemed to be smiling. Alisha wondered how many of them were tourists. She overheard a hawker outside a bar telling a young couple that there were more restaurants in the city now than there had been before Katrina. "Amazing, isn't it, how people bounce back after total disaster?" he was saying.

She turned away from him to hurry to catch up to Damien.

Soon she realized Damien was following one specific woman. Alisha fixed her eyes on the quarry ahead of him, a mid-thirties type in relaxed cut jeans and a T-shirt plain of slogans. Her hair floated in soft curls around her head and she walked with her hand in one front pocket of her jeans. Damien turned and caught Alisha's eye, and suddenly Alisha could see the scene through Damien's eyes, and knew what Damien knew. In the woman's pocket was her tip money for the night, and as she cut through the crowd her underlying thought was to keep the money safe. She was four blocks from her home on the second floor of a building off Royal Street. The woman turned and looked behind her and neither Damien nor Alisha could be seen.

Alisha felt Damien smile. He had worked his way into the woman's mind and made himself, and Alisha, invisible. Be ready, he seemed to say, into Alisha's mind. She brought herself up close behind him.

The woman turned down Rue St. Philip and began to whistle a tune. The street appeared deserted and Alisha guessed it really was, because Damien made his move.

"Excuse me," he said, in a lost-tourist voice, "but could you tell me . . ."

The woman turned to look at him and put her hand over her mouth. Then she said "William?"

And Damien said "Jennifer? Oh my goodness, I never . . . How strange to run into you like this!"

"William, I'm so happy to see you!" The woman threw her arms around Damien's neck and gave a happy little screech. Then she was kissing him, his cheeks, his lips. Alisha waited.

After a few moments, Damien bent his head to the woman's neck and she gasped, her hands rubbing Damien's back. Alisha knew Damien was feeding. She could smell the blood and felt the urge deep in her chest to do the same herself. She wanted to tell him to stop the charade, to stop messing with this poor woman's feelings—and her own. She knew he had not picked this scenario from the woman, Jennifer's, mind without cause, had not cast himself in the character of her old lover by coincidence. But she was caught up in the feeding surge. She could yell at him later.

Jennifer was swooning, now, repeating again and again "William, oh William," and clutching at Damien.

Damien pulled himself back with a deep breath. "Jennifer, you don't know how much I've missed you." He reached a hand toward Alisha. "But there's someone I'd like you to meet."

Alisha stepped forward.

"This is my fiancee, Alisha."

Jennifer seemed to freeze in place. Blood seeped a little where Damien had pulled himself away. "Come say hello, Alisha."

Alisha bent her mouth to the woman's neck. The acrid taste of her perfume disappeared as the blood began to flow. Jennifer stood statue-still and Alisha knew Damien held her in some kind of thrall. Who knew what Jennifer thought she was seeing at this point?

When Alisha pulled back, Damien held her close, holding her head to his chest while she let herself swoon a little on Jennifer's blood. When she looked up, Jennifer was standing off to one side, by herself, her hand over her neck and a wistful look on her face.

"Can she . . . ?"

"She doesn't see us, anymore," Damien said.

Jennifer's chest heaved suddenly and tears tracked her face. Her one hand went unconsciously to her full pocket, and she spun on one foot and ran up the stairs to her apartment. Alisha felt a sympathetic tear well up in her own eye, and she breathed slowly and evenly, until the moment passed, and she could step back from Damien confident and calm once again.

ALISHA HELD HER composure until they were once again alone in her hotel room. She sat in a chair by the window, her hands gripping the carved wood armrests, and snapped "So, tell me what you want to tell me."

"Alisha, Alisha," Damien came to sit on the edge of the bed closest to her. She heard the hiss of his trousers against the silky material of the coverlet as he sat. "I feel a little sorry for you. The Change doesn't seem to have gifted you with much."

"What is that supposed to mean?"

He held up his hands. "When you knew me, when I was alive, I was no one. I was nothing special. The Blood has made me something different, powerful." She saw a blossom of flame bloom behind his head and then disappear, and wondered if his choice of symbols was deliberate. "I was right to come to New Orleans. The veil is thin here," he said, and Alisha shivered, wondering if he had been able to read her thoughts before, "and I have been transformed."

Alisha waited for him to go on.

"But, you Alisha, you didn't even change your name. You're still wearing the same clothes."

"I like these clothes."

"You've forgotten, or maybe you never learned, just how much more life there awaits you now. I want to help you find out, I want to show you how much I've learned." Damien's eyes now blazed with the same flame that had illuminated his face earlier. Tiny fires leaped and jumped within his black irises. "Let me help you find the special power in *you.*"

Alisha folded her hands. "So you're offering me a place in your coven."

"Not just my coven," he said with a smile. "The ruling coven of New Orleans. The ruling coven of this hemisphere, in fact. It's quite a step up from your group of New England spinsters, let me tell you."

"No, Jeffrey, I won't let you tell me." She began to stand, then thought better of it and sat back again, her anger cold rather than hot. Fire. Fire had destroyed the coven in Portsmouth, not fighting or politics or psychodrama. Fire, set by outsiders, who might not have even known they were vampires. Ever since the fights over gay marriage had begun, they'd wondered if they should move to a less conservative area, but had done nothing, and then it was too late . . . She clasped her hands, clamping down on her emotions. "Do you remember why I left you?"

He pursed his lips and the fire in his eyes went out. "Yes. Because I was 'a no-good loser who was never going to amount to anything.'"

Alisha remembered saying those words. She remembered flinging them at him like razors, hoping to cut the clinging threads of his need for her. Clearly, she had not cut deeply enough. "Oh, Jeffrey, Damien . . ." She didn't know where to begin to explain.

Damien took a deep breath. "Look at me, Alisha. I'm not the miserable unfulfilled dreamer you knew."

Alisha could not look at him. She had been angry at him for manipulating the woman who had fed them, angry at him for manipulating her into coming all the way down here and promising a happiness he couldn't deliver. But now she felt more sad than angry, regretful rather than aggressive. She knew what he was going to say even before he said it.

"Take me back. Tell me we can be together again. Give me another chance."

She shook her head, feeling dizzy now, a déjà vu coming over her like they'd had this very argument once before, and maybe they had—her memory of her daylight years was fuzzy sometimes. "No, Jeffrey, you don't understand . . ."

"Then make me understand."

"I will!" She stood up then, her eyes wide and unseeing. The vertigo worsened but she stood her ground. "You're doing it now, even now, I can feel it."

"Doing what?"

"Using your . . . special powers . . . to try to enthrall me."

"I just want you to love me like you should have, then."

The room swirled and disappeared around her, but she formed herself around the beating heart of fresh blood she had drunk so recently. She pressed her hands against her stomach. He could not make her swoon like he had Jennifer. He could make her see things, maybe, but he could not make her forget who she was or where she had come from. "You've failed, Damien. You've failed at the one thing that now you should be able to do, the one thing which you needed to do all along, and which even now you haven't done."

"What is it!" he shouted, and the shout sounded like it came from far away.

"You never understood me, you never understood what I want or what I need." She felt herself beginning to spin, as she drew herself in. "And now, here, you can read my mind, you can feel my very thoughts, can't you?"

"Yes!"

"And yet, even with the ability to know my thoughts, you think you can win me over with scare tactics and displays of power and a cheap old boyfriend reunion scenario?"

"I just wanted you to feel my passion . . ."

"All that power and all you can do is fall back to your same old tricks? You never knew me, Jeffrey, you never knew anything but your own obsession for me and your own sense of self-importance. Our relationship was nothing but your attempts to show me how hard you worked for me, when really you did it all for yourself." Now

Alisha could see the faces of others all around her, women and men, staring, their eyes unblinking and their hearts not beating. The room disappeared completely and out of the vagueness that was left came the faces. She shrank under their gaze for a moment until she realized they were not looking at her.

They were looking at Damien. He was there, then, in his silly, archaic, brocade jacket, his fingers nervously plucking at his ruffles and his beard. "Alisha," he whispered. "Please don't do this."

"Please don't do what?" She grabbed his hands and held them in her own. "Tell you the truth? Jeffrey, listen to me, I'm only telling you the truth. Can't you see what you've tried to do to me here? Can't you see how wrong it is?"

He pulled his hands from hers. "Yes. I see I was wrong to invite you here, wrong to ever offer you a place with me, wrong to even try."

With the suddenness of a cliff drop, the vertigo stopped, and Alisha found herself in the dark. She blinked her eyes but the darkness was complete. She could not hear the echo of her breathing and reached out a hand to find she was in bed. Her own bed, it felt like, in the basement sleeping room at the house in Portsmouth. She felt for the edge of the bed, and swung her feet down and there were her slippers.

This can't be happening, she thought. *This house burned down. It was my night to go out, and I came back to find it burning . . .*

She felt another presence there with her then. "Who is it?"

"We come to thank you." The faces appeared out of the darkness one at a time, each flaring briefly and then disappearing. "Damien has not been one of us for very long, and we forgive him. But we thank you for showing us what he is."

"You're welcome," Alisha said, tears beginning to fall down her face.

"Why are you so sad?"

"This can't be real, this can't be happening. It's another trick of some kind. Or maybe I've lost my mind." She could smell the comforting smell of Belinda's laundry soap, mixed with the old-book scent of her bedroom.

"Your Jeffrey was wrong about many things, including one important thing," the voices told her. "The Ritual did not leave you unchanged. Outwardly and in your soul you seem the same, but your power is a special one for one who will live so long."

"I don't understand."

"The veils between life and death are the veils between yesterday and today, Alisha. You have the gift to part that veil. Use it well."

And then Alisha was alone.

No, not alone. She could feel, almost hear, the breathing of someone else in the house. Sharon, Sharon was asleep in the next room, her heart beating and her chest rising and falling, so she must have fed well tonight. If Sharon went out tonight, tomorrow would be Alisha's night . . .

Alisha burst out of her room into the hallway that separated the basement sleeping rooms. "Wake up, wake up!" One dim bulb lit the corridor.

The others came to their doorways groggy. Morning was approaching as a haze of gray on black. "What is it?" Sharon murmured and then yawned.

"I can't tell you how I know, but we have to leave the house tonight," Alisha began. *Jeffrey might have fancied himself devilish,* she thought, *but in the end he was our guardian angel.* Perhaps in the new future she was creating, he too, would be given another chance at redemption.

✝

THE MOST BEAUTIFUL MAN
IN THE WORLD

DON WEBB

>─!─◄►─•─Ο─•─◄►─!─≺

ER FAVORITE HUNTING GROUND WAS THE CAFE DU MONDE. SHE WASN'T the only one who preyed there, of course; there are great advantages to tourists as prey. It was an open-air cafeteria for vampires: as they wiped their powdered sugar from their chins and talked about how you couldn't get coffee like this back home, you could size them up. Ever since the place opened in 1862 it had served the needs of the city's undead.

There was a fellow there right now. He had had a hard night, maybe an argument with some friends, maybe a fight with his wife and so he had come down to Decatur Street to stare gloomily into his steaming coffee. He didn't even notice the fat pigeons that landed by the tables, keeping like the cafe itself a twenty-four-hour schedule.

She would wait till he decided to walk back to his hotel. He didn't look like someone that was staying in the Quarter, probably he had a room in one of the big hotels near the stadium. Sizing up prey was her second favorite part about being a vampire. She fantasized sometime about being a criminal profiler. Mrs. Sherman was *very* into criminal profilers. Not a lot of work opportunities for anyone who puts 240 down for age. Unlike some of her kind, she prided herself on keeping some tabs on the human world. It made the stalking better, it made the world more sensible, it made the feeding much, much better.

She was sitting in the shadows in the Square. Nine out of ten people couldn't see her. Some people regarded this as a feat of invisibility. She had thought so for years, until she had caught Norbert, that physics students from Tulane. He had known so much! He was the only victim that she had kept alive for a long time. They had had nearly eighteen months together. When she killed him, she had hoped that he would cross over. He was going to write a dissertation on the temporal biophysics of vampires. Of course, she had to kill him before he had submitted anything to his doctoral committee, such information might be useful to the crowd of wannabe Van Helsings that hovered around the vampire community like avenging angels. But it had made things so clear when he had told her . . .

Wait. He's leaving the cafe now. Let him pass. Walk up from behind.

"Excuse me sir? Are you on the way to the hotel?" she asked.

He turned and took in her auburn hair, her warm brown eyes, her diaphanous dress; and she had seduced him with a glance. It was too easy sometimes.

"Yes, Ma'am. Can I help you?" he said.

"I am worried to be out so late. I had seen you at the hotel earlier, and I was hoping you could walk me back. I would feel much safer," she said, already putting out her arm for him to take, which he did lightly, and with a smile thinking that he was the hunter, not the prey.

"Of course I'll walk you back, Ms.—?"

"Burgess," she said, "Sheila Burgess."

They walked and he began small talk. Had she been in the city before? Did she like Bourbon Street? Had she visited the Voodoo Museum? What about the cemetery?

He was boring, so she decided not to spend too long with him. She talked about her knowledge of architecture, about the wrought iron and balconies and the numerous hidden gardens and tiny retreats.

"In fact," she said, "there's a famous courtyard just up that alley. We could look over the fence at it."

They entered the alley.

He said, "I don't see any courtyard. I don't see any fences for that matter."

"Silly I just wanted you off the street for a minute, so I could have you for myself."

She put her arms up as if to draw him close for a kiss, and he bent down. When he passed close enough, she felt her will pouring into his body, holding him still for the feeding. The victim has to give himself willingly, but once the gift is made, he is hers.

Her fangs pierced the throbbing artery, and hot life poured into her in great spurts, filling her with what she needed.

Along with the blood came images, a dream-like stream of the victim's last thoughts and deeds and dreams. Nothing special here—he was a shoe-salesman, here for a business meeting, he couldn't sleep, he had a loveless marriage. His image of his wife was so weak that she couldn't see her at all.

The image stream was very unsatisfying, but it was the icing, and she fed for the cake. His blood was healthy, vital and tasty.

He lost consciousness, and fell out of her arms.

She took his wallet. She seldom needed or used cash, but she felt it lessened the chance of him reporting a vampire to the police. He wouldn't remember much, and the missing wallet would answer such questions as he might have or generate.

She stepped back.

There was time for another victim. She had fed, so it would have to be someone really special. There was a little all-night cafe in the garden district. She only went rarely, but she wanted something more exciting than the half-formed dreams of a shoe-salesman chasing around her head as she lay hidden away during the day.

She was about to fly, when she saw him—the most beautiful man in the world.

He had been watching her, standing less than five feet away. He looked full of admiration and maybe a little lust or love or some emotion that she knew from long ago but didn't have a name for now. He had long black hair, and eyes of cobalt blue. He had a slight tan, making him into some sort of pale-dark demigod.

"Hello, beautiful," he said. If anyone anywhere else had ever said that, she would have laughed, but she felt he meant it, and that she deserved it.

Her first thought was that he was also a vampire. From time to time the undead do seek each other's company, but such relationships are doomed because of the predator's need for resources. Always the hunger gets in the way, always eats love, friendship, art—whatever.

"Hello," she said.

The victim at her feet moaned. She looked down, then back to the beautiful man, but he was walking away.

"Who are you?" she asked.

"I am the shape of your dreams," he said.

She decided not to follow; she had to think. Vampires are a vulnerable lot because of the daily sleep, and the hatred of mankind for their captors.

She decided to call it a night, and flew home.

Home was a tiny boarding house in the garden district. The landlady knew what she was, and thought it was great. The landlady had hopes of being a great horror novelist, and felt the experience of having a vampire tenant would be good on her literary resume.

The landlady was an idiot and Sheila knew she would have to kill her someday. Inside the room with its heavy drapes and dust-covered blinds lay the coffin.

From *The Temporal Biophysics of Hemoglobin-Consuming Undead*

BY NORBERT NEILLY

(UNPUBLISHED THESIS) PG. 14

The attraction that human beings have toward vampires is not a simple sexual or aesthetic attraction; although such elements may certainly exist. I will show in this paper that the attraction is based on the normal movement of complex systems in time. In short humans are drawn to vampires because the vampire is more closely associated with the field-state called the *future*, than the present. There is a capacity discharge between the human and vampire that allows the human to have the same sort of experiences that they would normally associate with the *future*—that is to say intense fantasy activity or, if you will, daydreaming raised a quantum level. The vampire on the other hand has a discharge of the human's past in the form of memories and reveries. This relationship draws the human toward the vampire, by a simple intensification of the force that draws all of us toward the future every day. The vampire is drawn to the human, much as the mind is drawn to past events. This has profound effects on the psychology of both species, oftentimes in ways concealed by themselves. The first study of the micro-tubules which appear to be responsible was by Penrose (1994) and . . . .

All day long were half-formed phantoms for shoe-salesman life. When dusk came she wanted to wash out her brain. She would go clubbing and find someone interesting, someone that she could sink her teeth into her, as it were.

She choose a skimpy little outfit of green satin that showed all kinds of things when she wanted it to.

She stopped by her landlady's.

"You're going out tonight, aren't you?" her landlady asked with that flair for the obvious that seemed to be her most developed trait.

"Yes, Mrs. Sherman," Sheila said.

"How do you pick out you clothes for hunting?"

Sheila gave a brief description of the idea of looking sexy, when you want to attract men. This seemed novel to Mrs. Sherman, and Sheila wondered for the thousandth time how she had ever managed to find a Mr. Sherman in the first place. Of course Mr. Sherman was long gone by the time Mrs. Sherman had moved to New Orleans from Boston. Sheila often thought that everyone in the city except her was a transplant. Of course she was one of the very few that still regretted the Louisiana Purchase.

She had taken the name "Sheila Burgess" because she saw it on an envelope she found in Canal Street. Two men, Dick Clark and Ed Something-or-other, had been promising great wealth to Ms. Burgess. She had found Mrs. Sherman a short time afterward. It had been time to move the coffin again. Sheila moved every nine years, it relieved boredom, and perhaps stopped the stake-happy. Vampire hunters had never been a problem until about a century ago when Bram Stoker's novel had come out. That dreadful Rice woman, whom she had met at a party once, had made everything much worse by connecting New Orleans with vampire lore. Since her books the sale of cigarette cases with hidden mirrors had increased disgustingly.

There were great side-effects though, there were all these young people called Goths that wandered around the city *hoping* to be victims, and there were scads of would-be writers *hoping* to somehow tap into the success as though success were a vein. She wondered if she was the only vampire that had a literary landlord. Ah well, being a muse isn't so bad.

She told Mrs. Sherman that it was time to fly, and the middle-aged matron giggled with delight.

The club was for the Goth crowd. Normally they were pretty dull. The images and dreams that came along with their blood were full of black clothes, black walls, and the disgusting use of black makeup. This monochrome approach to life once again convinced Sheila that she was glad she was dead. However such clubs did collect a truly delectable food, the young would-be artist, whose blood was seasoned with the holy fire. She loved the blood of poets. One intense young man that she had lost control with and drained last year had the most searing dreams and images in his blood—so much so that she tracked down his works and read them. She was terribly disappointed; it seemed that his hunger for art was high, but that he regrettably knew nothing of the hard work—the precision that must match the passion.

She saw a likely fellow almost as soon as she passed in the Black Orchid's portals.

He was even handing a little book to a girl he was trying to impress, who was in turn doing her best unimpressed face.

She walked over.

"Are you the poet?" she said, her eyes big on the chapbook. *Bat Wings and Rose Petals* by Robert Severson.

He drew himself up, quite nice looking in his black velveteen suit. "I am the poet," he said. Then the veneer of arrogance broke with a smile, "It's my first book, would you like a copy?"

"Yes," she smiled.

Then they were talking and he was drinking coffee, and she wasn't drinking anything, but that wasn't too odd—half the patrons were trying to give out that they were vampires.

Then she glanced across the room and saw him.

He was in a blue shirt that matched his eyes, and wore a turquoise and silver pendant. He looked fierce and beautiful.

The poet had been speaking, and then noticed her distraction, and started to get up and leave.

"No," she said, "I thought I saw an old friend. I'm new to the city and had been hoping to run into Rebecca." A name picked quickly from the mental hat.

"Oh," the poet kept talking, and she decided to seduce him first, feed, and then track down the mystery man.

The poet was soon persuaded to taste the night air, and she soon tasted his rich redness. He was wonderfully full of dreams of pearls given to sweethearts, moonlit nights and white rose petals shaken onto black sheets, and storms in the ocean and Paris in the springtime. She had been to Paris as a little girl. It was different then, she had dreamt of going to see the Eiffel Tower.

He fell gently onto the street. She might drain him all the way to see if he had the strength to pass over. What was it Norbert said about that phase-transition?

He was watching. He had pressed himself against the wall of a building, being at one with its shadows.

When he saw that she saw him, he stepped forward smiling and open.

"Who are you?" she asked.

"John Seymour."

"That's very helpful. What are you?"

"A connoisseur of vampirism."

"What if I don't like to be watched?"

"You like to be watched, you dream about it, you fantasize about how good you are, and I must say you are, unlike many of the clumsy excuses for vampires I've seen, quite good, and quite beautiful."

"You're very gallant to have such a morbid hobby."

"It isn't a hobby. Here have a picture of me." He reached in his pants pocket and took out a snapshot. It was him, standing on Commerce Street in full daylight, reading a paper.

She looked up at him to ask another question, but found herself paralyzed for a moment. When it passed he was gone.

THE NEXT NIGHT, the mystery man was all she could think of. She stood at the street corner in the photo. Sometimes she would fly high above it and watch the streets and alleys. But he didn't come.

The night after that she tried hanging out at the Black Orchid.

The third night she was really hungry, but she made herself feed only in tiny amounts all over the city in the hopes she would find him looking at her.

She wanted him.

Not in the way she wanted a victim; although there was some of that.

She wanted him in the way she used to want a man, if after two hundred years of no human desires her memory was accurate.

It wasn't just sex, it was—well something more.

On the fifth night he found her. She had been heading to the Cafe du Monde. He was behind her on Decatur St.

"Ms. Burgess?" he asked.

His voice was warm like the gulf sea she had played in so very long ago.

"Yes," she said.

"Ms. Burgess, I thought about dropping by your home on Chambers St. today, but then I realized that you wouldn't be up."

Fear filled her; she should run; he knew where her coffin was. But his eyes were the eyes of starlight, and she could fear nothing.

"Ms. Burgess, or may I call you Sheila?"

"You may call me Violeta. I was born Violeta Zivie."

"What a beautiful name, the 'veiled one.' How fine for someone in whose aspect and her eyes the best of both bright do meet," he said.

"What do you want from me?"

"Everything, really. All the world and time. But I will start with a question: do you miss the day?"

Sheila thought of the warm sun—that great yellow that she had not seen since the early settlement here.

"Of course I miss the day."

"I can give you the day. Well, maybe I can give you the day."

"How?"

"I am your future, much as you are the future of men. I feed upon vampires, drawing their rich accumulation of the past. I don't have to feed often, once a decade perhaps. So I spend a long time looking for my prey. I've been watching you for three years, ever since you killed a student of mine at Tulane."

"Norbert. But I—"

"You needn't say anything. He died happy, which is a rare thing in the world of men."

"I had hoped he would pass over."

"I had hoped so too, I would have spent many long nights with him as we would bring science to bear on ancient magics. Oh don't look at me that way, I am not interested in putting blood in vials and testing my theories on dogs and mice.

There is a way to approach magic with science, already half in magic and wholly informed by wonder."

"Did you become what you are through your science?"

"No, I was you. I was brought to an even higher realm by a poor madwoman. She never knew what had happened to her, how she reclaimed the day by feeding on her own kind. Trying for self-knowledge began my science."

"If you drain me, I will be as you?"

"You might. Or you might be a husk that I leave on the street to wait the long centuries looking for one as beautiful as you."

"That doesn't offer me much hope."

"We have never been in the job of offering hope. Only possibility," he said.

"Norbert said that. He said that vampires offer dreams," she said. "What do you get if I die?"

"Nutrition and two hundred years of memories, not just yours, but of all those you have feasted upon."

"And I would get such dreams as you represent."

She thought about it only a moment, and then looking deeply into the cobalt of his eyes, decided they were so deep that the future must live there.

She stepped forward and put her arms around him. She kissed him once, then offered her neck.

"To the future" she whispered.

For George Alec Effinger

COLD TURKEY

NANCY A. COLLINS

><del>·‐·<>·‐O‐·<>·‐·<

THE RED RAVEN IS A REAL SCUM-PIT. THE ONLY THING MARKING IT
as a bar is the vintage Old Crow ad in the front window and a stuttering
neon sign that says lounge. The johns are always backing up and the place
perpetually stinks of piss.

She had to give the dead boy credit; he had the trick of appearing
human nailed down tight. He'd learned just what gestures and inflections to use in
his conversation to hide the fact his surface gloss and glitz wasn't there merely to
disguise basic shallowness, but an utter lack of humanity.

She'd seen enough of the kind of humans he imitated: pallid, self-important
intellectuals who prided themselves on their sophistication and knowledge of "hip"
art, sharpening their wit at the expense of others. Like the vampiric mimic in their
midst, they produced nothing but thrived on draining the vitality from others. The
only difference was that the vampire was more honest about it.

Sonja worked her way to the bar, careful to keep herself shielded from the dead
boy's view, both physically and psychically. It wouldn't do for her quarry to catch
scent of her just yet. She could hear the vampire's nasal intonations as it held forth
on the demerits of various artists.

"Frankly, I consider his use of photo-montage to be inexcusably banal—If I
wanted to look at photographs, I'd go to Olan Mills!"

She wondered where the vampire had overheard—or stolen—that particular
drollery. A dead boy of his wattage didn't come up with *bon mots* and witty remarks
spontaneously. When you had to spend a lot of conscious energy remembering to
breathe and blink, there was no such thing as top-of-your-head snappy patter. It was
all protective coloration, right down to the last *double entendre* and Monty Python
impersonation.

It would be another decade or two before the vampire dressed in black silk and leather with the stainless steel ankh dangling from one ear and a crystal embedded in his left nostril could divert his energies to something besides the full-time task of insuring his continuance. And for some reason she doubted the dead boy had much of a future in the predator business.

She waved down the bartender and ordered a beer. As she awaited its arrival, she caught a glimpse of herself in the mirror backing the bar. To the casual observer she looked to be no more that twenty-five. Tricked out in a battered leather jacket, a stained Circle Jerks T-shirt, patched jeans, mirrored sunglasses, and with dark hair twisted into a tortured cockatoo's crest, she looked like just another gothic college girl checking out the scene. No one would ever guess she was actually forty years old.

She sucked the cold suds down, participating in her own form of protective coloration. She could drink a case or three of the stuff with the only effect being she'd piss like a firehose. Beer didn't do it for her anymore. Neither did hard liquor. Or cocaine. Or heroin. Or crack. She tried them all, in dosages that would have put the entire U.S. Olympic Team in the morgue; but no luck. There was only one drug that plunked her magic twanger nowadays. Only one thing that could get her off.

And that drug was blood.

Yeah, the dead boy was good enough he could have fooled another vampire. Could have. But didn't

She eyed her prey speculatively. She doubted she'd have any trouble taking the sucker down. She rarely did, these days. Least not the lesser evolved undead that still lacked major psionic muscle. Sure, they had enough mesmeric ability to gull the humans in their vicinity, but little else. Compared to her own psychic abilities, the art-fag vampire might as well have been packing a pea-shooter. Still, it wasn't smart to get too cocky. Lord Morgan had dismissed her in such a high-handed manner, and now he was missing half his face.

She shifted her vision from the human to the Pretender spectrum, studying the vampire's true appearance. She wondered if the black-garbed art aficionados clustered about their mandarin, their heads bobbing like puppets, would still consider the pronouncements worthy if they knew his skin was the color and texture of rattan sailcloth. Or that his lips were black and shriveled, revealing oversized fangs set in a perpetual death's head grimace. No doubt, they'd drop their little plastic cups of cheap blush and back away in horror, their surface glaze of urbanite sophistication and studied ennui replaced by honest, old-fashioned monkey-brain terror.

Humans need masks in order to live their day-to-day lives, even amongst their own kind. Little did they know that their dependence on artifice and pretense provided the perfect hiding place for a raft of predators. Predators like the vampire pretending to be an art-fag. Predators such as herself.

Sonja tightened her grip on the switchblade in the pocket of her leather jacket. *Midnight! Time to drop your masks!*

"Uh, excuse me?"

She jerked around a little too fast, startling the young man at her elbow. She'd been so focused on her prey she'd been unaware of his approaching her. Sloppy. Really sloppy:

"Yeah, what is it?"

The young man blinked, slightly taken aback by the brusqueness in her voice. "I, uh, was wondering if I might, uh, buy you a drink?"

She automatically scanned him for signs of Predator taint, but he came up clean. One hundred percent USDA Human. He was taller than her by a couple of inches, his blonde hair pulled back into a ponytail. There were three rings in his right ear and one in his left nostril. Despite the metalwork festooning his nose, he was quite handsome.

Sonja was at a loss for words. She was not used to being approached by normal people in public. She tended to generate a low-level psychic energy that most humans found unnerving, if not antagonistic. In layman's terms, she tended to either scare people or piss them off.

"I—I—" She shot her prey a glance out of the corner of her eye. Shit! The bastard was starting to make his move, hustling one of the more entranced hangers-on.

"I realize this is going to sound like a really dumb, cheap come-on," he said, giving her an embarrassed smile. "But I saw you from across the room—and I just had to meet you. Please let me buy you a drink."

"I, uh, I—"

The vampire was escorting its prey outside, smiling widely as it continued to discourse on modem art

"There's something I have to take care of—I'll be right back! I promise! Don't go away!" she blurted, and dashed off in pursuit of her target for the night

SHE SCANNED THE parking lot, checking for signs of the vampire's passage. She prayed she wasn't too late. Once a vamp isolated and seduced a human from the herd, they tended to move quickly. She knew that from her own experience at the hands of Lord Morgan, the undead bastard responsible for her own transformation.

The vampire and its prey were sitting in the backseat of a silver BMW with heavily tinted windows; their blurred silhouettes moving like shadows reflected in an aquarium. There was no time to waste. She'd have to risk being spotted.

The imitation art-fag looked genuinely surprised when her fist punched through the back window; sending tinted safety glass flying into the car. He hissed a challenge, exposing his fangs, as he whipped about to face her. His victim sat beside him, motionless as a mannequin, his eyes unfocused and fly open. The human's erect penis jutted forward, vibrating like a tuning fork.

Sonja grabbed the vampire by the collar of his black silk shirt and pulled him, kicking and screaming, through the busted back windshield. The human didn't even blink.

"Quit yer bitchin'!" Sonja snapped as she hurled the snarling vampire onto the parking lot gravel. "Let's get this over with, dead boy! I got a hot date!"

The vampire launched himself at her, talons hooked and fangs extended. Sonja moved to meet the attack, flicking open her switchblade with a snap of her wrist. The silver blade sank into the vampire's exposed thorax, causing him to shriek in pain. The vampire collapsed, spasming as his system reacted to the silver's toxin.

Sonja knelt and swiftly removed the vampire's head from his shoulders. The body was already starting to putrefy by the time she located the BMW's keys. She unlocked the trunk and tossed the vampire's rapidly decomposing remains inside, making sure the keys were left in his pants pocket

She looked around, but there were no witnesses to be seen in the darkened lot. She moved around to the passenger side and opened the door, tugging the human out of the car.

He stood propped against the bumper like a drunkard, his eyes swimming and his face slack. His penis dangled from his pants like a deflated party balloon. Sonja took his chin between her thumb and forefinger and turned his head so that his eyes met hers.

"This never happened. You do not remember leaving the bar with anyone. Is that clear?"

"N-nothing h-happened," he stammered.

"Excellent! Now go back in the bar and have a good time. Oh, and stick that thing back in your pants! You don't want to get busted for indecent exposure, do you?"

SHE WAS BUZZING by the time she re-entered the bar. She liked to think of it as her après-combat high. The adrenaline from the battle was still sluicing around inside her; juicing her perceptions and making her feel as if she was made of lightning and spun glass. It wasn't as intense as the boost she got from blood, but it was good.

Someone jostled her, and Sonja looked down into the face of a drab, mousey woman, her face set into a scowl. She paused, studying the schizophrenia that radiated from the other woman like a martyr's halo. The scowling woman blushed, drew her shoulders in, ducked her chin, and hurried away, as if she'd suddenly woken up and discovered herself sleepwalking in the nude. Sonja shrugged and continued scanning the bar for the young man who'd spoken to her earlier.

Give it up, he's forgotten you and found another bimbo for the evening.

Sonja fought to keep from cringing at the sound of the Other's voice inside her head. She managed to go almost all night without having to endure its commentary.

She found him waiting for her at the bar. Sonja made a last minute spot-check for any blood or telltale ichor that might be clinging to her, then moved forward.

"You still interested in buying me that drink?"

The young man's smile was genuinely relieved. "You came back!"

"I said I'd be back, didn't I?"

"Yeah. You did." He smiled again and offered her his hand, "I guess I ought to introduce myself. I'm Judd."

Sonja took his hand and smiled without parting her lips. "Pleased to meet you, Judd. I'm Sonja."

"What the hell's going on here?!"

Judd's smile faltered as his gaze fixed itself on something just over Sonja's right shoulder. She turned and found herself almost nose-to-nose with a young woman dressed in a skin-tight black sheath, fishnet stockings, and way too much make-up. The woman psychosis covered her face like a caul found on a newborn infant, pulsing indentations marking her eyes, nose and mouth.

Judd closed his eyes and sighed. "Kitty, look it's over! Get a life of your own and let go of mine, alright?"

"Oh, is that how you see it? Funny, I remember you saying something different! Like how you'd *always* love me! Guess I was stupid to believe that, huh?"

Kitty's urge turned the caul covering her face an interesting shade of magenta. The way it swirled and pulsed reminded Sonia of a lava lamp.

"You're not getting away that easy, asshole! And who's this—your new slut?" Kitty slapped the flat of her hand against Sonja's leather-clad shoulder as if to push her away from Judd.

Sonja grabbed Kitty's wrist, being careful not to break it in front of Judd.

Come on, snap the crazy bitch's arm off, purred the Other. *She deserves it.*

"Don't touch me."

Kitty tried to yank herself Free of Sonja's grip. "I'll fucking touch you anytime I want! Just you stay away from my boyfriend, bitch! Now let me go!" She made to rake Sonja's face with her free hand, only to have that one grabbed as well, forcing her to look directly into her rival's face.

Kitty's features grew pale and she stopped struggling. Sonja knew the other woman was seeing her—truly seeing her—for what she was. Only three kinds of humans could perceive The Real World: psychics, poets, and lunatics. And Kitty definitely qualified for the last one.

She released the girl, who stood massaging her wrists, her gaze still fixed on her. She opened her mouth as if to say something then turned and hurried away, nearly tripping over her own high heels as she fled.

Judd looked uncomfortable. "I'm sorry you had to go through that. Kitty's a weird girl. We lived together for a few months, but she was incredibly jealous. It got to the point where I couldn't take any more of it, so I moved out. She's been dogging my tracks ever since. She scared off my last two girlfriends."

Sonja shrugged, "I don't scare easy."

HE WASN'T AFRAID of her. Nor did she detect the self-destructive tendencies that usually attracted men to her kind. Judd was not a tranced moth drawn to her dark flame, nor was he a renfield in search of a master He was simply a good-natured young man who found her physically attractive. The novelty of his normalcy intrigued her.

He bought her several drinks, all of which she downed without effect. But she did feel giddy, almost lightheaded, while in his company. To be mistaken for a desirable human woman was actually quite flattering. Especially since she'd stopped thinking of herself as human some time back.

They ended up dancing, adding their bodies to the surging crowd that filled the slam pit. At one point, Sonja was amazed to find herself laughing, genuinely laughing, one arm wrapped about Judd's waist. And then Judd leaned in and kissed her.

She barely had time to retract her fangs before his tongue found hers. She slid her other arm around his waist and pulled him into her, grinding herself against him. He responded eagerly, his erection rubbing against her hip like a friendly tomcat. And she found herself wondering how his blood would taste.

She pushed him away so hard be staggered backward a couple of steps, almost falling on his ass. Sonja shook her head as if trying to dislodge something in her ear, a guttural moan rising from her chest.

"Sonja?" There was a confused, hurt look on his face.

She could *see* his blood, beckoning her from just beneath the surface of his skin: the veins traced in blue, the arteries pulsing purple. She turned her back on him and ran from the bar, her head lowered. She shouldered her way through a knot of dancers, sending them flying like duckpins. Some of the bar's patrons hurled insults in her direction, a couple even spat at her, but she was deaf to their anger.

She put a couple of blocks between her and the bar before she stopped to catch her breath. She slumped into a darkened doorway, staring at her shaking hands as if they belonged to someone else.

"I liked him. I honestly liked him and was going to . . . going to . . ."

Like. Hate. What's the difference? Blood is the life, wherever it comes from.

"Not like that. I never feed off anyone who doesn't deserve it Never"

Aren't we special?

"Shut up, bitch."

"Sonja?"

She had him pinned to the wall, one forearm clamped against his windpipe in a choke hold before she recognized him. Judd clawed at her arm, his eyes bugging from their sockets.

"I'm . . . sorry . . ." he gasped out

She let him go. "No, I'm the one who should be sorry. More than you realize."

Judd regarded her apprehensively as he massaged his throat, but there was still no fear in his eyes. "Look, I don't know what it is I said or did back there at the bar that put you off . . . "

"The problem isn't with you, Judd. Believe me." She turned and began walking away, but he hurried after her.

"I know an all-night coffeehouse near here. Maybe we could go and talk things over there—?"

"Judd, just leave me alone, okay? You'd be a lot better off if you just forgot you ever met me."

"How could I forget someone like you?"

"Easier than you realize."

He was keeping pace alongside her, desperately trying to make eye contact with her. "C'mon Sonja! Give it a chance! I—damn it, would you just *look* at me?"

Sonja stopped in mid-step to face him, her expression unreadable behind her mirrored sunglasses. "That's the *last* thing you want me to do."

Judd sighed and fished a pen and piece of paper out of his pocket. "You're one weird chick, that's for sure! But I *like* you, don't ask me why." He scribbled something on the scrap of paper and shoved it into her hand. "Look, here's my phone number. *Call* me, okay?"

Sonja closed her fist around the paper. "Judd—"

He held his hands out, palms facing up. "No strings attached, I promise. Just call me."

Sonja was surprised to find herself smiling. "Okay. I'll call you. Now will you leave me alone?"

WHEN SHE REVIVED the next evening she found Judd's phone number tucked away in one of the pockets of her leather jacket. She sat cross-legged on the coarse cotton futon that served as her bed and stared at it for a long time.

She'd been careful to make sure Judd hadn't followed her the night before. Her current nest was a drafty loft apartment in the attic of an old warehouse in the district just beyond the French Quarter. Outside of her sleeping pallet, an antique cedar wardrobe, a couple of Salvation Army-issue chairs, a refrigerator, a cordless telephone, and the scattered packing crates containing the esoteric curios she used as barter amongst information and magick brokers, the huge space was practically empty. Except for those occasions when the Dead came to visit. Such as tonight.

At first she didn't recognize the ghost. He'd lost his sense of self in the time since his death, blurring his spectral image somewhat. He swirled up through the floorboards like a gust of blue smoke, gradually taking shape before her eyes. It was only when the phantom produced a smoldering cigarette from his own ectoplasm that she recognized him.

"Hello, Chaz."

The ghost of her former renfield made a noise that sounded like a cat being drowned. The Dead cannot speak clearly—even to Pretenders—except on three days of the year: Fat Tuesday, Halloween, and the Vernal Equinox.

"Come to see how your murderer is getting on, I take it?"

Chaz made a sound like a church bell played at half-speed.

"Sorry, I don't have a Ouija board, or we could have a proper conversation. Is there a special occasion for tonight's haunting, or are things just boring over on your side?"

Chaz frowned and pointed at the scrap of paper Sonja held in her hand. The ghost-light radiating from him was the only illumination in the room.

"What? You don't want me to call this number?"

Chaz nodded his head, nearly sending it floating from his shoulders.

"You tried warning Palmer away from me last Mardi Gras. Didn't work; but I suppose you know that already. He's living in Central America right now. We're very happy."

The ghost's laughter sounded like fingers raking a chalkboard. Sonja grimaced. "Yeah, big laugh, dead boy. And I'll tell you one thing, Chaz; Palmer's a damn sight better in bed than you ever were!"

Chaz made an obscene gesture that was tendered pointless since he no longer had a body from the waist down. Sonja laughed and clapped her hands, rocking back and forth on her haunches.

"I *knew* that'd burn your ass, dead or not! Now piss off! I've got better things to do than play charades with a dead hustler!"

Chaz yowled like a baby dropped in a vat of boiling oil and disappeared in a swirl of dust and ectoplasm, leaving Sonja alone with Judd's phone number still clenched in one fist.

Hell, she thought as she reached for the cordless phone beside the futon, *if Chaz didn't want me to call the guy, then it must be the right thing to do . . .*

THE PLACE WHERE they rendezvoused was a twenty-four hour establishment in the French Quarter that had, over the course of the last fifty years, been a bank, a show-bar, and a porno shop before becoming a coffee house. They sat at a small table in the back and sipped iced coffee.

Judd's hair was freshly washed and he smelled of aftershave, but those were the only concessions he'd made to the mating ritual. He still wore his nose and earrings and a Bongwater T-shirt that had been laundered so often the silk-screened image was starting to flake off.

Judd poked at the iced coffee with a straw. "If I'm not getting too personal— what was last night all about?"

Sonja studied her hands as she spoke. "Look, Judd. There's a lot about me you don't know—and I'd like to keep it that way. If you insist on poking into my past, I'm afraid I'll have to leave. It's not that I don't like you—I *do*—but I'm a very private person. And it's for a good reason."

"Is—Is there someone else?"

"Yes. Yes, there is."

"A husband?"

She had to think about that one for a few seconds before answering. "In some ways. But, no; I'm not married."

Judd nodded as if this explained something. It was obvious that some of what she'd said was bothering him, but he was trying to play it cool. Sonja wondered what it was like, living a life where the worst things you had to deal with were jealous lovers and hurt feelings. It seemed almost paradisiacal from where she stood.

After they finished their iced coffees they hit the Quarter. It was after midnight, and the lower section of Decatur Street, the portion located in the French Market, was starting to wake up. The streets outside the bars were decorated with clots of young people dressed in black leather, sequins, and recycled seventies rags. The scenesters milled about, flashing their tattoos and bumming cigarettes off one another, as they waited for something to happen.

Someone called Judd's name and he swerved across the street toward a knot of youths lounging outside a dance bar called the Crystal Blue Persuasion. Sonja hesitated before following him.

A young man dressed in a black duster, his shoulder-length hair braided into three pig tails and held in place by Tibetan mala beads carved in the shapes of skulls, moved forward to greet Judd.

Out of habit, Sonja scanned his face for Predator taint. Human. While the two spoke, she casually examined the rest of the group loitering outside the club. Human. Human. Human, Hu—

She froze.

The smell of *vargr* was strong, like the stink of a wet dog. It was radiating from a young man with a shaved forehead, like that of an ancient samurai. The hair at the back of his head was extremely long and held in a loose ponytail, making him look like a punker mandarin. He wore a leather jacket whose sleeves looked as if they'd been chewed off at the shoulder, trailing streamers of mangled leather and lining like gristle. He had one arm draped over the shoulder of a little punkette, her face made deathly pale by Face powder.

The *vargr* met Sonja's gaze and held it, grinning his contempt. Without realizing it, her hand closed around her switchblade.

"I'd like you to meet a friend of mine—"

Judd's hand was on her elbow, drawing her attention away from the teenaged werewolf Sonja struggled to keep the disorientation of having her focus broken from showing.

"Huh?"

"Sonja, I'd like you to meet Arlo, he's an old buddy of mine . . ." Arlo frowned at Sonja as if she'd just emerged from under a rock, but offered his hand in deference to his friend. "Pleased to meet you," he mumbled.

"Yeah. Sure."

Sonja shot a sideways glance at the vargr twelve feet away. He was murmuring something into the punkette's ear. She giggled and nodded her head and the two broke away from the rest of the group, sauntering down the street in the direction of the river. The nor paused to give Sonja one last look over his shoulder, his grin too wide and his teeth too big, before disappearing into the shadows with his victim

That's right. Pretend you didn't see it. Pretend you don't know what that grinning hell-hound's going to do with that girl. You can't offend loverboy here by running off to do hand-to-hand combat with a werewolf, can you?

"Shut the fuck up, damn you," she muttered under her breath.

"You say something, Sonja?"

"Just talking to myself."

After leaving Arlo and his friends, they headed farther down the French Quarter that few tourists wandered into after dark, populated with gay bars and less wholesome establishments.

As they passed one of the seedy bars that catered to the late-night hardcore alcoholic trade, someone's mind called out Sonja's name.

A black man, his hair plaited into dredlocks, stepped from the doorway of the Monastery. He wore a black turtleneck sweater and immaculate designer jeans, a gold peace sign the size of a hood ornament slung around his neck.

"Long time no see, Blue"

"Hello, Mal."

The demon Malfeis smiled, exposing teeth that belonged in the mouth of a shark, "No hard feelings, I hope? I didn't want to sell you out like that, girlchick, but I was under orders from Below Stairs."

"We'll talk about it later, Mal . . ."

Just then, the demon noticed Judd. "Got yourself a new renfield, I see."

"Shut up!" Sonja hissed, her aura crackling about her head like an electric halo.

Mal lifted his hands, palms outward. "Whoa! Didn't mean to hit a sore spot there, girly-girl."

"Sonja? Is this guy bothering you?" Judd was hovering at her elbow. He gave Mal a suspicious glare, blind to the demon's true appearance.

"No. Everything's cool," Sonja turned her bath on the grinning demon and tried to block the sound of his laughter echoing in her mind.

Who was that guy?"

"Judd—"

"I know! I promised I wouldn't pry into your past."

Sonja shrugged. "Mal is a—business associate of mine. That's all you need to know about him, except no matter what, *never* ask him a question. *Never.*"

They walked on in silence for a few more minutes, then Judd took her into his arms. His kiss was warm and probing and she felt herself begin to relax. Then he reached for her sunglasses.

She batted his hand away, fighting the urge to snarl. "Don't do that."

"I just want to see your eyes."

"No." She pulled away from him, her body language rigid.

"I'm sorry—"

"I better leave. I had a nice time, Judd. I really did. But I have to go."

"You'll call me, won't you?"

"I'm afraid so."

WHY DON'T YOU *fuck him? He wants it bad. So do you. You can't hide that from me.*

The Other's voice was a nettle wedged into the folds of her brain, impossible to dislodge or ignore. Sonja opened the refrigerator and took out a bottle of whole blood, cracking its seal open like she would a beer.

Not that bottled crap again! I hate this shit! You might as well go back to drinking cats! Wouldn't you rather have something nice and fresh? Say a good B-negative mugger or an O-positive rapist? There's still plenty of time to go trawling before the sun comes up. Or, you could always pay a visit to lover-boy.

"Shut up! I've had a belly full of you tonight already!"

My-my! Aren't we being a touchy one? Tell me, how long do you think you can keep up the pretense of being normal? You've almost forgotten what it's like to be human yourself. Why torture yourself by pretending you're something you're not simply to win the favor of a piece of beefsteak?

"He likes me, damn it. He actually likes me."

And what exactly, are you?

"I'm not in the mood for your fucking mind games!"

Welcome to the fold, my dear. You're finally one of us. You're a Pretender.

Sonja shrieked and hurled the half-finished bottle of blood into the sink. She picked up the card table and smashed it to the floor, jumping up and down on the scattered pieces. It was a stupid, pointless gesture, but it made her feel better.

SHE KEPT CALLING him. She knew it was stupid, even dangerous, to socialize with humans, but she couldn't help herself. There was something about him that kept drawing her back, despite her better judgment. The only other time she'd known such compulsion was when the thirst was on her. Was this love? Or was it simply another form of hunger?

Their relationship, while charged with an undercurrent of eroticism, was essentially sexless. She wanted him so badly she did not dare do more than kiss or hold hands. If she should lose control, there was no telling what might happen.

Judd, unlike Palmer, was not a sensitive. He was human, blind and dumb to the miracles and terrors of the Real World, just like poor, doomed Claude Hagerty. Rapid exposure could do immense damage.

To his credit, Judd had not pressed the sex issue over much. He was not happy with the arrangement, but honored her request that they "take it slow."

This, however, did not sit well with the Other. It constantly taunted her, goading her with obscene fantasies and suggestions concerning Judd. Or, failing to elicit a response using those tactics, it would chastise her for being untrue to Palmer. Sonja tried to ignore its gibes as best she could, but she knew that something, somewhere was bound to snap.

KITTY WIPED AT the tears oozing from the corner of her eye, smearing mascara all over her cheek and the back of her hand. It made the words on the paper swim and crawl like insects, but she didn't care.

She loved him. She really, truly loved him. And maybe now, after she did what she had to do to save him, he'd finally believe her. Proof. He needed proof of her love. And what better proof than to rescue him from the clutches of a monster.

Dearest Judd,

I tried to warn you about that woman. But you are blind to what she Really is. She is Evil itself, a demon sent from hell to claim your soul! I knew her for what she really is the moment I first saw her,

and she knew I knew! Her hands and mouth drip blood! Her eyes

burn with the fires of Hell! She is surrounded by a cloud of red

energy. Red as blood. She means to drag you to Hell, Judd. But

I won't let her. I love you too much to let that happen. I'll take

care of that horrible monster, don't you worry. I've been talking

to God a lot lately, and He told me how to deal with demons

like her. I love you so very, very much. I want you to love me too.

I'm doing this all for you. Please love me.

Kitty

JUDD WOKE UP at two in the afternoon, as he usually did. He worked six-to-midnight four days out of the week and had long since shifted over to a nocturnal lifestyle. After he got off work he normally headed down to the Quarter to chill with his buddies or, more recently, hang out with Sonja, until four or five in the morning before heading home.

He yawned as he dumped a couple of heaping tablespoons of Guatemalan into the hopper of his Mr. Coffee machine.

Sonja. Now there was a weird chick. Weird, but not in a schizzy, death-obsessed, art-school-freshman way like Kitty. Her strangeness issued from something far deeper than bourgeois neurosis. Sonja was genuinely *out there*, wherever that might be. There was something about the way she moved, the way she handled herself, that suggested she was plugged into something Real. And a frustrating as her fits of mood might be, he could not bring himself to turn his back on her and walk away.

Still, it bothered him that none of his friends—not even Arlo, who he'd known since high school—liked her. In fact, some even seemed to be *scared* of her. Funny. How could anyone be *frightened* of Sonja?

As he shuffled in the direction of the bathroom, he noticed an envelope shoved under his front door. He stooped to retrieve it, scowling at the all-too-familiar handwriting.

Kitty.

Probably another one of her damn fool love letters, alternately threatening him with castration and begging him to take her back. Lately she'd taken to leaving rambling, wigged-out messages on his answering machine, ranting about Sonja being some kind of vampire or succubus out to steal his soul. Crazy bitch. Sonja was crazy, too, but hardly predictable.

Judd tossed the envelope, unopened, into the trash can and staggered off to the bathroom to take a shower.

SONJA BLUE GREETED the night from atop the roof of the warehouse where she made her nest. She stretched her arms wide as if to embrace the rising moon, listening with half an ear to the sound of the baying dogs along the riverbanks. Some, she knew, were not dogs.

But the *vargr* were not her concern. She tangled with a few over the years, but she preferred hunting her own kind. She found it vastly more satisfying.

The warehouse's exterior fire escape was badly rusted and groaned noisily with the slightest movement, so Sonja avoided it altogether. She crawled, head-first, down the side of the building, moving like a lizard on a garden wall. Once she reached the bottom, she routinely pat-checked her jacket and pockets to make sure nothing had fallen out during her descent.

There was a sudden hissing sound in her head, as if someone had abruptly pumped up the volume on a radio tuned to a dead channel, and something heavy caught her between the shoulderblades, lifting her off her feet and knocking her into a row of garbage cans.

She barely had time to roll out of the way before something big and silvery smashed down where her head had been a second before. She coughed and black blood flew from her lips; a rib had broken off and pierced her lung again.

Kitty stood over her, clutching a three-foot long solid silver crucifix like a baseball bat. While her madness gave her strength, it was obvious the damn thing was *heavy*. Sonja wondered which church she'd stolen it from.

The dead-channel-crackling in Sonja's head grew louder. It was the sound of homicidal rage. Shrieking incoherently, Kitty swung at her rival a third time. While crosses and crucifixes had no effect on her—on any vampire, for that matter—if Kitty succeeded in landing a lucky blow and snapped her spine or cracked open her skull, she was dead no matter what.

Sonja rolled clear and got to her feet in one swift, fluid motion. Kitty swung at her again, but this time Sonja stepped inside her reach and grabbed the crucifix, wresting it from the other woman's hands.

Kitty staggered back, staring in disbelief as Sonja hefted the heavy silver cross. It was at least three inches thick, the cross beams as wide as a man's hand, and at its center hung a miniature Christ fashioned of gold and platinum. She was obviously waiting for Sonja's hand to burst into flames.

"What the hell did you think you were going to solve, clobbering me with this piece of junk?" she snarled.

Kitty's eyes were huge, the pupils swimming in madness. "You can't have him! I won't let you take his soul!"

"Who said anything about me stealing—"

"Monster!" Kitty launched herself at Sonja, her fingers clawing at her face. "Monster!"

Sonja hit her with the crucifix.

Kitty dropped to the alley floor, the top of her skull resting on her left shoulder. The only thing still holding her head onto her body were the muscles of her neck.

Way to go, kiddo! You just killed lover-boy's bug-shit ex-girlfriend! You're batting a thousand!

"Shit."

She tossed the crucifix aside and squatted next to the body. No need to check for vital signs. The girl was d-e-a-d.

What to do? She couldn't toss the corpse in the dumpster. Someone was bound to find it, and once the body was identified New Orleans Homicide would take Judd in for questioning. Which meant they'd be looking for *her*, sooner or later. And she couldn't have *that*.

I've got an idea, crooned The Other. *Just let me handle it.*

STEALING THE CAR was easy. It was a '76 Ford LTD with a muffler held in place with baling wire and a *Duke for Governor* sticker on the sagging rear bumper. Just the thing to unobtrusively dispose of a murder victim in the swamps surrounding New Orleans during the dead of night

She took an exit off the interstate leading out of New Orleans East. Originally it was to have connected a cookie-cutter housing development built on the very fringes of the marshlands to the outside world. The contractors got as far as pouring the concrete slab foundations before the oil slump hit. The condos were never built, but the access road remained, although there was nothing at its end but an overgrown tangle of briars and vines that had become a breeding-ground for snakes and alligators.

Sonja drove without lights. Not that she needed them. She could see just fine in the dark. Having reached her destination, she cut the engine and rolled to a stop. Except for the chiming of frogs and the grunting of gators, everything was quiet.

Sonja climbed out of the car and opened the trunk with a length of bent coat hanger. She stood for a second, silently inventorying the collection of plastic trash bags. There were six, total: one for the head, one for the torso, and one apiece for each limb. She'd already burned Kitty's clothing in the warehouse's furnace and disposed of her jewelry and teeth by tossing them into the river.

She gathered up the bags and left the road, heading in the direction of the bayou. She could hear things splashing in the water, some of them quite large.

She paused for a second on the bank of the bayou. Something nearby hissed. She tossed the bag containing Kitty's head into the murky water.

"Come and get it 'fore I slop it to the hogs!"

The assembled gators splashed and wrestled amongst themselves for the tender morsels like ducks fighting for scraps of stale bread.

Sonja was tired. Very tired. After this was over she still had to drive the car she'd stolen to a suitably disreputable urban area and set it on fire. She looked down at her hands. They were streaked with blood. She absently licked them clean.

When she was finished the Other looked through her eyes and smiled.

The Other wasn't tired. Not in the least

IT HADN'T BEEN a very good night, as far as Judd was concerned. He'd gotten chewed out concerning his attitude at work, Arlo and the others had treated him like he had a championship case of halitosis, and to cap the evening, Sonja pulled a no-show. Time to pack it in. It was four o'clock when he got home. He was in such a piss-poor mood, he didn't even bother to turn on the lights.

His answering machine, for once, didn't have one of Kitty's bizarro messages on it. Nothing from Sonja, either. He grunted as he removed his shirt. Was she mad at him? Had he said or done something the last time they were together that ticked her off?

It was damn hard to figure out her moods, since she refused to take off those damn mirrored sunglasses. Judd wondered how she could navigate in the dark so well while wearing those fuckers.

Something moved at the corner of his eye. It was the curtain covering the window that faced the alley. Funny, he didn't remember leaving that open . . .

She stepped out of the shadows, greeting him with a smile that displayed teeth that were too sharp. Judd felt his heart jerk into overdrive as the adrenaline surged into his system. He was ready to yell for help, then he recognized her.

"S-Sonja?"

"Did I scare you?" Her voice sounded like something out of *The Exorcist*. She sniffed the air and her smile grew even sharper. "Yes. Yes, I did scare you, didn't I?" She moved toward him, her hands making slow, hypnotic passes as she spoke. "I love the smell of fear in the morning."

"Sonja, what's wrong with your voice?"

"Wrong?" The Other thudded as she unzipped her leather jacket. "I always sound like this!"

She was on him so fast he didn't even see her move, lifting him by his belt buckle and flinging him onto the bed so hard he bounced. She grabbed his jaw in one hand, angling it back so the jugular was exposed. Judd heard the *snikt!* of a switchblade and felt a cold, sharp pressure against his throat.

"Do not struggle. Do not cry out. Do as I command, and maybe I'll let you live. Maybe."

"What do you want?"

"Why, my dear, I just want to get to know you better." The Other removed the sunglasses protecting her eyes with her free hand. "And vice versa."

Judd had often wondered what Sonja's eyes looked like. Were they almond-shaped or round? Blue or brown or green? He'd always imagined them as looking human, though. He'd never once pictured then as blood-red with pupils so hugely dilated they resembled shoebuttons.

The Other smirked, savoring the look of disgust on Judd's face. She pressed her lips against his, thrusting his teeth apart with her tongue, and penetrated his will with one quick shove of her mind.

Judd's limbs twitched convulsively as she took control of his nervous system, then went still. The Other disengaged, physically, and stared down at him. He couldn't move, his body locked into partial paralysis. Satisfied her control was secure, she moved the switchblade from Judd's throat.

"I can see why she finds you attractive. You're a pretty thing . . . *very* pretty." The Other reached out and pinched one of his nipples. Judd didn't flinch. "But she's much too old-fashioned when it comes to sex, don't you agree? She's afraid to let herself go and walk the wild side. She's so repressed." The Other shrugged out of her leather jacket, allowing it to fall to the floor.

"I will explain this to you once, and once only. I *own* you. If you do as I tell you, and you please me, then you shall be rewarded. Like this."

She reached into his cortex and tweaked its pleasure center. Judd shuddered as the wave of ecstasy swept over him, his hips involuntarily humping empty air.

"But if you fight me, or displease me in any way—then I will punish you. Like *so*."

Judd emitted a strangled cry of pain as he was speared through the pain receptor in his head. It felt as if the top of his skull had been removed and someone had dumped the contents of an ant farm on his exposed brain. His back arched until he thought his spine would snap. Then the pain stopped as it it'd never been there at all.

"Hold me."

Judd did as he was told, dragging himself upright and wrapping his arms around her waist. The Other knotted her fingers in his hair, pulling his head back so she could look into his eyes.

"Am I hurting you? Say yes."

"Yes."

"Good."

She smiled, exposing her fangs, and he realized that it was just beginning.

THEY FUCKED FOR three hours, the Other skillfully manipulating his pleasure centers so that he remained perpetually erect, despite his exhaustion. She randomly induced orgasms, often one right after another, numbering in the dozens. After the seventh or eighth orgasm, he was shooting air. She seemed to enjoy his wails each time he spasmed.

As dawn began to make its way into the room, she severed her control of Judd's body. He fell away from her in mid-thrust, his eyes rolled back behind flickering lids. The Other dressed quickly, her attention fixed on the rising sun. Judd lay curled in a fetal position amongst the soiled and tangled bedclothes, his naked body shuddering and jerking as his nervous system reasserted its control.

"Parting is such sweet sorrow," purred the Other, caressing his shivering flank. Judd gasped at her touch but did not pull away. "You pleased me. This time. So I will let you live. This time."

She lowered her head to his neck, brushing his jugular lightly with her lips. Judd squeezed his eyes shut in anticipation of the bite. But all she did was whisper, "Get used to it, loverboy."

When he opened his eyes again, she was gone. He was certain the door hadn't closed.

THE OTHER TOOK a great deal of pleasure in telling Sonja what it had done to Judd, making sure not to leave out a single, tasty detail as it re-ran that morning's exploits inside her head.

Sonja's response to the news was to scream and run head-first into the nearest wall. Then to continue pounding her skull against the floorboards until her glasses shattered and blood streamed down her face and matted her hair. She'd succeeded in breaking her nose and shattering both cheekbones before collapsing.

"GIRLY-GIRL! LONG TIME no see! What brings you into my little den of iniquity this time?"

The demon Malfeis sported the exterior of a flabby white male in late middle-age, dressed in a loud plaid polyester leisure suit with white buck loafers, a collection of gold medallions dangled under his chins, and he held a racing form in one hand.

Sonja slid into the booth opposite the demon. "I need magick, Mal."

"Don't we all? Say, what's that with the face? You can reconstruct better than that . . . !"

She shrugged, one hand straying to her swollen left cheek. The bone squelched under her fingertips and slid slightly askew. Heavy duty facial reconstruction required feeding in order for it to be done right, and she'd deliberately skipped her waking meal.

"You tangle with an ogre? One of those *vargr* punks?"

"Leave it be, Mal."

Malfeis shrugged. "Just trying to be friendly, that's all. Now, what kind of magick are you in the market for?"

"Binding and containment."

The demon grunted and fished out a pocket calculator, his exterior flickering for a moment to reveal a hulking creature that resembled an orangutan with a boar's snout.

"You heard me. I wish to have myself bound and contained."

"Sonja . . ."

"Name your price, damn you."

"Don't be redundant, girlchick."

Sonja sighed and hefted a knapsack onto the tabletop., "I brought some of my finest acquisitions. I've got hair shaved from Ted Bundy's hair just before he was to go to the chair, dried blood scraped from the walls of the Labianco home, a spent rifle casing from the grassy knoll, and a cedar cigar box with what's left of Rasputin's penis in it. Quality shit. I swear by its authenticity. And it's all yours, if you do this for me."

Malfeis fidgeted, drumming his talons against the table. Such close proximity to so much human suffering and evil was bringing on a jones. "Okay, I'll do it. But I'm not going to take responsibility for anything that happens to you."

"Did I ask you to?"

"ARE YOU SURE you want to go through with this, Sonja?"

"Your concern touches me, Mal. It really does."

The demon shook his head in disbelief, "You really mean to go through with this, don't you?"

"I've already said so, haven't I?"

"Sonja, you realize once you're in there, there's no way you'll be able to get out, unless someone breaks the seal."

"Maybe."

"There's no maybe to it!" he retorted.

"The spell you're using is for binding and containment of vampiric energies, right?"

"Of course. You're a vampire."

She shrugged. "Part of me is. And I'm not letting it out to hurt anyone ever again. I'm going to kill it or the trying."

"You're going to starve in there!"

"That's the whole point."

"Whatever you say; girly-girl."

Sonja hugged herself as she stared into the open doorway of the meat locker. It was cold and dark inside, just like her heart. "Let's get this show on the road."

Malfeis nodded and. produced a number of candles, bottles of oil, pieces of black chalk, and bags of white powder from the gladstone bag he carried. Sonja swallowed and stepped inside the meat locker, drawing the heavy door closed behind her with a muffled thump.

Malfeis lit the candles and began to chant in a deep, sonorous voice, scrawling elaborate designs on the outer walls of the locker with the black chalk. As the chanting grew faster and more impassioned, he smeared oil on the hinges and handle of the door. There was an electric crackle and the door glowed with blue fire.

Malfeis's incantation lost any semblance of human speech as it reached its climax. He carefully poured a line of white powder, made from equal parts salt, sand and the crushed bones of human babies, across the threshold. Then he stepped back to assess his handiwork.

To human eyes it looked like someone had scrawled graffiti all over the face of the stainless steel locker, nothing more. But to Pretender eyes, eyes adjusted to the Real World, the door to the locker was barred shut by a tangle of darkly pulsing veve, the semi-sentient protective symbols of the *voudou* powers. As long as the tableau remained undisturbed, the entity known as Sonja Blue would remain trapped within the chill darkness of the meat locker.

Malfeis replaced the tools of his trade in his gladstone bag. He paused as he left the warehouse, glancing over his shoulder.

"Goodbye, girly-girl. It was nice knowing you."

"I'M LOOKING FOR Mal."

The bartender looked up from his racing form and frowned at Judd. After taking in his unwashed hair and four-days' growth of beard, he nodded in the direction of the back booth.

Judd had never been inside the Monastery before. It had a reputation as being one of the more sleazy—and unsavory—French Quarter dives, and he could see why. The booths lining the wall had once been church pews. Plaster saints in various stages of decay were scattered about on display. A madonna with skin blackened and made leprous by age regarded him from above the liquor supply behind the bar with flat, faded blue eyes. She held in her arms an equally scabrous Baby Jesus, its uplifted chubby arms ending in misshapen stumps. Hardly a place to party down big time.

He walked to the back of the bar and looked into the last booth. All he saw was a paunchy, middle-aged man dressed in a bad suit smoking a cigar and reading a racing form.

Excuse me . . . ?"

The man in the bad suit looked up at him, arching a bushy, upswept eyebrow;

"Uh, excuse me—but I'm looking for Mal."

"You found him."

Judd blinked, confused. "No, I'm afraid there's been some kind of mistake. The guy I'm looking for is black, with dredlocks . . . "

The man in the bad suit smiled. It was not a pleasant sight. "Sit down, kid. He'll be with you in just a moment."

Still uncertain of what he was getting himself into, Judd slid into the opposite pew.

The older man lowered his head, exposing male pattern baldness, and hunched his shoulders. His fingers and arms begin vibrating, the skin growing darker as if his entire body had suddenly become bruised. There was a sound of dry grass rustling under a high wind and thick, black dredlocks emerged from his scalp, whipping about like a nest of snakes. Judd was too shocked by the transformation to do anything but stare.

Mal lifted his head and grinned at Judd, tugging at the collar of his turtleneck. "Ah, yes. I remember you now. Sonja's renfield."

"My-My name's not Renfield."

Mal shrugged. "So, what brings you here, boychick?"

"I'm looking for Sonja. I can't find her."

"She doesn't want to be found."

"I have to find her! I just have to! Before she does something stupid. Kills herself maybe."

Mal regarded the young human for a moment. "Tell me more."

"Something—happened between us. She feels responsible for hurting me. She gave me this letter a few days ago." Judd fished a much-folded envelope out of his back pocket and held it out to Mal. "Here, you read it."

The demon fished the letter out of its envelope like a gourmet removing an escargot from its shell. He unfolded the paper, noting the lack of signature and the smears of blood.

Judd,

I can never be forgiven for what was done to you. I was not the one who did those things to you. Please believe that. It was her. She is the one that makes me kill and hurt people. Hurt you. I promise I'll never let her hurt anyone, ever again. Especially you. I'm going to do something I should have tried years ago, before she became so strong. So dangerous. So uncontrollable. She's sated right now. Asleep in my head. By the time she becomes aware of what I'm planning to do, it'll be too late. I'm going to kill her. I might end up killing myself in the bargain, but that's a chance I'm willing to take. I won't let her hurt anyone again, damn her. I love you, Judd. Please believe that. Don't try to find me. Escape while you can.

"She doesn't understand!" Judd was close to tears as he spoke. "I *do* forgive her. I *love* her, damn it! I can't let her *die!*"

"You know what she is." It wasn't a question.

Judd nodded. "And I don't *care*."

"And why have you come to me?"

"You know where she is, don't you?"

Malfeis shifted in his seat, his eyes developing reptilian slits. "Are you asking me a questions?"

Judd hesitated, recalling Sonja's warning that he should *never*, under any circumstance, ask Mal a question.

"Uh, yeah."

Mal smiled, displaying shark's teeth. "Before I respond to any questions put to me, you must pay the price of the answer. Is that understood, boychick?"

Judd swallowed and nodded.

"Very well. Tell me your name. All of it."

"Michael Judd Rieser. Is that it? That's all you want? My name?"

"To know a thing's name gives one power over that thing, my sweet. Didn't they teach you that in school? Come to think of it, I guess not."

"What about my question? Do you know where Sonja is?"

"Yes, I *do* know." The demon scrawled an address on the back of the letter Judd had given him. "You'll find her here. She's inside the meat locker on the ground floor."

"*Meat locker?*"

"I wouldn't open it if I were you."

Judd snatched up the address and slid out of the pew. "But I'm *not* you!"

Malfeis watched Judd hurry out of the bar with an amused grin. "That's what *you* think, boychick." He leaned back and dosed his eyes. When he reopened them, he had shoulder-length hair pulled up in a ponytail, a ring in his nose, and four-days' growth of beard.

IT WAS COLD. So very, very cold.

Sonja sat huddled in the far corner of the meat locker, her knees drawn up to her chest. Her breath drifted from her mouth and nostrils in wispy flumes before condensing and turning to frost on her face.

How long? How many days had she been in here? Three? Four? Twenty? A hundred? There was no way of telling She no longer slept. The Other's screams and curses kept her awake.

Let me out! Let me out of this hell-hole! I've got to feed! I'm starving!

"Good."

You stupid cunt! If I starve to death, you go with me! I'm not a damned tapeworm!

"Couldn't prove it by me."

I'm getting out of here! I don't care what you say!

Sonja did not fight the Other as it asserted its ascendancy over her body. The Other forced her stiffened limbs to bend, levering her onto her feet. Her joints cracked like rotten timber as she moved. She staggered in the direction of the door. In her weakened condition she had difficulty seeing in the pitch black of the meat locker. She had abandoned the sunglasses days ago, but as her condition worsened, so did her night-vision.

Her groping hands closed on the door's interior handle. There was a sharp crackle and a flash of blue light as the Other was thrown halfway across the locker. She screamed and writhed like a cat hit by a car, holding her blistered, smoking hands away from her body. This was the twentieth time she'd tried to open the door and several of her fingers were on the verge of gangrene.

"You're not going anywhere. Not now. Not *ever!*"

Fuck you! Fuck you! I'll get you for this you human-loving cow!

"What? Are you going to *kill* me?"

Sonja crawled back to her place in the corner. The effort started her coughing again, bringing up black, clotted blood. She wiped at her mouth with the sleeve of her jacket, nearly dislocating her jaw in the process.

You're falling apart, You're too weak to regenerate properly . . .

If you hadn't pounded your head against the fuckin' wall trying to get out in the first place—"

You're the one that got us locked up in here! Don't blame me!

"I *am* blaming you. But not for that."

It's that fucking stupid human again! You think you can punish me for that? I didn't do anything that you hadn't already fantasized about!

"You *raped* him, damn you! You almost killed him!"

I didn't, though. I could have. But I didn't

"I loved him!" Sonja's voice cracked, became a sob.

You didn't love him. You loved being mistaken for human. That's what you're mad about; not that I molested your precious lover boy, but that I ruined your little game of Let's Pretend!

"Shut up."

Make me.

JUDD CHECKED THE street number of the warehouse against the address that Mal had given him. This was the place. It was one of the few remaining warehouses in the district that had not been turned into trendy yuppie condo-apartments. There was a small sign posted on the front door that read Indigo Imports, but nothing else. A heavy chain and double padlock secured the entrance and all the ground floor windows had burglar bars. There had to be *some* way of getting in and out.

He rounded the side of the building and spotted the loading dock. After a few minutes of determined tugging, he succeeded in wrenching one of the sliding corrugated metal doors open wide enough for him to slip through.

The inside of the warehouse was lit only by the mid-afternoon sunlight slanting through the barred windows and the whole place smelled of dust and rat piss.

The meat locker was on the ground floor, just where Mal said it would be. Its metal walls and door were covered in sworls of spray-painted graffiti. What looked like a huge line of coke marked the locker's threshold. Judd grabbed the door's handle and yanked it open. There was a faint crackling sound and a rush of cold, foul air. He squinted into the darkness, covering his nose and breathing through his mouth to try and mask the stench.

"Sonja?"

Something moved in the deepest shadows of the freezer.

"J-Judd? Is that you?"

"It's me, baby. I've come to get you out of here."

"Go away, Judd. You don't know what you're doing."

Judd stepped into the locker, his eyes adjusting to the gloom. He could see her now, crouching in the far corner with her knees drawn against her chest, her face turned to the wall.

"No, you're wrong, Sonja. I know *exactly* what I'm doing."

"I let her hurt you, Judd. I could have stopped her, but I didn't. I let her—let her—" Her voice grew tight and her shoulders began to shake. "Go away, Judd.

Go away before I hurt you again."

Judd kneeled beside her. She smelled like a side of beef gone bad. Her hands were covered with blisters and oozing sores. Some of the fingers jutted at odd angles, as if she'd broken them and they had healed without being properly set. She pulled away at his touch, pressing herself against the wall as if she could squeeze between the cracks if she tried hard enough.

"Don't look at me."

"Sonja, you don't understand. I *love* you. I know what you are, what you're capable of—and I love you *anyway*."

"Even if I hurt you?"

"*Especially* when you hurt me."

Sonja turned her head in his direction. Her face looked like it had been smashed then reassembled by a well-meaning but inept plastic surgeon who only had one blurry photograph to go by. Her eyes glowed like those of an animal pinned in the headlights of an oncoming car.

"What?"

Judd leaned closer, his eyes reflecting a hunger she knew all too well. "At first I was scared. Then, after awhile, I realized I wasn't frightened anymore. I was actually getting into it. It was like the borders between pain and pleasure, animal and human, ecstasy and horror, had been removed I've never known anything like it before! It was *incredible*! I love you, Sonja! All of *you*!"

She reached out and caressed his face with one of her charred hands. She'd turned him into a renfield. In just a few hours the Other had transformed him into a junkie, and now she was his fix.

"I love you too, Judd, Kiss me."

SHE SAT BEHIND the wheel of the car for a long time, staring out into the dark on the other side of the windshield. Nothing had changed since the last time she'd been out here, disposing of Kitty.

She pressed her fingertips against her right cheek, and this time it held. Her fingers were healed and straight again as well. She readjusted her shades and opened the car door and slid out from behind the wheel of the Caddy shed bought off the lot, cash-in-hand.

Judd was in the trunk, divvied up into six garbage bags, just like Kitty. At least it'd been fast. Her hunger was so intense she'd drained him within seconds. He hadn't tried to fight when she buried her fangs in his throat, even though she hadn't the strength to trance him. Maybe part of him knew she was doing him a favor.

She dragged the bags out of the trunk and headed in the direction of the alligator calls. She'd have to leave New Orleans, maybe for good this time. Kitty might not have been missed, but Judd was another story. Arlo was sure to mention the missing Judd's weirdo new girlfriend to the authorities.

It was time to blow town and head for Merida. Time to go pay Palmer a visit and check on how he and the baby were making out.

Palmer.

Funny how she'd forgotten about him. Of all her human companions, he was the only one she'd come closest to loving. Before Judd.

She hurled the sacks containing Judd's remains into the water and returned to the car. She tried not to hear the noise the gators made as they fought amongst themselves.

She climbed back into the car and slammed a cassette into the Caddy's tape-deck. Lard's *The Last Temptation of Reid* thundered through the speakers, causing the steering wheel to vibrate under her hands. She wondered when the emptiness would go away. Or at least be replaced by pain. Anything would be preferable to the nothing inside her.

I don't see why you had to go and kill him like that. We could have used a renfield. They do come in handy, now and then. Besides, he was kind of cute . . .

"Shut up and drive."

✝

PAS DU MORT

LISA LEPOVETSKY

>─┼─◄♦>─○─<♦>─┼─◄

THE DANCE. *THE DANCE WAS EVERYTHING—HER WORK, HER BLOOD, HER life, And now they were going to take her life away, give her place of honor to a younger dancer, the wispy, blond Donna Chai, a simpering child who scampered across the stage like an overgrown grasshopper, Moira's world was suddenly unfamiliar, threatening—nameless evils wailed in the dark corners for her. All her signposts were turned upside down. She would have to find her way home alone.*

MOIRA'S FIRST IDEA for the vampire dance came as she toured the New Orleans cemeteries. St. Louis Number One, the oldest cemetery in the city, seemed to crumble around her even as she wandered the hot, narrow walls between crypts with a little group of tourist. Jason Sitare, her dance company's director and choreographer, was spending the first few days in New Orleans auditioning new dancers—and retraining at least one dancer for Moira's solo, her *pas seul.* That gave the rest of the company time to tour the city before rehearsals started. On a whim, Moira had decided to take the two-hour city tour, which included a walk through the cemeteries.

Martin, the bearded tour guide, indicated points of interest in a bored sing-song voice as his charges huddled together in the steamy late-afternoon drizzle. The damp air seemed to swallow sounds, and his voice had a flat, distant quality, though he stood less than ten feet from her.

"And behind you," he sighed, flipping his dark ponytail over his shoulder, "is the crypt of the famous voodoo queen Marie Laveau. As you see, people leave trinkets and gifts of food for her, and write coded messages on the walls. You might call it voodoo graffiti."

Martin's little joke fell flat, but he didn't seem to notice or care. He turned toward the back of the cemetery, his black umbrella obscuring his next few words, and the tourists hurried forward so they wouldn't miss anything. Moira hung back.

She wanted more time to examine Marie Laveau's tomb. She walked slowly around the small building, trying to decipher the patterns of crosses and circles chalked on the sides. All she could make out was some message about the birth of anarchy.

Returning to the front, Moira noticed a brass plaque set in the cement wall. As she bent to read it, her eye caught a dark movement around the corner of the small stone crypt. Moira glanced up; but saw nothing. A shudder passed through her as she remembered the warnings she'd heard about muggers lurking in the New Orleans cemeteries, waiting to prey on solitary tourists. She couldn't hear the guide anymore, or see her group.

She straightened, trying to remember which way they'd gone. They couldn't have gone far—the cemetery was only a block or two deep. She should be able to find them easily, but her heart thudded deafeningly in her ears as she listened for them. Moira had a terror of becoming lost ever since she'd wandered away from her mother in a large department store when she was six. Her mother had finally found her cowering beneath a rack of long, black fur capes. Moira had been praying the big people wouldn't notice her and take her to the dark places her mother had warned her about. Then she'd never find her way home.

She'd thought she conquered the old fears, but those horrors crowded in on her again like vultures around a dying doe.

"Mama, Mama, please find me," she whispered, feeling her childhood terror plucking at her nerves. But she was on her own. Not only was Mama not in New Orleans, but she'd been in her grave for seven years now.

Moira tried to draw deep, calming breaths, but the air seemed too dense to drag into her aching lungs. She heard a soft rustling noise behind her and whirled, hoping the guide had found her. Nobody was there. The air was empty, except for that sense of something moving just beyond her field of vision again, something dark and feathery that she'd just missed seeing. She thought she heard someone laugh softly—or was it the faraway call of a bird?

Moira looked up toward the gray skies, as though she'd find some message written in the clouds, some map showing her where to go. Of course, acre was nothing up there but a lone black bird drifting slowly above the cemetery. But she suddenly heard Martin's voice off to the left.

"And if you'll just step this way, ladies and gentlemen . . . "

With tears of relief filling her eyes, Moira hurried in that direction, finding the group behind a long row of what the guide was describing as "oven crypts," because their curved openings in the brick wall looked like nothing more than bread ovens. It was when Moira glanced up over Martin's head, looking for the bird she'd recently watched, that she saw the weeping statue. High on a pedestal, a gray silhouette against grayer clouds, a woman knelt, her head bent in sorrow, a granite cape drifting around her in pale, unmoving waves.

There was something familiar about the delicate features, nearly hidden by the folds of the cloak. After a moment, Moira realized with a cold start that the statue had Donna Chai's face. Well, the nose was a bit more aquiline, the lips a bit fuller, but the resemblance was striking. On closer inspection, Moira thought the woman's face didn't quite mirror grief—the hint of a dark smile seemed to tug at the corners of the stone lips.

At the same moment, Martin was discussing the popular theory that vampires roamed the streets and cemeteries of New Orleans.

"Of course," he said, "I can't say whether or not there are such things as vampires, in New Orleans or anywhere else." However, his rehearsed smile and raised eyebrows spoke loudly, saying, *We both know there are no such things, but let's play the game, okay? Then we can all go home.*

"Several popular fiction writers from the area have stirred interest in vampires, those evil, undead creatures who travel only by dark and prey on the living by drinking their blood."

Moira stopped listening to Martin's droning voice as he described books and films about vampires along the bayou. Her attention was riveted on the stone woman who seemed to float in the air above the cemetery—the delicate positioning of her arms, the curve of her spine, the way her bowed head tilted ever so slightly to one side, as though listening for a healthy heartbeat.

And suddenly she could see herself spotlighted on stage, dressed in black— no, deep, bloody crimson, her dark hair loose and liquid down her back, dancing her way through the life of a vampire in the City of the Dead, New Orleans. The director had complained only last week of being tired of Moira's Saint Joan number. She needed something new, something to make them remember how good she was, to make them forget about the golden girl Donna Chai. Her vampire number was the perfect solution, Moira's gift to the city of New Orleans and her rebirth as *premier danseuse.*

Moira fairly trembled with anticipation. She couldn't wait to get back to the theater and start working on it She would use the "Totentanz," the Death Dance from Berlioz's *Symphony Fantastique*, letting the haunting dark notes fly around her, clothe her in their sensual, dangerous rhythms. And she would dance as no one before her had ever danced, creating a world that would at once fascinate and terrify her audience.

As soon as the bus driver dropped her of at her hotel, she grabbed her dance clothes and took a cab to the rehearsal hall. She searched the practice rooms until she found the music director. He said he had the music she wanted, and she changed into her leotard while he cued it up for her.

She found an empty mirrored room, and pressed the play button on the tape recorder . . .

SIX HOURS LATER, Moira collapsed onto a metal folding chair near the door, panting and dripping with sweat. Her lungs ached and every muscle in her body trembled with the strain of her nonstop effort. But she'd finished the overall design of her vampire number, her *Pas du Mort*—and it was good, very good. She could feel it.

Moira's legs and arms had seemed to know where they should be with very little input from her brain. She had felt the Berlioz clutch her like strong fingers from the first chords, bending her body in serpentine rhythms, arching her back arid neck until the sinews felt as though they would snap. Moira had seen the music swirling around her like dark graveyard mists. It was as though her body had directed her thoughts, rather than the other way around. She still had a few steps to fill in, transition movements mostly, where the music changed, but the dance was essentially complete now. If she had to perform it tomorrow, she could.

Still, Moira couldn't rest. This was the most important dance of her life, and it had to be perfect. She couldn't afford the tiniest wobble, the least shift in balance, Though her whole body screamed for her to stop, her brain ordered her to continue practicing until her movements were flawless. Moira knew if she sat any longer, her muscles would begin to stiffen and the rest of the night would be lost. With tears in her eyes, she rose, rewound the tape, and began again.

BY THURSDAY, SHE was ready. The next night was the company's last night in the city, and Moira approached the director with her proposal,

"I have a surprise for you, Jason," she said coyly. "I've designed a new number for the show tomorrow."

He sighed and didn't look up from the papers on his desk. Not another *Saint Joan?*"

Moira cringed, but breathed deeply before answering. "No, this is something special, inspired by New Orleans itself. I call it *La Pas du Mort.*"

"Dance of the Dead?" Jason glanced up, a skeptical frown on his face. "Sounds a little melodramatic. How long have you been working on it?"

"Nearly a week," she lied, knowing he'd never believe the dance was finished if she told him she'd been working on it less than three days

His frown deepened. "Are you sure you're up to a new solo? You look kind of pale, tired."

Moira realized she was tired—exhausted, in fact, She hadn't slept more than four hours a night since she'd toured the cemetery. All her free time had been focused on her new dance. But she straightened her shoulders and tried to look as energetic as possible.

"I'm fine," she said. "Never better. Wait till you see this number—you'll love it. It won't take much preparation: I'll make my own costume, and I'll just need a simple set of some Styrofoam tombstones and dead trees. The fog machine will take care of any imperfections."

Moira hated the pleading note behind her voice. She'd never had to beg for a dance before.

"What about music? Lighting?"

"I've already set it up—no problem. There's just one catch."

Jason sat back in his chair and laced his fingers behind his head, "Catch? I don't like the sound of that."

"I don't want anybody to see the dance before Friday."

"Not even me?"

"Not even you."

"I don't know, Moira . . . " Jason was shaking his head.

"Jason, have I ever let you down?" Moira held her breath as Jason seemed to take forever to answer. In the end, he didn't.

"All right," he said, bending over his papers again. "But it'd better be as good as you say." He glanced up once as she turned to go, and spoke very quietly. "Don't let me down."

THE NEXT NIGHT, the house was full. Jason had made up a huge poster advertising Moira's vampire dance as the company's "gift to the good people of New Orleans." The management had even set up a row of folding chairs in the back of the theater, to accommodate their accidental oversell.

Donna Chai opened the show with her homage to the life of Isadora Duncan. In her green gossamer shift, she fluttered between vine-laden pedestals like a damsel-fly. Watching from the wings, Moira grudgingly admitted to herself that the girl had talent. She felt fear cramp her belly at the thought. Her eyes shifted to the audience, and her gaze was caught by a copper-haired woman and two men—one dark, one blond—sitting in the front row. There was nothing unusual about them; they were dressed in evening clothes like everyone else, and they weren't more or less beautiful than those around them. But they were very pale, and the reflected spotlight made their skin look almost translucent.

And they weren't looking at Donna Chai, or even the stage. All three were looking straight at Moira. Their eyes held an intensity that seemed to bore into her, to merge with her soul as she stood rooted to the spot. Moira felt her legs tremble. She wanted to run both from them and to them at the same time

Suddenly Donna's dance ended, and the dancers for the next number pushed past Moira, jostling her farther backstage. The spell was broken, and she returned to her dressing room to await her call. To his credit, Jason had scheduled *La Pas du Mort* last, as the crowning glory of the night's performances. The significance of this position was not lost on Moira—if she was anything less than perfect, she was through.

The evening dragged on endlessly until the stage manager tapped on her dressing room door and, without opening it, called, "One more number and you're on."

Moira's blood froze in her veins. She rose slowly from the dressing table, and watched herself in the long mirror as she drew on her black leotard. Her movements were graceful and sure, but she noticed a tremble in her hands as she wrapped the burgundy satin cloak around her shoulders. Long black feathers fluttered at the hem, and danced around the edges of the hood.

Moira had covered her hands and face in the palest foundation she could find, accenting the hollows of her cheeks and eyes with blue-gray shadow. She nodded with satisfaction at the woman who watched her from the mirror. She looked beautiful and gaunt, without being skeletal, and her dark eyes glittered almost feverishly from the pale depths of her face.

She whirled away from the mirror and headed upstairs to the wings. The Civil War number had just ended, and Moira watched the stagehands move the wood-and-Styrofoam cemetery into place. Despite the last-minute construction, the tombs and crypts looked amazingly realistic. Anticipation tingled along the edges of Moira's nerves and she drew a deep, shuddering breath. As the lights dimmed to blue, one long black light breathed ghostly life into the fog being pumped from the wings.

The first haunting strains of Berlioz's "Totentanz" rippled from the speakers, and Moira felt herself drawn toward the stage. She crept between the crumbling makeshift crypts, hunched into herself until she found the center of the stage, where light caught on the fog swirling around like a phantom almost ready to materialize. Then she crossed her hands beneath her face, staring into the audience, frozen for a long moment.

She heard a combined gasp as the black light turned her flesh purple and rippled along her cape. In that moment, her gaze found the three people she'd seen earlier. Their eyes were riveted on hers, and she felt something pass between them, some almost-painful thrill of electricity.

The jolt passed into her brain and coursed down her spine, settling like hot mercury in some deep recess she'd never known existed.

Then she was moving again—gliding, whirling, drifting in the whiteness, her body moving in ways even site couldn't believe. One moment her arms wrapped around themselves like hungry snakes, the next they flew out and up to become the branches of long-dead, long-forgotten trees. Her legs stretched tighter and leapt farther than she could have imagined, and she could sense the audience holding its collective breath at every arabesque. They were hers, and she was in love with her power. She dared not look at the two men and one woman sitting in the center of the front row, however, or she knew somehow she'd be lost.

All too soon the dance ended, and the last strains of the insane music faded into the rafters. All the lights dimmed, leaving only the black light illuminating Moira's upturned face and clenched hands. Then, suddenly, that too disappeared. For a long breathless moment, the night lay in complete silence. Moira's ragged breathing sounded like a tornado in her ears.

Then the applause began and the lights came up. The pale trio were standing front row center, and soon others rose behind them until the entire audience was on its feet, applauding wildly and cheering. Moira saw tears streaking the cheeks of many. She sank into a low curtsy, her head, down and arms outstretched as though gathering the adulation of her public.

Three dark red roses landed at her feet, and she knew immediately: where they'd come from. She grabbed them and curtsied once more, then ran into the wings.

Jason bowed as Moira ran past, and Donna Chai reached out to hug her. But Moira pushed her away and flew down the steps. She slammed the door of her dressing-room behind her, and collapsed onto the floor, her stomach heaving drily and all her muscles cramping violently. She felt as though she were in the throes of a virulent flu. Her skin hurt and her head seemed to wobble heavily on her neck. Moira tried to weep, but was unable to manage even a tear.

Then someone was lifting her from the floor, standing her on her trembling legs. Cold hands grasped her upper arms firmly but tenderly, and a deep male voice spoke.

"You were magnificent tonight. We knew you would be."

The voice seemed to come from inside her as well as from outside. She lifted her face and saw before her one of the two men who'd been sitting front row center. His eyes seemed to have a life of their own. As she gazed into them, Moira thought she saw something move in their depths, like a small creature trying to escape. After a long time, he blinked.

She glanced around them, and saw his two companions standing on the other side of the room, their arms around one another. The blond man licked his lips.

Moira's voice croaked painfully through her throat, "What are you doing here?"

"We've come for you," the dark man before her said, his lips barely moving.

The woman brushed her red curls from her face and smiled. "We've known you were ours from the moment we found you in the cemetery."

"The cemetery? You were there?" Moira recalled the whispered laughter and the sense of being watched. She shook her head, trying to make sense of it all.

"We were there," the dark man said, "and now we're here. You called us, and we came."

"I didn't call you. I don't even know you." Moira tried feebly to pull away, but the thin cold fingers gripped her tighter.

"You called us with our dance," he said. "Your body speaks more clearly than your voice, don't you know that? You've always known us. You've waited your whole life for us to come take you with us."

He bent his face to hers, biting hard into her lower lip. Blood pooled into her mouth.

The pain was excruciating, and yet exquisitely beautiful. She felt her own blood stream down her chin, both from the front of the wound where his long wet tongue flicked out to catch it, and from the overflow inside her mouth. She swallowed, tasting the salty copper flavor of her own blood—and something else, something bitter that seared the delicate lining of her mouth.

She gasped from the pain and tried to jerk her head away, but his tongue hooked behind her front teeth and held her. His hands flew to the sides of her head and pulled her lips against his. The thick tongue snaked into the back of her mouth, choking her and coating her throat with something that seemed to freeze and burn her flesh at the same time.

But suddenly, Moira didn't want him to stop, She wrapped her arms around him and drew him close to her, aching for the icy chill of him inside her. She heard soft laughter from across the room, and ignored the small voice deep in her brain warning her one last time that she'd never known until now what it really meant to be lost.

✝

FAREWELL TO THE FLESH

JOHN HELFERS

>—·—‹+›—•—O—•—‹+›—·—‹<

SETH WATCHED IN AMUSEMENT AS THE BLACK ROBED FIGURE TO HIS right raised a gleaming dagger over the unconscious woman on the stone slab beneath him.

Chanting in a low monotone, the hooded form held the dagger aloft while his other hand gripped a golden, gem-encrusted cross, held upside down, over the woman spread-eagled on the stone, the ropes encircling her wrists attached to large iron rings set in the rock.

Upon seeing the cross, the rest of the similarly-clad group of cult members standing in a loose circle around the sacrificial table bowed low, their chants mingling with their leader's. Seth bowed also, following their example, but he only mouthed the simple lines, a small part of his mind registering the cultists' mispronunciation of some of the ancient phrases. *Amateurs*, he thought, his eyes locked on the priceless artifact the cult leader was gesturing with.

"Yog-Sothoth, I ask that you come forth from the spirit world and take your rightful place in this vessel which has been consecrated for you. Arise, Yog-Sothoth, and begin preparing this realm for passage into the next world, the coming of the cleansing, the purification of the holy, and the destruction of those who would oppose you."

Like me, Seth thought. He had been on the trail of these cultists for a few weeks now, ever since they had "acquired" the cross, and had followed them to their lair primarily to find out what they were up to. After following them out to the cemetery, it had been child's play to snatch one of them and masquerade in his robes for the evening's ceremonies. He had been rather disappointed to learn that they were garden-variety satanic worshippers, attempting to summon some kind of ancient overlord to grant them dark powers over the rest of humanity. Seth would have sighed at the ridiculousness of it all, if he still breathed. *Stupid amateurs*, he corrected himself.

The cultists were now swaying back and forth, and their leader's voice, degenerating into a frenzied intonation of ancient incantations, had reached a fever pitch. Still holding the cross over his head, he plunged the dagger down towards the woman's chest.

Then Seth moved.

Faster than anyone could see, he rose to his feet, stepped towards the cult leader, and redirected the dagger blade away from the woman and into the man's stomach. There was a moment of shocked silence as everyone in the room sensed that something had gone very, very wrong.

Seth's hood had fallen from his head after he had gotten up, and as he looked into the leader's shocked eyes, he smiled, letting the light from the two torches that illuminated the chamber fall upon his elongated canines.

"Not tonight," he whispered, twisting the blade in his victim's abdomen as he plucked the cross from the man's trembling hand. Without a sound, the cultist slipped quietly to the floor, too surprised to even moan, and passed into unconsciousness.

Seth didn't look back, but glided to the torches at the far end of the room and smothered both of them with his robe, plunging the chamber into complete darkness.

The next minute was a frenzy of crazed noise. Screams and scrabbling of the remaining cultists trying to find their way out of the sacrificial room that had suddenly become a deathtrap punctuated the heavy thuds of bodies being thrown against stone walls, thick wet sounds of torn flesh and snapping bone, and the gurgles and moans of the dying.

When it was over, Seth walked to the door, mindful of the newly-made mess on the floor, unbolted it, and threw it open. Moonlight flooded the room, illuminating the carnage he had left. The silver light revealed a large pentagram drawn inside a circle around the stone coffer, with several parts erased by the smears of blood that covered the floor.

Seth paused by the door for a moment, looking outside to see if the commotion had attracted any attention. *Not likely, given where we are,* he thought. The odor of the nearby ocean was so pervasive that he didn't need to breathe to smell it.

He examined the cross in his hand, inspecting it for damage. Finding none, he tucked it into a pocket of his suit and walked back to where the head cultist lay, surrounded by a widening pool of his own blood. Kneeling beside the body, Seth removed the dagger from its temporary sheath and leaned down to drink his fill.

When he was finished, he looked at the knife, turning it over in his hand. It was a *kris*, or wavy blade, forged out of some dull gray metal. The handle appeared to be carved into the shape of a merman-like creature with scales covering its entire body. Its outstretched arms formed the guard, with scaled hands at each end, and its head, with its bulbous eyes and gaping, fang-filled mouth appeared to be swallowing the base of the blade. Although Seth didn't remember wiping the dagger off, the blade was clean, as if the knife hadn't even been used.

It wasn't immediately familiar, which was strange in itself. Usually Seth knew any kind of artifact on sight, but this one was foreign to him. *I wonder if Giancarlo knows anything about this,* he thought. Holding the knife gave him an unusual feeling, as if there was another presence in the room. Shaking his head, Seth chided himself for his nervousness. *It just isn't everyday that I find a unidentifiable piece of artwork, that's all.*

He used the dagger to cut the ropes that bound the girl to the stone slab, slinging her body over his shoulder. She moaned as he hoisted her up, and he checked to make sure that she hadn't woken. He could feel the warmth of the blood coursing through her, smell the nearness of it, the vitality of it even more potent than the lake of spilled liquid in the bloody chamber, and although he had just fed, the hunger pangs stirred feebly in him, the all-consuming need always making its presence known. Seth knew this would happen, and he was able to ignore the incessant thirst with relative ease.

Carrying his load to the door, Seth stopped and took one last look behind him. "When bad cultists go worse," he said, shaking his head and exiting the room, closing the door behind him.

Outside, Seth looked around, checking the cemetery for any signs of life. He glanced back at the mausoleum he'd just left and was gratified to find no signs of disturbance. *Given the state of this place, it'll be several days, perhaps even a week or two, before these guys are found,* he thought. Shifting the girl to a more comfortable position, he carried her across the cemetery to his rented Lincoln Town Car parked on the road. He opened the door and set her down in the front seat, tossing the dagger on the floor as well. He then walked to the large van the cultists had driven to here, opened the driver side door, and scanned the car's interior, finding a woman's black leather purse on the passenger seat. He grabbed it, making sure there was nothing else there to connect her to the bloodbath in the mausoleum, then closed and locked the van's doors. Walking back to the car, he got in and drove away.

Once out of the cemetery, he got onto highway 90 and accelerated east, towards the distant city. Driving through the low marshlands and the thicker swamps, Seth headed for the bright light that hung over the buildings that formed the low skyline. Streetlights, bonfires, spotlights, flashlights, headlights, and anything else that would repel the night were bouncing off the clouds of the overcast night and giving the city a glowing halo, a halo that Seth knew this particular city did nothing to deserve.

From here he could hear the noise as well as if he was standing on the corner of Bourbon Street listening to the jazz go down. Parades, parties, block-long celebrations weren't uncommon as the laid-back people of Louisiana shook off their usual easy-going attitude, partied like there was going to be no tomorrow, and lit up the night with their festivities. And of course, since it was the year of the millennium, New Orleans was welcoming the next thousand years with the *carnivale* to end all carnivals.

He grinned. *I love New Orleans in February,* he thought. *The exuberance, the decadence, the intensity of it all. That, and it's one of the few times I can roam a city freely, without having to worry about keeping my guard up. After all, there are enough fake vampires roaming around, what's one more, even if I am real?*

A low moan from the passenger seat attracted Seth's attention. He looked over at the woman slumped next to him, her blonde hair hanging over her face. *Ah yes, what to do with you?* he thought, reaching for her purse with one hand. A quick flip of her pocketbook revealed that Seth had rescued was Diana Corgan, and that she lived in the French Quarter.

Which will be impossible to drive to for the next week or so, he thought. *Better to take her to the church. I'm sure the good father can put her up for the evening.* He skirted around the city to the south side, about a kilometer away from the docks, and pulled into the parking lot of a large church. He drove around to the back of the building and parked the car near a pair of double doors lit by a single light bulb. Just outside the church doors, Seth paused for a moment, listening to the loud celebrations, the blare of trumpets and cheers of the crowds watching parades, the constant reminder of the humanity surrounding him. *Ah, Mardi Gras,* he thought.

With the cross in his hand, and the still-unconscious woman over his shoulder, Seth entered the church.

The small entryway he found himself in was dark, but a dim glow led him into the main chapel. The cavernous room was lit by dozens of candles surrounding the altar, where a lone priest knelt, deep in prayer. Seth made no noise as he crossed the room to the first row of pews and gently set the woman down. He stood in the aisle beside her and waited for the priest to finish.

After a few seconds the shorter man raised his head, kissed the cross on his rosary, and got to his feet. When he turned around, he started at seeing the tall, pale man standing in the aisle of the church.

"Don't you ever knock? I didn't like it the first time you did that, and I don't like it now," the priest said, fingering his rosary as he slowly walked closer.

"I know, Father," Seth said, "Please forgive me. I meant no offense." Seth usually disliked priests, primarily because of their opinion of him, but Father Giancarlo was different. He still believed in the power of his faith, and he didn't try to bluster and threaten Seth every time the vampire accepted a Church assignment. The fact that each had saved the other's life fourteen years ago, the last time Seth had been down south, had only cemented their friendship. The arrangement suited both men just fine, and whenever Seth was in town, he always tried to visit his old friend.

"Besides, I had a very good evening, so I hardly think you can blame me for using a little levity to spice up the night," Seth said, holding up the cross so the reflected candlelight twinkled as it dangled on its chain.

"The cross of Coronado," the priest breathed. "Finally back to its rightful owners after more than fifty years of searching." He reached out to reverently cup the cross in his hands. "I suppose I do not want to know how you recovered this?"

Seth shook his head. "You're too young. Let's just say that there's one less group of cultists running around tonight."

"I don't suppose I can get you to take confession for what you've done?" the priest asked.

Seth smiled, not showing his teeth. It was an old joke between them, with Father Giancarlo often saying that it was the one thing that would assure him canonization. Although they had often discussed history in past visits, Seth had never mentioned his past deeds, and the priest had never asked. "Father, I've been around since the Church tried to excommunicate Queen Elizabeth the First. I'm afraid the list of my misdeeds would cause you to expire of old age before we got halfway through."

Father Giancarlo grunted. "When I heard you had come to New Orleans to investigate this matter personally, I almost didn't believe it. But here you are. Although I agree with what you are doing, I cannot condone it. Nor, by the same token, can I stop you. By the way, what name are you using this time?"

When Seth told him, he nodded. "The ancient Egyptian god of adversity, eh? It suits you."

Since Seth had been walking the earth for more than six centuries, he had created several identities for himself to aid in his unique line of work. His passion for recovering and protecting art had taken him to all corners of the world, and he was known to many people under many different names. The last time he had been in America was when he had saved the statue of Sitting Bull from what he had thought was a group of racist skinheads. They had turned out to be vampire hunters who had baited a trap for him. After disposing of them, he'd been hunting the rest of the group for the past year, but had come back when he had stumbled onto the lead for the cross. Now that his obligation was over, he would probably resume his search.

"Who's this?' Father Giancarlo asked, motioning to the young woman sleeping on the bench.

"That was going to be the cultists' sacrifice for the evening. I was hoping you might be able to watch over her after I . . . speak with her."

"I will take care of her. Do you wish to be left alone?" the priest asked.

"I don't see why it would matter. This will give you something to talk to your superiors about. Just watch," Seth said as he leaned close to the unconscious woman. "Diana, open your eyes."

The young woman's eyes snapped open, and she lifted her head and sat up straighter on the bench. He gaze was not focused on either Seth or Father Giancarlo, but on a point very far off in the distance, at something only she could see. She appeared relaxed and calm, almost as if she might have been attending church, if this had been Sunday.

"Diana, listen to me. You have been out all night enjoying yourself during Mardi Gras. You will go directly home, where you will fall asleep and not awaken until noon tomorrow. You will not remember anything that happened tonight. When you awaken tomorrow, you will assume that you had too much to drink and passed out at home. The instant this man wakes you tonight, you will thank him, get up and go to the cab outside this building, and instruct the driver to take you home. Sleep now," Seth said. He straightened and looked at Father Giancarlo. "There is one more thing."

The priest sighed and shook his head. "With you, there always is. What is it?"

Seth produced the dagger and held it out. "I would like any information you have as to which culture this weapon comes from."

Father Giancarlo took the strange knife and examined it closely. "This is interesting. Where did you acquire this?"

"Like I said, the cultists were going to sacrifice the girl, and this was the dagger they were going to use."

"There seems to be a lot of this kind of black magic and sacrificing going on, especially during Mardi Gras. In the past few years it seems that every crackpot claiming he's seen visions of Satan or what-have-you has started his own little church of fanatics." The priest held the dagger up to the light. "The merman motif would fit a number of old South Pacific polytheistic religions that often believed in the existence of a "water god," Father Giancarlo said, "but they died out or were converted long before metalworking was known to them. What sacrificial weapons have been found were always made from stone or wood. I'll check the church's databases and see if we can come up with anything. I'll let you know what I turn up. Can I still reach you at the same number?"

"I'll get your message," Seth said. "Right now it's time for me to go."

"Understood, my friend," the stocky priest said. "The Church and I owe you another debt, as usual."

"Your friendship is payment enough for me," Seth said with a smile. He offered his hand, and the two men shook. "Go with God, Father."

"I always do," Father Giancarlo said. "I'll call a cab for our sleeping friend here."

"When it arrives, just wake her, she'll do the rest on her own. I'll be seeing you," Seth said as he headed for the back door. "Let me know what you find."

"Of course . . ." the priest barely said before his unusual companion was gone. "May the Lord keep and protect you as well, my friend," he whispered, but only the statue of the Virgin Mary heard him in the now silent cathedral.

SETH AWOKE THE next night with a strange desire to experience the nightlife of New Orleans. Outside, the party was in full swing, as usual, and the cheerful music and celebrating voices combined to produce a melancholy effect in him.

As much as I have experienced, and as long as I have survived, sometimes I still do not think that I have lived one-tenth as much as a single person out there. I wonder if they ever stop to think about just what it is they have, and whether they appreciate it. Probably not during this week, and especially not in this city, he thought while showering. Although his body didn't sweat or exude any kind of oil, Seth enjoyed some of the rituals of humanity, feeling that these simple experiences gave him a little more kinship with them. He also liked to thumb his nose at some of the ancient myths regarding his kind. *Can't cross running water, my ass.*

The hunger hit him just as he was toweling off, the need coursing through his body, reminding him, as it did every night, of the price he was paying for the endless days to come. *And yet I feel it is worth it,* he thought as he staggered into his hotel bedroom, heading for the large locked cooler that was plugged into the wall. Opening it revealed the one thing he never traveled without, his own portable blood supply. Seth reached for one of the long plastic pouches and slit it open, pouring the unlife-sustaining contents down his throat. *Some fearsome predator of the night I look like now,* he thought while he drained the bag, then took another. Only after that one was dry did the hunger agony abate somewhat, but Seth knew that he couldn't be around a lot of people tonight, in case the hunger came upon him again. *With so much prey available, I might not be able to stop myself,* he thought. *Better to spend my night alone, for safety. Again.*

Replacing the blood bags in the chest, Seth dressed and picked up his cell phone to check his messages.

"Seth, this is Marten. I've wrapped up our business in Istanbul, and will be heading back by the time you hear this. None of the leads panned out. I'll have the report ready for you when you get back."

Seth smiled. Marten was his number two man, his contact between himself and many top people in the art world. Their paths had crossed several years ago in Italy, when Marten had been cat-burglaring for wealthy collectors who simply had to have original works of art for their private enjoyment. Seth had been hired to stop whoever had been stealing the priceless works of art. Seth had won that one, and, instead of turning Marten over to the authorities, had made him a very lucrative offer instead, one that in effect, couldn't be turned down. Over the years Marten had become more and more indispensable to Seth, serving as his eyes and ears during daylight. They had been in the Middle East together, but Seth had come back to America when the Church had contacted them. He played the second message.

"Seth, this is Father Giancarlo. I need to speak to you as soon as possible about that dagger you found. Come to the church after dark, and tell no one about this." The time stamp on the message told Seth that Giancarlo had called at about 3:00 p.m.

That sounds like something to take my mind off my troubles, Seth thought. He drained another blood bag to ward off the thirst for awhile longer, grabbed his keys, and headed out the door.

DRIVING OVER IN his car, Seth mused on the apparent oddity of where he was going. *A vampire* going to *a priest, in a church, no less.* He shook his head at the false superstitions regarding his kind. *Holy water, crosses, the sacrament, garlic, all nonsense.* Vampires still had a few vulnerabilities, such as sunlight, a stake through the heart, and the need for blood. *Despite what the movies claim, we have fewer weaknesses than anybody thinks. But, the more misinformation that is spread about us, the better.* He pulled into the church parking lot, got out of his car, and headed inside.

As soon as Seth walked into the church, he knew something was wrong. It was too quiet, as if when the doors had shut behind him, they had cut off all sound from the church.

He stood there a moment, testing the air, and it was then that the smell registered. A familiar scent hung in the air, a thick coppery odor that the vampire knew intimately. Seth was in the foyer before the main hall, and he strode forward without pausing, pushing the entry doors open and stepping inside.

At first glance, all seemed to be in order. The candles in the vestry were flickering, their soft golden light holding the darkness at bay. The holy water font burbled quietly in the corner, recirculating the blessed liquid for the faithful to anoint themselves with. Moonlight drifted down though the large stained glass window at the other end of the church, painting the carpeted floor in a wash of silver and multi-colored light.

But the scene above the altar at the far end of the cathedral made Seth stop dead in his tracks. The beautifully carved and gilded cross suspended from the ceiling was coated in blood, which slowly oozed down its sides to puddle on the floor. The altar itself was also splotched with crimson, as if someone had been held there while being bled. But it was the figure hanging above that caused Seth's hands to clench into helpless fists and a snarl to escape his lips.

On the cross hung the body of Father Giancarlo, upside down, his arms dangling limply. Each leg had been stretched to an end of the crosspiece and nailed there. His throat looked like it had been ripped out, but Seth couldn't tell for sure, because his chest had been torn open, leaving a raw, eviscerated mess from his stomach to his neck. His once-immaculate shirt was soaked with congealing blood, a red collar where there used to be a white one. His eyes were still open and staring, a shocked look on his normally calm face.

Before Seth could take a step forward, he felt the cold metal circle of what was undoubtedly a gun muzzle press into the back of his neck. A low voice to his right started to ask, "Tell me why—"

Seth snapped. His right arm blurred upwards, striking the man's wrist with enough force to send the pistol flying straight up. Swiveling to face his attacker, his left hand, already curled into a fist, slammed into the man's solar plexus, causing his body to shake as if he had been suddenly electrocuted.

Seth grabbed the man by the throat and lifted him effortlessly into the air with his left hand. Without looking, he reached out with his right hand, caught the pistol as it fell, and put to the man's forehead.

"—I shouldn't kill you right now?" Seth growled. "Believe me, if you had anything to do with my friend's death, you won't be alive long enough to hear the answer."

"But if you kill him, I won't help you find out who killed my brother," a new voice said from the front of the church.

For a moment there was almost complete silence, broken only by the gasping sounds coming from the man Seth was holding in the air. He looked over towards the grisly tableau to see a tall woman with cappuccino skin dressed in a long cashmere overcoat standing in front of the altar. She was flanked by two even taller men, both dressed in immaculate suits and expensive leather overcoats. Seth's keen eye also noticed the slight bulges under their arms.

"Ramon is my personal assistant. Killing him will not get our relationship off to the best start," the woman said.

"As I recall, he was the one who put the gun to my head. I don't like being threatened," Seth said.

The woman motioned for her guards to stay where they were, then started walking down the aisle towards Seth. "If you are who I think you are, I know you had nothing to do with Batiste's death. My brother spoke very highly of you, Seth."

"I knew Father Giancarlo for over fourteen years, and he never mentioned having a sister," Seth said, turning to face her. He still held Ramon a foot off the ground, oblivious to the small choking noises he was making.

"Our mother married again after Batiste's father died," the woman said while coming closer. "Her first husband was pure Italian, her second was a *mulatto* French Creole. I am the result of the latter. Although my brother loves—loved—me very much, he could not talk about me often, for fear of jeopardizing his position in the Catholic Church. You see, I am a *mambo*, a voodoo priestess. There were those in the Church who felt my brother already conspired too close with—unnatural things. I had no wish to add fuel to their fire."

"Oh? Then why the hired muscle? I wouldn't think bullets would help you against spirits. Or priests, for that matter," Seth said.

"My . . . family is responsible for much of the illegal activity that goes on in New Orleans. I am not involved in that aspect of my family's business, but rival houses would try to use me for their own ends. Perhaps you've heard of the Giancarlo house in Italy. They're quite notorious over there."

Seth hid his smile. *As a matter of fact, I have*, he thought. It had been at the patriarchal head of the Giancarlo family's mansion where he had found Marten and recovered several dozen paintings they had stolen. He was well aware of their reputation both in Europe and the United States. Seth had suspected his friend's history, but, like Father Giancarlo, had never brought it up. *That's probably why he never spoke about his past. Another thing we had in common*, Seth thought.

"Do you think you could put Ramon down now? I don't like that shade of purple he's turning. If you still need a hostage, I am close enough now. Although after watching you in action, I have no doubt you could kill all three of my guards before I could reach the door."

Seth regarded her for a moment. Close up, she looked to be about thirty-five, with a emerald-eyed gaze intent enough to rival his own. Abruptly, Seth released Ramon, who fell to the ground, his hands massaging his throat. The scowl on his face was directed at his former captor, who ignored him.

"So why did you come here?" he asked.

The woman didn't answer for a moment, her eyes looking down at Seth's chest. He followed her gaze to the pistol he was still holding. "Oh," he said, letting it dangle by the trigger guard and holding it out to Ramon, who retrieved it gingerly. "Well?"

"I'm assuming it was for the same reason you're here. Occasionally my brother would consult me for information on some of the more—esoteric items the Church would find or recover during their work. I found a message on my answering machine this afternoon about a sacrificial dagger he had been researching. He asked me to stop by tonight, as he had wanted to introduce me to a friend. I assume he meant you."

"Some reception," Seth said.

"Well, when we walked in and discovered that," she said, waving at the scene behind her, "we weren't really trusting anybody anymore. I'm sorry."

"About what happened to me, or about your brother?" Seth asked.

The woman's eyes flashed as she glared at him. "Don't patronize me. It tears me apart to see my brother desecrated like this. I respected his choice, just as he respected mine. When his killers are found and justice is done, then my grieving will begin. But for now, my only thoughts are to find whoever did this, and destroy them."

Seth nodded. "I'm sorry. Believe me, we both want the same thing, and I won't rest until I find those responsible."

"Whomever it was, they were obviously here for a reason," the woman said. The dagger is gone. I've looked everywhere for it, with no luck."

"But how did they know? No one knew I was coming here. The cultists I took it from were all dead, I made sure of it," Seth said.

"Are you sure that was all of them? Did anyone see you coming or going?" the woman asked him.

"No, I was alone, except for . . . her," Seth answered.

"Who?"

"The cultists' sacrifice. A woman," Seth said. "If the cultists did manage to track me to here, then they may go after her again."

"It's possible they have her already. You'd better go to her, make sure she's all right. I have several leads of my own to check up on. You have a number where I can reach you, correct?"

Seth handed over a card with a number printed on it, nothing more. "You can reach me at this number for the next three days. What about you?"

The green-eyed woman rattled off a string of numbers that Seth immediately committed to memory. "What do I call you?" he asked.

"Dominique," was her answer. "Call me when you've located her."

"Of course. One thing I have to do first," Seth said. He ran towards the altar and cross, right past the two bodyguards. Springing onto the marble platform, he leaped straight into the air, landing lightly on the crosspiece of the cross. As gently as possible, he removed Father Giancarlo's body from the cross and, holding it in his arms, jumped to the ground.

Seth walked towards the bodyguards and addressed the one nearest to him. "Give me your coat."

"What for?" the bodyguard asked, "he's dead already."

Seth smiled, baring his fangs at the man. "Care to join him?"

The man's eyes widened, but he still looked over at Dominique, who nodded slightly. With a shrug, he wriggled out of his overcoat and dropped it on the floor in front of him.

Seth tenderly wrapped Father Giancarlo's body in the coat, making sure his eyes were closed before covering his face. "*In pace requiescat*, my friend."

Seth rose and turned to Dominique. "I have no doubt that you will see to his burial. When you leave, make sure no one else comes in," he said, then ran out of the church to his car, heading for the home of Diana Corgan.

THE STREETS OF New Orleans were packed with partygoers, the city disgorging thousands of people into the clogged avenues for celebration, parades, bands, and just having a good time. All of which made traveling even remotely close to the city nearly impossible. Seth had to bite back his frustration at his snail's-paced approach to the neighborhood where Diana Corgan lived.

After an hour's travel, he finally inched his way into the French Quarter, pulling up to a massive house that looked like it had been split up into several separate apartments. Seth recalled Diana's apartment number from her driver's license, then left his car sitting in the street, trusting the carnival to flow around it if need be.

He slipped through the deafening crowd, dodging well-wishers, drunken revelers and endless offers to join the merriment, and headed up the stairs to the entrance. Once inside, the noise abated somewhat, but the pulsating throb of the celebration in progress followed him up the stairwell to Diana Corgan's third-floor apartment.

When he reached the landing, the first thing he noticed was the open door with a faded number 2 on it. He tried to listen to see if anyone was inside, but couldn't make out anything; the noise from the street below swallowed any sounds from the apartment.

Seth edged over to the wall next to the doorway, looking through it at the part of the room he could see. What appeared to be a living room was decorated in thrift-shop modern, with an easy chair, coffee table, and part of a couch that had all seen better days visible in the room. Through an archway on the far side of the room, Seth saw a small room that looked to be part of the kitchen. A door beside it was closed.

Seth reached out and pushed the door open all the way, listening to it thud into the wall. He then stepped inside, scanning the rest of the living room. Finding nothing, he headed for the closed door. As he approached, he noted another familiar smell in the air, along with two distinct perfumes, one of which he had smelled before. He listened at the door, then, hearing nothing, pushed the door open.

The scene that greeted him could have been a twin of the one in the church, only this time the body was lying on a bed. This one was a young woman with short brown hair and a gaping red hole where her chest used to be. *It's not Diana*, Seth thought in relief. Looking around, he found no signs of a struggle. *Of course that doesn't mean anything*, he thought. *Perhaps she was taken by surprise. But where's Diana?*

The answer to that question was nowhere in the rest of the apartment. The perfume smell was stronger in the living room, but when Seth tried tracing it, he lost the scent in the hallway. He went back to the apartment, looked around one final time, then pulled out his digital phone and dialed Dominique's number.

"Yes," her cool voice answered.

"They've already been here," Seth said. "Her roommate's dead, and Diana's nowhere to be found."

"If they have her already, then I know where to find them. Meet us at the cemetery you found her at last night."

"Of course, they'll try to complete the ceremony. Why do they still need her?"

"Because you let the ceremony go on for as long as you did, now it can only be completed with her as the vessel," Dominique said. "A mistake we won't let happen again."

"You've got that right," Seth said, ignoring the dig. "I'll see you there."

DURING HIS DRIVE to the cemetery, Seth thought about what had happened the previous night. *I suppose what she said might be true. I don't know that much about magic as Dominique does. But whatever they were up to, it can't be any good. Assuming they could have actually pulled their little ritual off in the first place.*

By the time Seth pulled his car up to the cemetery, it was just before midnight. The cultist's van was still parked where it had been the night before. The cemetery, a place where Seth had confidently walked last night, was now layered in a thick gray fog that obscured the dozens of mausoleums that dotted the landscape. Strangely, the murky vapor only extended to the stone wall of the cemetery, and did not spill onto the road.

As Seth got out of his car, he felt a peculiar energy in the fog, a palpable power radiating from the unusual mist in the graveyard. As he approached, the fog seemed to solidify before him, completely blocking any view of the building beyond it. Seth shook his head, stepped forward, and vaulted the fence.

The fog engulfed him. Seth had no idea where he was in relation to anything around him. A quick glance behind him confirmed that he could no longer see the road or his car. Seth took a step forward, than another. The fog coalesced on his clothes and face, soaking him with cold stale droplets of water. Seth kept walking forward, waiting for something to happen.

When the fog moved, it almost took him by surprise. Gray tendrils of water vapor pushed against his face, pouring into him through his nose and mouth. Seth didn't struggle or fight, he just stood there, feeling the now condensed water dripping into his lungs. After a few minutes, the liquid filled his body completely.

Seth let his body go limp, and the fog lowered him gently to the grass. It then began to dissipate, breaking up and vanishing into the night as if it never existed. Seth lay motionless and watched until every trace of the unnatural vapor had disappeared, then he rolled to his hands and knees and began expelling the water from his body. *Once again, being a vampire does have its advantages, such as not having to breathe*, Seth thought as he spat the water out.

When he was done, he looked up and spotted the mausoleum he had been at the night before. His heightened senses picked up the low sound of voices across the graveyard, and he headed towards it.

He hadn't gone more than a few yards when he saw the familiar shape of the marble building looming in the night before him. The voices were louder now, and Seth could see shadows and flickering light in the entryway to the mausoleum. Seth crept to the entryway and looked inside.

Once again, the players from last night had resumed their familiar roles. Diana Corgan, her eyes wild and staring, lay bound once again on the stone table. Above her, dagger in one hand, cross in another, was the cult leader from the previous evening. His face was now an ashen gray, and he moved stiffly, like a puppet whose controller hadn't mastered the strings yet. *He was dead, I know he was, and I didn't turn him into a vampire*, Seth thought. *And anyway, why is he here, but the rest of the bodies aren't?*

However, an even bigger surprise was seeing Dominique and her two looming bodyguards standing next to the cult leader, watching him prepare for the ritual.

I might have known, Seth thought, gauging the distance from himself to Dominique. The torchlight cast flickering shadows that would easily hide his approach. Glancing over at the small group clustered around the stone altar one last time, Seth slipped noiselessly into the tomb.

He flitted from the door to behind one of the bodyguards in the space of a single heartbeat. Grabbing the taller man's head, Seth twisted it with all his strength, breaking the man's neck in a single movement. As the bodyguard started to collapse, Seth moved to the second man and crushed his throat with a single swift blow. By the time the first man had hit the floor, Seth had grabbed Dominique by the neck and prepared to end her life as well. At least, that's what he tried to do.

As he laid his clawed fingers on her skin, his hand felt like it had grabbed the sun. Snarling in pain, he pulled his arm back and recoiled from the shock of the burn. He steeled himself to try to strike her again, but before he could, he felt a cold hand encircle his neck in a vise-like grip and lift him off the ground. Seth tore at the imprisoning fingers, trying to free himself, but they might as well have been forged of solid, unyielding steel. In answer to his efforts, the hand simply increased its grip, cracking Seth's neck vertebrae. Suddenly his body went limp, unable to move, only this time he wasn't faking it. His head remained upright, held there by the implacable hand clutching his neck.

"So glad you could join us, Seth," Dominique's icy voice held a note of triumph. "I took the precaution of upgrading my bodyguards and my personal *gris* to something that could handle you should you actually appear here. It's too bad about Ramon, but I have no doubt he'll still serve me even better than before.

"I'm very pleased the fog didn't kill you. It only confirmed my suspicions of what you really are."

Seth's mouth opened but no sound came out. Dominique noticed and spoke to the thing holding him. "Ramon, loosen your hold on his neck so he may speak."

Behind her, the cultist continued his chant, speaking, and then answering himself in a language long dead:

> *"Iä! Iä! Iä! Fthaghn fealth nostro carneilgn dosum*
> *Y'targh vorbelg hah'thelth nutarngh esqis*
> *Sothoth-Yog cyrnlea sulnabis queth'nas pax*
> *Apsoh noxtra pacuon daggheth yan'noth es risciven!"*

Seth tried his throat once again and found it in working order. "Surely you don't believe in all this crap."

Dominique smiled. "Of course, and soon you will too. Just before my resurrected servant there completes his sacrifice, this time without interruption, I will step in and summon the greatest of the elder gods to this plane. I have you to thank for making this all possible."

Seth thought frantically, trying to buy time until he could figure out a way to get free. "Why? Why here and now?"

"Mardi Gras is the largest, longest non-secular celebration on the continent. Do you know how much spiritual energy is being given off in this city? The celebration, the revelry, the fucking, the fighting. All of that, a psychic explosion on the megaton scale, if you will, that before was just going to waste, but now, channeled through our young victim here, it will be used to power the opening of the gate across the dimensional universe, where Yog-Sothoth will feel the vortex opening and come to me."

Dominique held up the Cross of Coronado, its gems winking in the torchlight. "How fitting that an artifact of my brother's pitiful religion provided the final key to unlocking the gate to the Old One's power. Two thousand years ago, a god supposedly walked this earth. Tonight, on this anniversary of his arrival, a new supreme being will come forth to supplant him."

Great, New Orleans rings in the millennium by unwittingly summoning the ultimate party crasher, Seth thought. "But if you already had the girl, why go to the trouble of luring me here?" he asked.

"We didn't have the body, the other group of cultists did," Dominique said. "I had investigated this scene today at my brother's request, where I noticed that the pentagram had been partially erased, which meant that some of Yog-Sothoth's power had escaped, and reanimated whatever inert matter it could use, such as the cult's high priest. I knew that it would want the ceremony completed, and that the zombie would eventually come back here. As for you, your body, once properly prepared, will make a most suitable vessel for the avatar of Yog-Sothoth to reign upon this world." Dominique's eyes shone with the fever of the insane. "I would love in tell you more, but my time is almost at hand. Be ready to bring him closer, inside the circle when I tell you" she commanded her mindless zombie.

By now the marble tomb throbbed with otherworldly energy. Dominique removed her robe revealing her brown skin covered only by loincloth. Unholy ritual markings covered her breasts, arms and stomach. "Prepare the sacrifice," she told the high priest.

The gray-skinned cultist had thrown back his hood, revealing dull watery eyes and a thin line of yellow drool hanging from a corner of his mouth. He used the dagger to slit Diana's blouse open, then carved an upside down cross on her chest, the blood welling out to form the holy symbol in crimson. The priest quickly backed away, out of the summoning circle to next to Dominique.

Immediately the air above her actually seemed to solidify, thickening and coalescing into a swirling cloud of noxious smell and impenetrable solid blackness. In the middle of this cloud there was a bright blue pinpoint of light which began to grow larger.

As soon as she saw it, Dominique took the dagger from the cultist's hand and, shouldering him aside, held it ready. The cultist staggered away from the stone slab and stood, staring at nothing.

The point of light was now basketball-sized, and a cold wind was rising inside the mausoleum, causing the torches to flicker, their light insignificant next to the unearthly illumination coming from the center of the room. Seth felt that same strange presence he had noticed when he had held the dagger the night before, only this time it was much stronger.

His spinal cord had regenerated, but Seth didn't know how that was going to help him. Dominique's damned zombie was holding him by the back of his neck, making it impossible to get the leverage to do any significant damage. *Besides, I couldn't even pry open his hand, even with my strength. What good would a punch do?*

Dominique began the final stage of the summoning chant. "*Iä! Iä! Iä -ka! Yog-Sothoth nyarlop kaz'yeth vezuan ftheagh ust'yre!*"

The pinpoint of light suddenly expanded, throwing out bright blue beams that anchored themselves to twelve equidistant points around the stone slab. The wind was howling now, an eldritch scream that nearly drove all coherent thought from Seth's mind. He watched in wonder as the blue light became a pulsing, crackling ball that hovered in the air over the altar and the mercifully unconscious Diana Corgan.

Seth watched in horror, the first time he had experienced that emotion in decades, as a huge, obscenely twisted shadow fell over the blue light. Writhing, slime covered tentacles slowly pushed out of the blue rift that had been torn between this world and some other unspeakably grotesque dimension, tentatively exploring the new realm they suddenly found access to. Seth knew that whatever those tentacles was connected to was about to poke its head, or whatever passed for it, through the portal.

If I don't do something right now, I'm going to see the rest of this thing, and that will be all she wrote for me, N'awlins, everything, he thought. Summoning up all of his remaining mental faculties, he directed them at the zombie holding him with all his strength. Usually he preferred to talk to whomever he was trying to control, but in dire emergencies he could expend the majority of his power in a single mental command that would almost automatically be obeyed.

But not this time. When Seth tried to enter the zombie's mind, he felt a solid wall of mental shielding protecting the creature. *Dominique's defenses. Now we're in serious trouble.*

The tentacles gripped the edges of the glowing blue portal and started pushing on it, enlarging it so the rest of its unearthly body could begin coming through. A gout of foul-smelling ichor spurted from the portal to land, smoking and hissing, on the stone floor of the mausoleum. The hideously distended head of whatever nightmarish monstrosity Dominique had conjured up was about to emerge from its extradimensional womb on the other side of the universe.

One last chance, Seth thought. With all of his remaining strength, he sought to control the cultist who was standing, slack-jawed, beside Dominique. With an effort, he pushed his way into the man's mind, finding it an empty shell. Seth could feel the immense power of the entity that had given the man his unnatural life screech in outrage as he gained control. *I hope this works,* he thought, as he gave the man one command with all of his strength.

It did. Just as Dominique turned to command the zombie to bring Seth to her, the cultist jerked, then lurched forward and pushed her as hard as he could. Dominique staggered forward, through the protected circle, and squarely into the blue portal that had now grown to envelop the entire stone altar. Her agonized scream as the blue beams lanced through her knifed into Seth's ears like a scalpel sliding through his brain. The blue light immediately started to recede, and the tentacles, sensing something had gone wrong, jerked back inside, the last two wrapping around Dominique and lifting her, still screaming, through the blue portal with them. The blue light shrank to a pinpoint again, then vanished.

At once, everything was still and quiet again. Seth fell to the floor, twisting and rolling to come up on his feet and face whatever it was that had held him.

Collapsed in a boneless heap was the bodyguard whose neck he had broken, his hand still outstretched in a pincer grip. Seth looked around to see the other bodyguard and the cultist, both dead as well. Of Dominique, Diana Corgan, or the thing from beyond this world, there was no sign.

Seth got up after a minute, feeling his neck vertebrae stretch and pop as they regenerated themselves. He walked over to the cultist and took the golden cross out of his hand and held it for a moment, shaking his head.

"You've been bought dearly tonight," he said, wrapping the cross's chain around his hand. He slowly walked around the summoning circle, looking for the sacrificial dagger, but could find no trace of it.

"I hope it's with Dominique in whatever hell she finds herself in," he said. Leaving the mausoleum, Seth ran back to his car, got a container of gasoline, and liberally soaked the three remaining bodies. A lighter found in one of the bodyguard's pockets set them all ablaze. He would call it in to the police later. Much later.

As Seth walked to his car, he stopped for a moment, fancying he could hear the party still going on in New Orleans. He looked over at the bright lights of the distant city and thought again of the thousands of innocent people there, living their lives, unaware of what they had, and how easily it could be taken from them.

They'll never know how close it all came to ending tonight. No one deserves to know that, he thought. *But I will. Tonight, and forever.*

How I envy you, Father Giancarlo.

I already wish I could forget.

✝

A TEMPORARY VAMPIRE

BARBARA EMRYS

>─┤◆>─◆─O─◆─<◆├─<

THUS FAR WE HAD DRIVEN PAST ANNE RICE'S MANSION IN THE Garden District, where a limo in front had caused avid but disappointed speculation, and toured French Quarter scenes approximating killings by Lestat, Louis, and Claudia. In one of these, "Lestat" stalking a young woman was re-enacted. A woman dressed in nineteenth-century garments—to we would know it was not an actual attack on a tourist—strolled past a streetlight and into darker shadow. She looked over her shoulder twice, but in the wrong direction, for we had noticed the gleam of a pale face at another angle to her. She walked on a bit faster now, but still as she passed the alley, he had her, "Lestat" drew her to him, one hand over her mouth, and she fainted away. Then there was perhaps a full minute of him feeding, the bite and then lapping and sucking. There was red paint in abundance over her blouse. Then he let her go, limp, to the ground and looked straight at us as though still hungry. While the group reacted, he seemed to fade into nothingness. Perhaps there way a swirl of sparkly mist before the last spot was extinguished.

I appreciated this "Vampire's New Orleans" tour the same way a houngan appreciates a stop at the voodoo shop with a midnight trip to the swamps. Still, New Orleans was new to me, as was the American south; many evening tours had similar themes and I found the antics of the aficionados amusing enough.

I had successfully avoided the four single women and also the lonely older couple, and stuck with a younger version of them, recently married, for whom the tour was clearly a turn-on. Their exchanged glances and their constant bodily contact were feeding from the mild perversity. They used me as distraction that further heightened their tension and I, as it were, basked in their glow.

Then we made a final stop, end of the line, in Jackson Square. The daylight mimes had been gone long since, but one had lit her poses by torches of the sort made for patios in drizzly weather. In the intermittently revealing light she stood on a small platform draped in crimson satin, but she wore, of course, black. A softly draped dress as black as smoke. Her glorious hair spilled over it like liquid gold. She should have been too lovely to mime the vampire, but the effect was stunning. One saw the golden hair first, then the dark red mouth and the long incisors.

I realized belatedly that she was part of the tour.

Her "fangs" looked so real they must have been expensive prosthetics. Her long white arms came up slowly, languorously, and reached out to our whole group, yet to each of us alone. Her eyes looked at no one, and so everyone. When coins were tossed, she sank into a crouch and pulled her lips back. The young husband next to me gasped half aloud in sheer pleasure.

There are mimes that essentially clown and there are mimes that add to reality. For the first time that night, even in this haunted city, she made the dead real.

Except for myself, which would not have been mime. Yet as I watched her strike pose after voluptuous and feral pose, it was as though only the two of us knew, and all these others were ignorant.

By now our little group had drifted away; the younger and older couples headed for bed, the single women for the bars. None had any interest in the mime beyond momentary titillation. They tossed coins and a few bills and departed. Others had gathered, however, principally men by ones and twos, to whom she played as shamelessly as a stripper for the money they dropped into the collection box.

And yet she still was inside the role, I found it unsettling, and I waited at a small distance until she shook off the vampire and stepped down. She threw a short cloak over her shoulders and tied back her hair then tipped the money into her bag. Perhaps she had palmed the teeth; I couldn't tell.

The change was enough that the last of the men sheared away. She cast one glance at me and discounted me as a threat. She walked briskly away towards Canal and at a distance, I watched her enter a car drawn up there. The motor fired and the car drew away.

I continued walking but turned through the French Market towards Café du Monde, where I took the merest taste of chicory coffee and sugar powder, and pondered what I had seen. Already I hoped she would appear again the next night.

AND MYSELF? I am the man at the far end of the bar, back to the wall, watching the rest of you. In the dim lighting you notice only the well-cut leather jacket and my distinguished silver highlights. Or else I'm the lone wolf strolling down Bourbon Street eyeing the passing parade but not entirely part of it. Hands in my pockets, shoulders relaxed, perhaps moving to the beats drifting out of clubs. Maybe you catch my eye and smile at me, and I smile back and walk on. Or maybe I stop and buy you a frozen daiquiri in a plastic cup and we walk deeper into the darkness, and in the morning you have a bruised throat or wrist or elbow, exactly like when you gave blood. You hardly remember me and vow to drink less. I have made that vow also.

Once I had a family of sorts among the living, who knew me and were not afraid, but that was long since. Once I was not alone in my rambles, but he too, my Aubrey-analogue, is gone. I have come here as people shop for a retirement home or relocation with movable employment. I walk around thinking, is this a place for me? I was undecided before I saw the vampire mime.

THE NEXT NIGHT I was early enough to watch her arrive and set up. The torches were already in place and the platform and collection box. Perhaps the tour provided them. But she spread the silken drape, removed her cloak and dropped some money into the box. I walked around the square. There was no car waiting yet. Likely it would return. As I turned back I saw her staring into the darkness I passed through. Her body language changed as she stared, no longer arm and purposeful, but sinuous and sinister. Was it possible, I wondered, that she was vampire?

As she began, I made my way through the tour group to drop a bill into the collection. I could smell her perfume, a rich, spicy odor, and her sweat. She was alive. She was superb. Each pose she held perfectly as a statue, without visible muscle tension, then shifted at the reward of money. But none of it was mechanical or false. If she had learned not from experience and certainly not most films, might she have learned from—a mentor, say?

People came, saw, paid and left. She had to have noticed me but she gave no sign at all, and I left before she was done, to prowl restlessly through the warm night among the still-crowded streets. I fed at last from one so totally inebriated that any memory would seem by morning fantastic. Lying down for the day, it was her face, gold-framed, that filled my mind. I wanted her. Wanted her in my life. She was young and interesting. If she did not have a mentor—might she want one?

THE LIVING TALK of more than one life in the same body, a concept I never understood until I had been . . . "turned," I believe is the current parlance. But my existence now is like that. There was my young life before, and my mature life, and then my lives after: my wild early years among Boston immigrants; my sober Massachusetts years in which I much identified with the region's historical persona of guilt and bloodlust, my family years in Chicago with significant others, living and not; the companion years of making my grand tour. Now there were years alone and wandering with the impersonal intimacy of feeding and the illusion, sometimes, of friendship that is in fact passing acquaintance. How many more lives will I live in this body? I wonder. Is this a new one beginning?

I WALKED SLOWLY from my large hotel (evening room service upon request) to Jackson Square in a light, misting rain. She was unlikely to pose in it. I sought out the Pirate's Alley bookshop, still open to sell Faulkner, Chopin, and even Rice. I handled one of her novels, wondering if this had been a source book for the mime, Faulkner I've never been able to read, but if I lived in New Orleans, perhaps I would come to understand him. I met Hawthorne, who's more to my taste, and once discussed original sin with him. Nothing in the concept explains my state. No snakes involved, no fall from grace. I was not even precisely murdered, nor—at least once I understood my condition—have I often done more than steal blood. But then, I had a mentor.

The rain had stopped and the sky partly cleared, I saw at a distance the mime approaching. Her hair was covered by the hood of her cape and a man walked with her, carrying the stage and the torches. He too, I saw as they neared me, was alive, his skin as dark as sky. He set up the platform and lit the torches. I followed when he left, but he led me only to the same sedan that had picked her up before. He drove away before I could locate a taxi, but I could arrange for one by the time she left.

Tonight, walking across the square towards her back, I perceived her audience. As on the other nights, men and a few couples had gathered. I stopped in the shadows behind her and watched their faces. Lust, as I had expected, and perverse thrill. Even the women present, who perhaps wanted to be her wanted the vampire lover too. Only one face among them did not shine with desire. One nondescript man, brown hair, pale face, unremarkable clothing, watched with predatory anticipation. I thought he had been there the first night too, but I was not sure.

He was not vampire either. Light reflected off his sweating face and, as I came nearer, alcohol breathed off him. I joined the small group and looked up at her, and her pose was off slightly, stiffened and just a bit forced. She too had noticed him and he worried her. And worried as I was also, I felt elation. Better than anyone else, better than her driver (or friend, partner, lover), I could protect her from this.

People came and went. Not much money tonight. The hunter approached her too closely, offering a folded bill as he might to a lap dancer. She went to attack pose, admirable fangs bared, nails clawing. He laughed, but stepped back, and I closed with him, a sharp point pressed to his side.

"Come with me," I whispered, and pulled him away.

Again she broke her pose enough to watch us pass into a shadowy street. Once away he turned to grapple with me and I bit him quickly, taking enough blood to render him unconscious. I took his wallet for good measure.

By the time I had cleaned my face and hands and covered my shirtfront, she was gone. Stand empty, torches out, as though she'd never been there at all. The familiar isolation washed over me.

LETITIA CONDIT, AGED twenty-two, was making her move. Actually, her first move had been to go to college, even though her family, who didn't have a nickel, couldn't see the point. During the year she'd majored in theatre and gotten by on scholarships and part-time work, and during the summers, on top of a full-time job, she'd gone to what its students called the "University of Silence," the mime school.

Her mama had thought maybe she could do a cute little routine at the fair, at least until she had kids, or maybe be a clown for kiddie birthday parties. Her daddy had never had a clue what she was doing. Now she had graduated, it was time for the next step, which was professional experience. She'd always seen that her best choice was character parts, but they were more limited for women mimes. She'd avoided the sexy parts like Lady Godiva (but you have the hair for it, her teacher said) or any other role that wasn't dignified.

She had made a perfect Virgin Queen as her final project, performing it three times, once at the school and twice in the Quarter. Payment produced regal gestures and a cynical smile, and no actress had ever done them better. But through the persona trance she'd heard the audience, what there was of it, wondering who she was supposed to be and making wrong guesses, or half-assed ones: "Maybe she's that Queen—Elizabeth? Or was that Anne Boleyn?" One had actually said, "Naw, I think it's the Pope."

A sexier character, but not about sex per se, was required and so she had studied the Quarter and its hordes. And come up with the vampire. The sexual implication was there, but the power was hers, and she liked that balance. And the tour company had bought it as closure for their jaunt. They didn't care if she went on longer, after their group had broken up. They even supplied the torches and the platform, and she called Kip on her cell phone when she was ready to leave. Kip was a tour guide and too religious to approve of her persona, but he was reliable back-up.

He was what made it possible, in fact, to face down the skankier or drunker men, and feel safe walking away with up to 100 dollars a night, on top of what the tour paid her. She was making her living with her art, and this satisfied her more than anything she'd ever done. Never mind that Kevin, the jerk, had broken up with her over it. What had she ever seen in Kevin? Well, he had been good in bed. But she performed better with her bed empty anyway, even if she was lonely afterwards, back in her tiny apartment.

Some nights she was too restless to sleep afterwards, and some of those nights she concocted plans, because this was a summer gig. When the rains came, she needed another move altogether. It was possible to move the act into a bar, but that felt too close to other acts. She'd talked to a manager at one of the likelier places, but even he had suggested removing some clothing along the way.

Some nights she went for a walk into the Garden District: She always walked to St. Charles and by Anne Rice's house as a kind of talisman, sympathy for the vampire. Loners, they were, outcasts, some of whom hadn't chosen their lot. All of it went into her performance. And that was where she'd first seen the guy, the one she thought of as "the Count."

He had drifted out of tree shadow into streetlight and moonlight as effortlessly as a ghost. For a second she thought she had seen a ghost—Lafayette Cemetery was only blocks away. She drew back into shadow herself, though she'd been convinced he knew she was there, even though he never looked her way. He'd been staring at the Rice house as though taking a personal picture. He stood there motionless white the usual carload of drunken kids piled out and struck what they thought were vamp poses while taking cell-phone pictures of each other and laughing hysterically. Then he seemed to be done, wheeled round and walked towards the trolley line in a brisk, human manner.

He wore ordinary clothes, too; a dark jacket. With a T-shirt beneath, and dark pants. He looked . . . actually, in that thin-faced, sad way, like a sexy mask of tragedy. He looked . . . unhappy. A touch of weariness, a hint of boredom and, most of all, loss of hope, of goals. A face that didn't want to give up, on a person that had, Letty knew herself an acute observer, as mimes must be. Because of all this, because of the night and the place, and because he had a certain something about him, she thought of him as the real deal. The Count. Some nights his image had fueled her performance.

And now he'd turned up in her audience. Letty had been disappointed, actually, to see the elegant, slim man on a vampire tour. Almost disappointed that he watched her. And when he turned up again, she thought he was just another guy ogling her boobs and not noticing her art. But again there was something. Maybe it was just her imagination, but his interest felt personal. More like a talent scout than a masher. Interested in *her*. She should be so lucky.

Tonight, though, the guy she thought of as the stalker was back. Letty had talked with other female mimes about the attention you drew and how to deal with it. That's why she'd insisted on Kip to pick her up, which he was heartily sick of doing, but even he understood the reason. After a performance she was strung up but distracted at the same time. And this one guy, she could see in his face that he thought he owned her. He was around last week; and then she thought he'd quit, but tonight he was back. She put her anger into the poses and he didn't even get it. He came up in her face, trying to break her out of the pose and into just another money-hungry woman . . .

. . . and the Count took hold of him, said something and pulled him right away. Neither of them came back. Letty made one final pose and stepped down. She dumped the money in her bag, slung it across her chest, threw the cloak around her and walked in the direction the two men had disappeared.

No one there. She looked down alleys and side streets. No sign of them. She was just about to speed-dial Kip when she saw to her left a body propped in a doorway. Letty approached cautiously, but the figure didn't stir. It was the jerk, the one who'd been after her, but he was out cold. And on his neck and shirt there was blood. She reached one finger and touched it. Sticky blood. The feel of it ran through her veins like ice. She stood up and jogged away fast, back to the square, to the lights.

There was her platform, her torches, as though nothing had occurred. She called Kip, who was already, he said, on the way. She walked down the most brightly lit side of the square, through a fog of beer and saltwater catch, towards the river. She shivered in the car, too sunk in speculation to notice the taxi that followed her. In her apartment, she locked herself in, no thought of walking the district tonight. She did not see the man with the well-cut clothing and the distinguished white at his temples alight from his taxi and take note of her name and address on the bell. But later, when he dialed the number he had obtained via the concierge, her message machine recorded his voice.

WHEN LETTY PLAYED back the message, she couldn't help being intrigued. It wasn't the talent-scout break she'd been hoping for, but a freelance journalist who might get her a feature story—with pictures—was nothing to sneeze at. And besides, he had the most gorgeous voice, deep and resonant, that made every word he said pack extra meaning. He wasn't from here. He sounded like New England, maybe, but not in awhile. When he said, "I believe it might benefit your career," she believed it would, and so she called back.

After some phone tag late in the day, she agreed to meet him after her performance for a very late supper. In his favour, the restaurant he named was not a bar or a gumbo palace but a reputable bistro that people went to for the cuisine more than the ambiance. And he had said he would come to the performance; she felt better meeting him first, though it might be safer to meet him at the restaurant, entirely on her own. You couldn't be too careful, no matter how terrific his voice sounded.

The appointment gave some extra fire to her performance that night. No let-down going home alone, no nervous wandering in the dark. She was making her move towards the professional future she wanted the way a vampire wanted blood. Letty ran the whole range of poses she'd developed, flowing from seductive lover to sinister embrace to bared fangs, the crouch over a body, cowering back as from a cross, turning at bay, and back to a come-on glance over one shoulder with just the hint of fang showing. Maybe because she was so pumped or maybe because it was Friday night and the tour was full, she had her best crowd in awhile and the collection box filled up nicely.

And the Count was there. Standing as he had other nights at the back of the group, applauding when others did, smiling with pleasure at each pose, though he had seen them all before. Maybe she ought to be afraid of him too, but she just wasn't. He kept his distance, anyway. The man who'd crowded her last night wasn't there and she'd seen no mention of a murder in the *Times-Picayune*. The jerk had gotten into a fight, most likely. She hoped he wouldn't be back.

By the time she finished and stepped down, her jaw ached from the fitted fangs and from holding the positions, but she knew she had done it flawlessly. She took out the teeth and pulled her hair back, part of the ritual. And when she turned, there was the man she called the Count. Letty was tall herself, but he *was* taller, and he still moved like water. When he spoke, she realized immediately that he was her supper date.

And that put her in a quandary. Of course she knew he had seen her perform before. But the Count had been there three nights running and last seen in the company of the jerk who ended up bleeding in a doorway,

She said, "Aren't you a little old for a journalist?" All her doubt went into it.

"I believe writers are all ages, but for me it's a second career." He shifted so that the light shone on his face. A pale face, which inspected her caution. "I can meet you at the restaurant—or somewhere else if you prefer."

"Junkanoo," Letty said. "On Toulouse. In half an hour—I want to change first."

He knew where it was and walked away to secure a table. Letty made her way to a nearby poor-boy place with spacious women's facilities. There she changed into pants and rook off her theatrical make-up in favour of natural lips and just a little powder and eyeliner. She folded away her persona and looked at herself. Still a bit flushed from the performance and from her hopes for publicity too. And from the fact that it was the Count, be honest. It was exciting to find out about the mystery man. She repacked her costume in her large shoulder bag, along with the folder of publicity stills she'd brought along, and walked to the restaurant.

"JUNKANOO, ALWAYS CARNIVAL," the sign read. Spicy Caribbean food, and the walls hung with costumes, photos, and masks. A lot of the masks had horns. The journalist—Nathan Court—had got one of the window tables. These were visible, but quieter and more private in terms of sound, at least. Old-fashioned manners—he got up to pull out her chair—but he asked her what was good here instead of taking command. They ordered glasses of red wine, a plate of calamari, and a bowl of stew for Letty. She regarded him across the small table. If she stretched out her arm, she could touch his long-fingered hand.

"So, you're a freelancer, you said—does that mean you don't know where a story about me might appear?" She asked it just to show she was no innocent.

"It means I'm not working on assignment, yes. But there are editors I've written for before and I queried the subject as soon as I knew you'd talk to me. I've written for the airline magazine *Great Southern*. They like the New Orleans angle, but the appeal is broad enough too."

The wine arrived and Letty took a sip. "Well, O.K. What do you want to know?"

How one became a mime, where she'd studied. Predictable background. Over the calamari and gumbo, though, he asked, "Why a vampire? Is it just the Anne Rice influence?"

So she explained, even though the food cooled, about personas and the difficulty of dignified ones for women mimes.

"Vampires are dignified?"

"Sure, think of Count Dracula. Never a hair or a gesture out of place." And she explained the power angle. "The vampire's not a really inviting role, come down to it. Not the way I do it anyway."

"Yes, the way you do it, I see the dignity. I see the danger. And the isolation of mime feeds those, doesn't it? When you're up there, I mean, you are apart."

He stared at her eyes, not her chest, and stared so intently that he ate hardly anything, but then he was also taking notes. They discussed the isolation of mimes, feeding the crowd's response not into reaction but into the strength of the poses.

"And where did you get your poses? I'm just curious. They aren't the standard movie vampires—unless you go back to Dracula. Not the camp ones, certainly."

Letty finished her wine and refused the waiter's offer of another glass while she thought how to put it. "I saw certain movies. *Daughter of Dracula*—have you seen that one? She's so deadly, but vulnerable too. And an early version of *Carmilla*. But mostly I read."

"*Dracula?*"

"Sure. And *Carmilla*, who's the first female vampire. She wanted her victims willing—at least some of them. Wanted them to be a little in love with her. And also Mina Harker in *The League*—"

"—*of Extraordinary Gentleman*. Peta Wilson was excellent at showing the power subtly. That moment when she turns, wiping blood off her mouth—"

"Yes, that's one. I actually tried to work up a pose for it, but it's not very clear what's going on out of context and I didn't want to fool with fake blood."

"When I first saw you," he said, "I almost thought you could be vampire."

Not *a* vampire, she noted. He must read too. "I'm a temporary vampire," Letty said, and he laughed with her. "When I saw you," she said, "I thought you were a ghost."

He was all attention. "When did you first see me? Where?"

"One night by the Rice house," she said. "At least I think it was you. You sort of floated over to it and watched awhile, then left."

"Ah," he said. "I do go for walks. Like yourself, perhaps? And then I write."

"A night person," Letty said, studying him. "And you live here, in the city?"

"I live many places," he said, and Letty heard the bitter undertone. "I've been here for a few weeks."

The waiter had brought the bill, and the room was far more subdued. Nathan Court insisted on paying it and had just begun to make an appointment to go over the draft article with her. Letty was hoping he'd be here at few more weeks, at least, They both had grown accustomed to people passing near the bay window, and did not immediately react when a body appeared in peripheral vision, but this one stopped, inches away.

Nathan looked up and froze, and then Letitia looked. The jerk from last night, dressed like a vampire or an undertaker in stark black, turned his glare from Nathan to her, and smiled gloatingly.

And then he was gone. "That's the guy—what did you do to him last night?"

Nathan looked disturbed, but kept his voice even. "I told him to back off, to leave you alone."

"And I saw him later, unconscious in a doorway, with blood on him."

"I'm not surprised. He's a violent type."

"And you—are you a violent type?"

"Letitia—"

She got up, rummaging in her bag for the cell phone. "Do the article—do whatever you want, but leave me out of the rest—"

She was out on the street, leaving him to deal with the bill. She punched speed-dial for a cab; and almost ran for the next main street. There was a large black car parked at the corner and, as she hurried past, the driver's door opened so fast it hit her. She stumbled back against a balcony post, and he was on her, hands around her neck, hot breath in her face. "You monster's whore—"

Letitia kicked his shins and clawed at his eyes, but his fingers closed steadily and her vision shrank into one little ball of light and consciousness. She couldn't scream, couldn't get enough breath. The way he leaned towards her against the door, they could be embracing, and no one was going to . . .

Suddenly she could breathe again. She slid to the ground, panting, and watched the two men come to grips. No one could mistake this for an embrace. Her attacker, the larger and heavier man, had one hand around Nathan Court's throat, holding him off. And Nathan's body changed, as though he now were miming, heavier and more centered, but fast. Letitia began to inch backwards, away from their straining bodies, keeping her eyes on them. "Monster," the guy hissed, "you blood-sucking—"

Nathan opened his lips and the fangs showed dearly, a set that put her own to shame. He sank them deep into the wrist at his throat and there was no pretend about it. The attacker screamed in pain and, among the passers-by, someone yelled, "I've called the cops!"

It galvanized both men. Nathan let go of the hand and drew his head back again, but her attacker's hand now held a glinting blade and he drove it home in Nathan's chest. Instead of reeling back, Nathan head-butted the taller man in the nose then punched him in the throat, Almost absently, his left hand pulled out the knife. There was surprisingly little blood, less than she'd seen last night.

He was a vampire. He had blood on his mouth. She saw the tip of his tongue lick it away.

"Letitia—" He put the knife in his pocket and kept his back towards the people still watching at a distance and holding up cell phones for pictures. "Call 911. You were attacked—he's been hanging around. A bystander punched him. I wasn't here. Clear?"

He was a vampire. He saw she knew. "I can't stay. It's too close to dawn for a police station, and besides—"

Now they heard a siren. Letitia nodded, unable to make a sound. She looked away towards the flashing light and, when she looked back, he was gone. Her obvious trauma, once the police arrived moments later, convinced them more than any explanation, but by the time they drove her to the station, she had come up with one.

She was a street performer, yes. She'd answer all their questions. With the tour, and she recited contact information. Sometimes men in the audience were drunk. Sometimes they acted out. She described the man's actions the night before, omitting Nathan. Tonight the same man had followed her from a restaurant where a journalist had been interviewing her. Yes, she had the journalist's number at home. She'd been calling a taxi when she was attacked. She described everything except the bite and who had intervened. A stranger, she said, who'd gotten a lot more than he bargained for.

Letitia knew that bystanders must have seen him speaking to her. He'd said, she told the police, that he couldn't get involved. Didn't explain otherwise. Just said, "You'll be all right now," and took off. He might know martial arts. An effective fighter, anyway. The bite wound she didn't know anything about, except—the guy seemed to be nuts on the subject of vampires: Kept saying she was the monster's, uh, girlfriend. Maybe he actually believed she was a vampire. People believed all kinds of things.

At long last they released her. She had called Kip and had called the tour, and their lawyer would contact her tomorrow. Today, almost. And she was excused from performing that evening, though they hoped she'd be able to complete her contract. In an early, faint dawn she took a taxi home, and let herself into the apartment.

The first thing she saw was the note. It was stuck with tape to the doorknob. Letty peeled it off and locked herself in. Her heart sped up the second she opened it.

Letitia

    Forgive me for coming here. I was in no state to cross a hotel lobby. I apologize for frightening you. I mean you no harm and I am helpless until sundown in any case. I'll go then.

    I imagine the police will want to interview me. Tell them you've left me a message—and really leave one, in case they check.

    As I told you, the article is real. I'll email it to you and let you know when it comes out.

    I wish we'd had more time together before you found out about me. You must be very shocked and I only add to that by being here. Please use my room at the hotel—the key is on your half table—if you've no one to stay with today.

    I wish . . . I wish many things,

Nathan

She dropped the letter and darted to her bedroom. No, not there. He had better manners than to sleep in her bed like Goldilocks. She almost laughed. And, of course, he was in her costume room, along with all her personas, a sewing machine and her make-up table. He had unrolled the futon she kept in there and lay like a corpse upon it, on one side, face turned away from her. She noted that he'd drawn down the shades and pulled the curtains closed as well. Of course he had.

She tiptoed across the room. She couldn't help feeling as though she'd wake him. She snapped on a light and sat at her make-up mirror and looked at him. He was even more corpselike. Eyes closed, oblivious. Vulnerable. She could call the police, stake him, roll him out in the yard, whatever she chose. He had trusted her. He had saved her.

And thinking through this, she realized she was not afraid of Nathan Court, Yankee vampire transplanted south. What kind of woman, after all, poses as a vampire? What kind dips her fingers in the blood on a man's shirtfront in a dark doorway? Not the easily spooked.

Letitia left the light on—wasn't going to disturb him—and put away her costume. Then she creamed her face at the dressing table, which also reflected his motionless form. Not breathing, either. Probably didn't eat, except blood. Was he going to need some when he woke up? Unknown whether he could have sex like in the books. Lots of unknowns.

Cross those bridges later. She went to her room and changed into a long T-shirt and brushed out her hair. Made some hot chocolate. She didn't feel alone, the way the usually did, even though her houseguest was completely out of it. Dead to the world, in fact. She snorted into the cocoa, and then yawned.

She set down the mug and got out spare blankets from the hall that she tucked around the curtains. Then she lay on the floor beside him, her body mirroring his. Slightly on one side, one arm under his head and half stretched out, the other curled. His body did not look relaxed into sleep. He seemed to be holding a pose impossibly long. Letty made her own breathing minimal. The sleeping vampire: too static to perform. But she'd like to move the way he did; the suddenness and apparent of effort were worth her study.

If the article was real, so was the journalist. And how different was that from an agent? They both knew what sold and dealt with marketers. She would explain that to him tonight. After he'd talked to the police. It would make sense: danger had thrown them together. You found out about each other fast that way. Got involved fast. But he'd need to sleep in the other room after tonight, so she had access to her stuff. It was going to take some rearrangement. She left the door open, brushed her teeth and got into bed, and, because she was only a temporary vampire, set the alarm for noon.

✝

THE VAMPIRE IN HIS CLOSET

HEATHER GRAHAM

><+<)><+(+)><+<)><+(+)><+<

THE VAMPIRE WAS REAL. CHRIS KNEW IT THE SECOND HE THREW OPEN the lid of the coffin. Before the creature opened its eyes, Chris knew that it was real. No regular corpse could have looked so very alive. Well, rather dead, too, of course, but alive, as well. The creature's skin was pale, but still, it had a glow of life. And it seemed as if the lungs were moving, as if the heart were beating.

The eyes suddenly flew open, and Chris felt his own heart begin to thunder and soar. They were black eyes, obsidian black, as black the night beyond them. They were spectacular eyes, large, hypnotic, fine eyes, rimmed with red, as if rimmed with blood.

And then, it began to smile. Smile, and stare at Chris's throat, where the rampant beating of his heart was giving tell-tile signs at his vein. Blood was racing throughout his system. For a hungry vampire, that pounding of his pulse must have been quite a sight.

"Hello," the creature said, and its smile deepened cunningly.

Chris had expected a hoarse rasp. Or perhaps an accent. Something Romanian, exotic. This vampire had the faintest hint of a Southern accent.

Well, this was New Orleans.

Still, Chris had seen every single vampire movie it was possible to see. He waited for the creature to say something like, "I vant to drink your blood," but the creature did not do so.

It stared at Chris. Then it rose to a sitting position very slowly within the boundaries of its coffin.

"Well, sir, you have awakened me." There was the slightest pause. "You must know that I am a vampire," it said, Still, that soft accent. The voice was husky, masculine. Chris imagined that most women, Magda included, would find it a sensual, alluring voice.

In fact, this vampire was one alluring fellow. Like the Bela Lugosi Dracula, or maybe more like Frank Langella. He certainly was not the hunched, ugly creature once played by Klaus Kinski. With his obsidian-dark eyes and jet hair, a face constructed of clean lines and very classical features made him very handsome, despite the paleness of his flesh.

And when he stood, rising out of his coffin with a swift, smooth movement, he was tall, broad-shouldered; well-proportioned: In short, he was amazingly charismatic, Chris found himself studying the creature, enrapt himself, and very nearly losing hold of the Cross of Damocles that he held within his fingers.

"A thirsty vampire . . ." the creature said, those obsidian eyes boring directly into his—

Chris remembered himself in time. He fumbled in his pocket and swept forward the Cross of Damocles.

Instantly, the creature threw up its arms, cowering away from Chris.

"By Satan himself! You carry THAT talisman!" The vampire cried.

Chris stared at the cross with the same amazement with which he had first stared at the vampire. Oh, yes, he had believed. As long as he could remember, he had believed. He had Seen the Bela Lugosi movie first, he thought, and then later on he had read Bram Stoker's book, hanging on every word. And he had become more and more convinced that Bram Stoker had been writing due to some real-life experience. Vampires were real, vampires did exist.

As he had grown older, he'd learned to curb his beliefs. But he'd loved the stories. So much so that he'd learned to write them himself, and in time, he had done quite well with it. He'd started with "The Vampire That Ate New York," and he'd gone through many of America's major cities since. But his success had made him restless. He needed something more. He needed something real.

One night in a Houston bar he'd heard about the house right by the Garden district in New Orleans. It was called "The Castle" because it was a castle—the original owner had ordered every single brick and stone over from Europe. It was going amazingly cheaply because it had a history of the macabre; suicides within the walls, disappearances on dark and rainy nights, and the like. Rumor had it that the last owner—a German man—had stayed only a matter of weeks, then returned suddenly to Europe, leaving word that the property should be condemned.

If there were such a thing as a living—or non-living—vampire, as it were, then Chris was certain that he had found where that vampire should exist. And so he had determined that he would buy the house.

It hadn't been easy. Magda liked Houston. And after ten years of marriage, it seemed that Magda had learned the art of getting her own way. But this time, Chris had been determined. He'd gone so far as suggesting that he and Magda call it quits at last, and go their separate ways. Magda had been startled into a rare silence. As far as buying The Castle went, Chris was quite determined. Since his vampire books kept Magda living the life style that Magda found so enjoyable, she had at long last given in.

And once in the house, well . . .

Chris had dug and torn through it, but he had known where to look from the beginning. There had been a cellar in the house, rare for New Orleans, where people were buried above the ground to avoid the water table. Well, it was a half-cellar, really. The castle had been built up on a landfill to allow for it.

And it was perfect. It was dank and dreary, and there were spider webs galore. Chris loved it. He had immediately set up his word processor and printer and his beloved books and posters of Vampira and Elvira. His determination had done him very well. In the very first week he found the first of what he called "the Van Helsing papers," although there was no evidence that they had been written by anyone named Van Helsing. Chris was still convinced.

The papers had been old, yellowed. They had been written in a script that had begun neat and legible, and become more and more flowing and illegible as they continued.

He—it—the creature!—had been the one to have the castle built. He—it— the creature!—must now be contained. And the Cross of Damocles, blessed by five popes and containing the flesh of the martyr John, could contain the creature. Anyone holding the cross had power over the creature, and anyone who learned the secrets of the cross could actually bind the creature to his will. Of course, care must be taken. The gravest care. For the creature, too, had powers. The only real way to be safe was to keep the creature locked in his sepulcher, with the cross in the brick, as the writer of the papers had left it. For the vampire, awakened, might make demands. And for his life, and his sanity, the man to awaken the beast might well have to meet those demands . . .

But no. After he had found the papers, Chris had found the Cross of Damocles, laid over a. wall of brick. And he had torn down the bricks, found himself in a large closet with a smell of dust and mold and a coffin dead center in the small space.

And now . . .

The vampire.

"You are real!" Chris gasped.

"Indeed yes, I'm real. Thirsty, aggravated—no, truly annoyed. What is the meaning of this interruption? Really!" The vampire actually had a very deep drawl. And he was deeply distressed. He slammed clown the lid of his coffin and hiked himself atop it, sitting so that his elbows rested on his knees, and his chin rested on his folded hands. "You seem to have no intention of letting me take one good bite out of your neck for a long drink, so why disturb me?"

I don't want to become a vampire!" Chris said. But I have given some consideration to your needs: I managed to buy some blood—"

The vampire instantly perked up. "Human, I hope?"

"Yes, human," Chris told him. He strode out of the closet, careful to keep a tight hand on the cross. On his desk he found the sanitary plastic container of bright red blood and turned to hurry back to the vampire. He didn't heed to hurry. The vampire was right behind him. In seconds he had taken the bag from Chris. He swallowed down the container to the last drop.

He was incredibly neat. Not a speck of blood touched his frilled white shirt, black evening cape, lips, or chin.

"Ah, that was good!" he said softly. "Not as good as taking it fresh from the neck, mind you, but delicious after all these years, nonetheless. Thank you. Now," he stared steadily at Chris, "just what can I do for you?"

"Well," Chris began, "I'm a writer—"

"Ah!" The vampire said, and it seemed that he needed no more. He walked around the desk and sank into Chris's swivel chair, making himself very comfortable. "Like that Bram Stoker fellow."

"You knew him" Chris gasped, excitedly leaning against the table. The cross was in his hand. It nearly fell. Both Chris and the vampire noticed it. The vampire, watching Chris, smiled cunningly once again.

"You must be careful. Mister, er . . . ?"

"Lambden. Chris Lambden," Chris supplied, "And you, what is your name, what should I call you?"

"Well, call me 'Count,' of course," the creature said.

"Then you are him, the original—"

The creature was shaking his head. He swept out his hand, indicating that Chris should take the comfortable old stuffed armchair in front of his desk. "You were considerate of me. I'll give you something of a story, if you wish." He leaned back, casual, elegant, eyeing the room, very conversational. "I hear them say that Bram based his story on Vlad Dracul, the Impaler, the ruler who killed so many thousands of his enemies, and was still, in his way, a hero to his people." He shrugged. "Well, yes, that is true, you see, for a gypsy witch whose only son was caught on Vlad's skewers cast a curse upon him, and so he became the first of a long and illustrious line of vampires."

"Lord!" Chris gasped, falling into the indicated chair.

The vampire winced. "Must you?" He demanded.

"Does Vlad the Impaler still live?" Chris asked. He blushed. "Well, not live, exist?"

The vampire shook his head. "No, no, I'm afraid not. Alas, I never knew him myself."

"Then how—"

"How did I become a vampire?" He picked up a pencil and idly tapped it upon the table. "Ah, let's see. It was in the early eighteen hundreds . . . before or after the War of 1812, I'm not really sure." He shrugged, "It makes little difference now. I was a younger son of a French aristocrat, come to New Orleans to make my fortune. But then I was down in the bayou one night with the love of my life, when suddenly— swoop—out of the trees it came!"

"It?"

He shrugged. "The one they actually called Count Dracula, one of Vlad's family, so he was always telling me. Personally, I think that it was all boast."

"Really?" Chris sat perfectly still, mesmerized. "What then?"

"Well, they made a party of it you see. Dracula pounced down upon my dear Deanna, and when I hastened to her rescue, he set upon me instead!"

"And you died and became a vampire!"

"No, no, no, not directly!" the creature said, annoyed. "Whatever have you been reading and how dare you write about us when you seem to know so very little!"

"Sorry," Chris apologized.

"Now, pay attention. If the neck is ripped to shreds and too much blood is taken, the victim dies—goes to heaven or hell—and that is that! To create a vampire is an art! An art in form, and in seduction. Blood must be taken three times, from the same spot. Then a new creature may be born. Be serious, Mr. Lambden! The world would have run amuck with vampires years ago if it were so very easy for one to become one of the 'undead'!"

"Yes, I imagine you're right," Chris agreed. He stared at the creature across his desk. It seemed that he was becoming more and more—normal! He had such an easy way about him. And Chris had already learned so much . . .

But just when he was about to ask another question, a loud voice called his name. It was melodic, it was feminine, but it was loud.

"Chris! Christopher! Do you know what time it is! You've got to come up here right away! The people from the magazine will be here first thing in the morning and we're to be the cover!"

The vampire arched a brow. Chris leapt to his feet "Get back into the closet!"

"How rude!"

"Please, quickly!"

The creature had just disappeared behind the rubble of bricks when Magda appeared at the top of the stairs that lead down to the half-cellar.

"Chris! Did you hear me?"

Oh, yes, he certainly had. He smiled at her. Really, she was such a vision. Magda had this wonderful head full of near-platinum blond hair. It hung over one eye like that of a sex-goddess from the thirties. She had huge blue eyes and an angelic face, and a form that was certainly the best that money could buy. In the pale light filtering in from the kitchen, she seemed to fit the castle, fit the gothic mood of this very night. She was beautiful in a white silk gown that fluttered softly in the air-conditioned night.

"Chris?"

"I'm coming, Magda," he promised her.

She remained there, watching him. Then she shivered, "However can you spend so much time in this awful, dreary place? Honestly, Chris, I should leave!"

"Magda, I'll be right up. I won't ruin the interview, I promise."

She started to speak again, then spun around and disappeared. Chris watched after her. She was really so lovely. Once, he had loved her with all of his heart. He wasn't sure exactly what had happened.

He thought that it had something to do with her mouth.

"She is charming! She is elegant! She is fire!"

Chris almost jumped a mile. The vampire was directly behind him again.

"She is my wife!" Chris said sharply. *And she's a shrew,* he added in silence to himself. It didn't matter. Not tonight. Tonight, he had found his creature.

"Back to your coffin," Chris commanded. "I've got to go up to bed."

"Ah! With that image of grace and beauty!" The vampire said. "So seductive!"

Chris grunted. He didn't tell the creature that the last thing Magda had on her mind was seduction. She simply didn't want his face appearing on the cover of a national magazine if he had bags under his eyes. "Come on now, please? Back. I don't want to have to touch you with the Cross of Damocles—"

The warning was enough. The vampire gasped, swept his cloak before his face, and headed back for the closet. He started to crawl in when Chris noticed for the first time that he had not been lying alone.

A woman lay to the far side of the coffin. Like the vampire, she was pale. Ivory skin glowed softly by the jet-black beauty of her hair.

"My Deanna!" said the vampire.

"Wow!" Chris murmured, "Two vampires—why didn't she awaken?"

"She's not a vampire," the creature informed him loftily. "Only I can awaken her."

"Then she's a very well preserved corpse?" Chris asked.

The vampire sighed with vast impatience. "She hovers between the land of the living and the dead. You see, Dracula first took her blood, then I did the same. But then, I did not drink her blood a third time. Alas . . ."

Alas, what?" Chris demanded.

"Well, the world was filled with beautiful women. So she lies with me while I wait . . ." He shrugged, and grinned. "I shall either make her my consort at last, or choose another. One of these centuries."

He'd had enough of the conversation. He crawled into his coffin, studying Chris.

"Have you plenty of material for your book?"

"Oh, no. We've just begun. I'll be back tomorrow night, I promise."

"Good. I've much more to tell you." The vampire closed his eyes, then opened them again. "Ah, it does feel good to rest on a full stomach once again!"

Chris closed the lid of the coffin. He left the closet behind, replacing most of the bricks and setting the cross within them. He hurried up the stairs then, just as Magda began to call to him again.

Chris decided to shave before going to bed, since the reporter and photographer were coming very early. He paused with the razor just above his cheek and studied his reflection. He was just thirty-five, really in his prime. He was a nice six-foot-two, with sandy hair, green eyes, a decent jaw line and shoulders that had carried well into not just high school but college football, even if he hadn't had the talent or the desire to carry his athletics into the pros.

Magda would have liked that. She found quarterbacks—winning quarterbacks, that was—to be the epitome of honor, glory, and the American male.

He sighed and set down his razor. Where had he gone wrong? Then he started to wonder what his life would be like if only he'd married a brunette. Like the one lying in the coffin with the creature. In her death-like sleep she had appeared so soft and sweet and gentle.

"Chris!"

While Magda . . .

He wasn't going to think about it now. Not when his life had taken this marvelous turn. There was a vampire in his closet.

The next morning the reporters came. Magda was stunning in an outfit by Dior. The reporters stayed most of the day, and he and Magda gave them a wonderful interview. The reporters gushed. They were such a beautiful young couple even if he did write such very weird things.

Just before dusk, the reporters left. So did Magda. There was a cocktail party at the DeVantes. She was going, even though Chris was determined to refuse.

She was so very blond and pretty as she prepared to go. Chris felt a twist within his heart. He even forgot his vampire for a moment.

"Magda, do you really have to go? We could just stay home together tonight. We could watch TV, rent a movie."

"Don't be silly, darling!" She charged him, "I must go—keep up our social standing. Darling, I'm doing this for the both of us!"

She left Chris watched her leave, feeling another pang of nostalgia. Then he remembered his creature.

And he hurried back down to the cellar.

The vampire—or Count—as he preferred to be called, was quite a regular fellow. That night he talked about endless trips to Europe. He gave Chris a blow-by-blow description of the occupation of New Orleans during the war, then muttered something about the way that the Yanks had won.

"You mean the Civil War, right?" Chris asked.

"Why, what other war could you be talking about?" the vampire demanded.

"Oh, there were two major wars and any number of lesser wars since then!" Chris assured him.

"Tell me about your shirt," the vampire demanded.

Chris looked down at his chest. He was wearing his "Saints" T-shirt, Chris did his best to describe a rousing game of football in return. The vampire sighed. "I'd dearly love to see a game."

"You've never seen a professional football game?"

"My dear Mr. Lambden, I have been in this cellar since 1901."

"Well, there is television," Chris said.

"But you could take me out,"

Chris shook his head. "No. No, I definitely could not let a vampire loose in the streets of New Orleans!"

"I wouldn't be loose. You'd still have the cross,"

Chris shook his head, heard Magda muttering upstairs, and decided with a sigh that it was time to return his vampire to his closet.

But certain seeds had been sown, and Chris was just as curious as the vampire. He wanted to take him out.

Within a week, he had bought the vampire his own "Saints" T-shirt and a pair of black stretch Levi jeans.

The vampire wore them well. He was just admiring himself in Chris's swivel shaving mirror when they were both startled by an intrusion.

"Christopher Lambden, I swear that I'll have you institutionalized if you don't quit—oh!"

They'd been so absorbed in the new clothing that neither Chris nor the vampire had noticed the door at the top of the stairs open, or Magda come on in.

Magda hadn't expected company. Obviously. Her Mouth was left in a wide O. "Magda!" Chris said.

Magda recovered quickly. She offered the vampire one of her most engaging smiles. "Hello. I'm sorry. I didn't realize that Chris had company!" She smoothed her hands over her tight jeans, then walked on down the steps and extended perfectly manicured fingers to the vampire. "We haven't met. I'm Magda." Just Magda. Not Magda Lambden, not Magda, Chris's wife—just Magda. Well, that was her way.

She was an atrocious flirt. Once upon a time it had infuriated Chris. Then, somewhere along the line, he had ceased to care. Now, he was intrigued. He should have been jealous about his wife, he realized. He was more interested in her reaction to his vampire. "Oh, yes, Magda this is—"

"Drake," the vampire offered, elegantly kissing Magda's fingers. Obsidian eyes touched his wife's powder-blue gaze.

Chris made an instant decision. "I've invited him to a Saints game, Magda. I'd love you to come, too: Of course, I do understand how you feel, about games—"

I'd love to come," Magda insisted.

Chris smiled. "Fine."

It was a wonderful game. The home team won, the crowds were going wild. Chris had some difficulty convincing "Drake" that he couldn't take just one little bite out of one little cheerleader's neck, but really, all in all, "Drake" was very well behaved.

Magda kept him occupied.

Coming home was more difficult. Chris had to convince Magda that Drake would be perfectly happy sleeping in the cellar. He was firm. Magda was at last convinced.

Chris wedged the Cross of Damocles into a little niche in the door to the cellar.

Not that Chris mistrusted his wife, but he kept a sharp eye on her that night. When she rose and wandered down to the kitchen, he managed to sneak just ahead of her, and be there when she would have opened the door to the cellar.

"What were you doing?" he asked her,

"Oh, just checking on our guest!" she supplied.

Chris smiled, "I've checked on him. He's fine." Chris swallowed hard. You mustn't go in there, Magda."

"Why, Christopher—"

"Do you love me, Magda?"

"Well, don't be absurd! Of course, I do. Whyever else would I stay with such a strange bookworm if I didn't! I could be off seeing the world, Chris. Having a life like that of your friend! Dancing in Paris, going to the bullfights in Madrid . . ." Her voice trailed away.

Chris ignored the pathos, "Magda, if you love me, trust me. I can't stay awake forever. You must stay out of the cellar at night."

"Of course, darling, if that's what you want!" She turned, all innocence, and started back for the stairs, Chris followed her. He tried very hard to stay awake that night.

He awoke with the first pale streaks of dawn. He stretched his hand out on the bed. It was empty.

"Magda?"

He heard the shower running. He leaned back, breathing in with relief. Maybe she did love him. But did she love him enough?

It was not so difficult to explain to Magda that Drake slept by day—Magda liked to sleep by day herself, and when she wasn't sleeping, she liked to shop. She was gone that morning by ten.

Chris spent most of the day in the closet, just watching his vampires—no, his vampire and the vampire's almost-consort—sleeping. They didn't move. Not a muscle, not a breath.

That night, Magda was in a wonderful mood. She insisted that they show their visitor the *Vieux Carré*, or French Quarter. Drake was certainly ready.

"Have you seen it before?"

"Oh, yes, but it was quite some time ago!" Drake assured her,

They set out. They watched jazz bands and Drake stared with absolute fascination at all the strip joints. One buxom beauty, obviously just off work, passed their way.

"Just a sip!" Drake whispered to Chris. "One little sip of blood from one of those, er, ladies of the night!"

"No, I've a pint for you at home. Magda wants to stop for steaks. How shall we manage it?"

The vampire sighed, "You are full of myth and legend. I love a good steak. Just make sure that it's very, very rare!"

They had steaks, which Drake did seem to enjoy, although he turned his nose up at the crawfish appetizers. They came home. Once again, it was time for bed. Magda pulled out the sleeper in the cellar herself. She went upstairs.

"Into your coffin!" Chris commanded.

"But I'm not at all tired!"

Chris hesitated. "All right, then. Watch some television until morning. But remember, the cross will be lodged at the top of the door. Just as it was last night."

"Oh, I'll remember," the vampire promised. He had on a pair of Chris's best flannel pajamas. Like everything else, he wore them well.

Chris wedged the cross into the door, and went on up to bed.

Magda was at her dressing table, brushing out her hair. She eyed Chris in the mirror. Such a beautiful woman. She wore a nightgown with a lace edge around her throat.

"Coming in?" Chris asked her, plumping up her pillow.

"Of course," Magda replied. She set down her brush and slid in beside Chris There was a Band-Aid on her neck. Chris looked at her gravely. "Magda, you must stay away from Drake."

"And you mustn't be so jealous. He's your friend; you brought him into the house, remember?"

"What did you do to your neck?"

"Pardon? What?" Absently, Magda touched the Band-Aid. "Oh, nothing. It's a bug bite."

"Don't betray me, my love," Chris said.

"Chris, I would never!"

Chris kissed her. "Goodnight, darling," he told her "Remember, you must trust me, and be very, very careful."

"Of course."

He held her as he drifted off to sleep. *Stay with me, Magda!* he thought, hovering between wakefulness and darkness. Morning came. He stretched out his hands. She was gone.

But once again, he heard the spray of the shower.

She was becoming an early riser.

Drake was up and ready when Chris came down the stairs that night. He was wearing one of Chris's best tailored shirts and an Izod sweater.

He wore them well.

"I'm ready," he said. "What will it be tonight, a game, some music, a stroll?"

"Actually," Chris said sternly, "I was thinking about getting some work done."

"Oh," the vampire said with disappointment. Then he looked at Chris slyly. "Oh, well, I've nothing but years ahead of me."

"Now that's what I thought that we would talk about tonight," Chris said, sitting down behind his desk. "What does kill a vampire?"

"Surely, you know!" The vampire said.

"I want to hear it from you."

"After, perhaps, we could take a walk down Bourbon Street and stroll to the water. I've quite a desire to see the old Mississippi flowing by."

"After, perhaps," Chris smiled.

The vampire sighed patiently. "There's the stake through the heart. Everyone knows that."

"Everyone," Chris agreed.

"Bright sunlight. A few minor streaks of dawn will not do it, but bright sunlight. Vampires burn up like dry tinder in bright sunlight."

"I see."

"There's holy water—but you'd need a tub of it to really do the trick."

"A tub of holy water," Chris waited, "Is there anything else? A silver bullet, a—"

"Christopher," the vampire said indignantly. He was starting to sound an awful lot like Magda. "You're talking about werewolves. If you want to know about werewolves, you'll have to have one."

Chris smiled. "Fine. You want to see Bourbon Street, let's see Bourbon Street."

"Where's your wife? Is she coming with us?"

"I don't know. Magda seems to be a bit under the weather lately. Very sleepy. You wouldn't know anything about that, would you?"

"Not a thing," the vampire said, entirely innocent. Chris smiled. He could almost see the sly smile the minute he turned his back.

They walked through the *Vieux Carré* once again. That night they stopped for Cajun food at K. Paul's. Chris ordered the vampire the hottest thing on the menu and sat back with delight as he watched the creature swallow glass after glass of water.

Magda didn't notice. She was busy talking away. The vampire knew Paris like the back of his hand. He could rattle away in French, He even kissed Magda's finger tips in the middle of the meal.

But he was getting very sloppy, Chris thought. Because during that kiss, Chris could see the glittering tip of his fangs. He came so close to an honest-to-God bite. Right there. In the restaurant.

They stared at the mighty Mississippi, and then they wandered back to the car. Soon they were home again.

They bade the vampire goodnight. .

And upstairs, Chris bade his wife goodnight. "Remember, Magda, stay away from the cellar."

"Of course," she murmured.

She fell asleep so very quickly.

There was a much larger Band-Aid on her neck now.

Chris roused himself. He silently descended and opened the cellar door, slipping the Cross of Damocles into the pocket of his robe. In silence, he came down the steps.

The vampire didn't notice him. Still in Chris's shirt and sweater and jeans, he was seated before the television set, entranced as Bela Lugosi played Dracula. Every once in a while, he gave off a disgruntled sniff.

Chris walked around in back of him and sank into the swivel chair behind his desk. The vampire didn't notice him.

Chris waited.

At exactly 2 A.M. the cellar door opened. Magda, a vision of innocence and purity in her ivory and lace nightgown, appeared at the top of the stairs.

"Drake!" she called softly,

Chris watched as the vampire smiled. A slow, cunning, entirely-pleased-with-himself smile. He rose. "My darling!" he called to Magda.

Magda came running down the steps and into his arms. "We've simply got to quit meeting like this!" Magda said.

Oh, Magda, darling! Always a cliché, Chris thought.

"Christopher suspects."

Well, of course, he suspects, what am I supposed to be, stupid? Chris wondered in silence.

"My darling, Magda! After tonight, it will not matter anymore," the creature told her. It struck Chris that they were absurdly normal-looking standing there, the vampire in his clothing, Magda all decked out to seduce. People didn't change— times changed.

"Oh, after tonight, it will matter more than ever!" Magda whispered. "Drake, I want the things that you talk about all the time. I want to travel, to roam the continents! I want Paris in April, a London shopping spree. All the exotic places you come from—"

"Hell, he comes from New Orleans!" Chris broke in, unable to take it any longer.

His vampire, his wife, both stopped and stared at him.

"Chris!" Magda said in alarm.

The vampire smiled, holding Magda close against himself "It's too late, Christopher. You thought yourself so clever. Well, I've had her twice. And now, she is mine."

"Oh, Christopher, I am so sorry, but I am his!" Magda insisted. She didn't seem to understand quite how she was "his." "Dear Christopher, I do love you but I want to be with him, I want to fly . . ."

"Do you fly?" Christopher asked, interrupting his wife but addressing the vampire politely.

"Chris—" Magda began again.

"He's a vampire, Magda," Chris told her bluntly.

Magda didn't believe.

"Christopher, Christopher, always into your strange fantasies! Can't you just accept it? Someone else came along. Someone fascinating, intriguing!"

"So you'd really rather be with him. Even if he is a vampire?"

"If he were Satan himself," Magda replied impatiently.

Chris lifted his hands and hiked his shoulders in a shrug, looking at his vampire.

"Who am I to stand in your way? Go ahead. Go right ahead."

Magda started when the vampire flatly showed his fangs with no finesse or pretense whatsoever. "Chris!" She managed to croak. "He is a vampire!"

"Better than Satan, I imagine," Chris consoled her philosophically. The fangs were at her throat.

"Chris—!"

"Sorry, darling, I'm doing this for both of us!'

The vampire was, as usual, fastidious. Not a drop spilled upon Magda's flesh, or wet his lips, when he was done.

Magda fell to his feet like a rag doll.

"Is she . . . ?" Chris said.

"Yes. She'll come to soon enough, a vampire. So sorry, old boy. But you were asleep at the helm, as they say."

Chris shook his head, "So sorry, old boy, but you must have been asleep at the helm."

"Pardon?"

"I awakened you," Chris reminded him. "And you betrayed me three times."

"Three times—?"

"The three times it took to make Magda into a vampire. She was my wife, remember?"

The vampire narrowed his obsidian eyes. "Now wait a minute—"

"If you don't play by the rules, I won't either," Chris. Warned him "You must now obey my three commands!"

The vampire scowled, starting for him. Chris produced the cross, and the creature stepped back.

"All right, what do you want?"

"I want you to leave, tonight. You'll take Magda, of course, and since I don't want any problems with the police, you'll make a show of going."

"And where am I going?"

"Europe, of course. "I'll see that your coffin is sent on ahead. That's one."

"And two?"

"No more people! I'll keep you well supplied with blood from the blood bank. I don't like to boast, but I am a fairly wealthy man."

The vampire was looking truly sulky now. "Just a little sip of the fresh stuff now and then?"

"No. Never."

The vampire smiled suddenly. "I'll outlive you, Christopher."

"Maybe. Maybe not. I like to whittle on wood while I'm thinking out my plots. I'll have plenty of stakes at hand, for anytime I might need them."

Magda was starting to come around. "I feel so very strange!" she said.

"There's one more command," Chris told the vampire,

"Yes?" The vampire was truly irritated now.

"I think that you should awaken Deanna. You can leave her with me. You and Magda are going to need all the room you can get in that little coffin. Trust me— she kicks!"

The vampire muttered something, then directed his forefinger toward the closet and the coffin.

"I don't see her," 'Chris 'said.

"She'll be up and about in just a few minutes," the vampire assured him. Magda still seemed disoriented. It didn't matter. The vampire dragged her up beside him.

"What . . . ?"

"We're leaving," the vampire said curtly.

"By the front door, please," Chris said. He followed the two of them up the stairs. Then out to the street. As the vampire had been commanded, he made a show of leaving.

But once he and Magda were down the street, he had had enough. He swept up his arm dramatically, just like Lugosi had done in the movies. He turned into a bat. Magda gave out a little cry, but in seconds, she was a second black creature of the night beside him.

"Oh, no! What did you do to me!" Magda wailed. Her voice had grown sharp.

"Paris!" The vampire muttered back. "You wanted to go to Paris."

"And I wanted to fly first class!" Magda whined. "On an airplane! With champagne—"

Chris started to laugh softly. The vampire certainly had his hands full.

There was a soft noise behind Chris, at the doorway to the castle. Deanna. The name leapt unbidden to his mind, and for a moment, little chills swept along his spine. What had the vampire left him? Would he turn to find a withered crone? A skeleton frame with cloth that decayed, quickly becoming ashes in the wind?

He turned. His chills dissipated.

It was, indeed, Deanna. No skeletal form, no mound of ash. She offered him a breathtaking, tremulous smile. She raised her hands, and looked at them in the moonlight, then she smiled his way again.

"I'm human!" she whispered.

"Yes."

"And you . . . well he is gone . . . and you, you must have saved me." She offered him a wistful, crooked little smile. "You must be my hero."

Hero? He'd never really thought of himself in such a manner, but it was nice to be able to do so, "I did manage to have you awakened," he said.

Her smile deepened. What a beautiful face she had. She trembled slightly. "I think that you're a hero," she said softly. The she shook her head ruefully. "A hero I could easily learn to love. For eternity."

"Oh, no. Not eternity," Chris corrected her. "Just a normal lifetime," he said very quietly.

"Oh, yes! A normal lifetime!" she agreed.

She was decidedly old-fashioned looking in her long, outdated gown, but that could be fixed. Magda had left behind closets full of clothing.

"You'll have to forgive me, it's been a long, long time since I went to sleep. What year is it?"

Chris told her.

She gasped, and looked into his eyes. She seemed to like what she saw. "I'm afraid I'm very behind the times," she apologized. "You'll have so much to tell me . . ."

Her voice trailed off. She looked as if she might fall. Chris hurried up to her side. "Let me take you into the house."

"The house looks familiar . . ."

"Yes, it should be familiar to you. Of course, it has changed. Over the years," Chris told her. "Come, let me show it to you. My name is Christopher Lambden, and I write books about—" He hesitated.

"Yes?" She said, smiling softly, waiting.

"Westerns," he said. "I think I'm going to write westerns from now on."

About the Authors

✝

Poppy Z. Brite is the author of several novels, including *Lost Souls*, *Drawing Blood*, *Exquisite Corpse*, *Liquor*, *The Value of X*, and *Prime*. Her short fiction has appeared in magazines and anthologies, been collected into several single-author volumes, including *Swamp Foetus*, *Are You Loathsome Tonight?* and *The Devil You Know*. She has also edited two volumes of vampire erotica, *Love In Vein* and *Love in Vein II*. Currently she lives in New Orleans with her husband Chris, one old dog, way too many cats, and an albino king snake.

Nancy A. Collins is the author of several novels and numerous short stories, and served a two-year stint as a writer for DC Comics' *Swamp Thing*. She is a recipient of the Horror Writers Association's Bram Stoker Award, The British Fantasy Society's Icarus Award, and a past nominee for the Eisner, the John Campbell Memorial, World Fantasy and International Horror Guild Award. Best known for her ground-breaking vampire character, Sonja Blue, her works include the *Vamps* YA series, *Knuckles and Tales*, and *Sunglasses After Dark*. Her most recent work is the Golgotham series, scheduled for release by Penguin/Roc in 2010. She is also planning a new Sonja Blue novel, the first in nearly a decade. Ms. Collins makes her home in Cape Fear, appropriately enough, with her fiancé and their Boston Terrier, Chopper.

Ferelith Dawson lives and writes in New York State.

Russell Davis has written numerous short stories and novels in a variety of genres under several different names. Some of his most recent work can be seen in the anthologies *Fellowship Fantastic*, *Man vs. Machine*, *Under Cover of Darkness*, and *Imaginary Friends*. He lives in Nevada, where he writes, rides horses, and spends time with his family.

India Edghill's (Jennara Wenk) interest in vampires dates to the stormy evening she made the mistake of reading Dracula and wound up staying up all night looking nervously over her shoulder. Her interest in history is also long-standing; her father was a major history buff whose favorite authors were Will and Ariel Durant. India inherited his love of research and history, and wound up writing historical fantasy stories and historical novels. India's novels include *Queenmaker: A Novel of King David's Queen*; *Wisdom's Daughter: A Novel of Solomon and Sheba*, and *Delilah*. Some of her short stories can be read on her website: www.indiaedghill.com.

Barbara Emrys teaches a class on horror literature at the University of Nebraska-Kearney. She has made "A Temporary Vampire" into a novel now in search of a publisher.

Heather Graham, the *New York Times* and *USA Today* best-selling author, sold her first book, *When Next We Love*, in 1982. Since then, she has written more than one hundred novels and novellas, including the launch books for Dell's Ecstasy Supreme line, Silhouette's Shadows, and Harlequin's mainstream fiction imprint Mira Books. A founding member of the Florida Romance Writers chapter of RWA since 1999, she has also hosted the *Romantic Times* Vampire Ball, with all revenues going directly to children's charity. She is pleased to have been published in approximately twenty languages, and to have been honored with awards from Waldenbooks, B. Dalton, Georgia Romance Writers, *Affaire de Coeur*, *Romantic Times*, and more. She has had books selected for the Doubleday Book Club and the Literary Guild, and has been quoted, interviewed, or featured in such publications as *The Nation*, *Redbook*, *People*, and *USA Today* and appeared on many newscasts including local television and *Entertainment Tonight*. Married since high school graduation and the mother of five, her greatest love in life remains her family, but she also believes her career has been an incredible gift, and she is grateful every day to be doing something that she loves so very much for a living.

John Helfers is a full-time writer and editor living and working in Green Bay, Wisconsin. During his career, he has worked on anthology and novel projects with many bestselling authors. He has written and edited both fiction and nonfiction, including *Tom Clancy's Net Force Explorers: Cloak and Dagger*, *The Alpha Bravo Delta Guide to the U.S. Navy*, and the forthcoming nonfiction anthology *From the Jaws of Death*. His most recent nonfiction project, *The Vorkosigan Companion*, co-edited with Lillian Stewart Carl, was nominated for a Hugo Award in 2009.

Lisa Lepovetsky holds a Master of Fine Arts degree in writing, and teaches writing and literature classes for both Penn State University and the University of Pittsburgh. She has been widely published in many anthologies and periodicals, including Ellery Queen's Mystery Magazine. Lisa has written three full-length plays, published a novel, *Shadows on the Bayou*, and creates murder mystery theaters.

Billie Sue Mosiman, nominated for both the Edgar and the Stoker awards, is the author of thirteen novels and numerous short stories. Her collection of short stories is titled *Dark Matter*. She lives in Texas with her husband, Lyle, and a Shih Tzu called Domino. She is working on a new dark fantasy novel.

Jennifer Stevenson lives in the Chicago area with her husband of thirty years. Her stories have been published in a number of anthologies. "Solstice" was published as a chapbook by Green Man Review. *Trash Sex Magic* is her first novel. She is currently working on The SeX Files, a series of sexy, funny fantasies for Ballantine Books, beginning with *The Brass Bed*, and continuing with *The Velvet Chair* and *The Bearskin Rug*.

Cecilia Tan is the author of many books including the paranormal romance *Mind Games*, the erotic short story collection *White Flames*, and the Magic University series of erotic fantasy. She is the editor of many volumes of vampire stories, including *Bites of Passion, Erotica Vampirica, Blood Surrender, A Taste of Midnight, Women of the Bite*, and others. Find out what she is up to at ceciliatan.com.

Don Webb is a four-time loser—he has been nominated for and didn't win the International Horror Critics Award, Rhysling Award, Shirley Jackson Award, and a Hugo Award for fan writing. His work has been included in a Norton Anthology and also in *Trucker's USA*. He has worked in a corndog factory, shot fireworks professionally, and written a book on the Greek Magical Papyryi. He was born on April 30. Send Gifts!